THE
PARIS SPY'S GIRL

BOOKS BY AMANDA LEES

WW2 Resistance Series

The Silence Before Dawn

Paris at First Light

The Midwife's Child

AMANDA LEES

THE
PARIS SPY'S
GIRL

bookouture

Published by Bookouture in 2024

An imprint of Storyfire Ltd.
Carmelite House
50 Victoria Embankment
London EC4Y 0DZ

www.bookouture.com

ISBN: 978-1-83790-627-7
eBook ISBN: 978-1-83790-626-0

This book is a work of fiction. Whilst some characters and circumstances portrayed by the author are based on real people and historical fact, references to real people, events, establishments, organizations or locales are intended only to provide a sense of authenticity and are used fictitiously. All other characters and all incidents and dialogue are drawn from the author's imagination and are not to be construed as real.

For Lisa, without whom I wouldn't be here and nor would this book.

PROLOGUE

She paused in the doorway, one hand on her hip, the other holding a champagne glass, her low-cut dress leaving nothing to the imagination. The diamond that dangled between her breasts caught the light from the chandeliers, sparkling almost as brightly as the green eyes that scanned the room, settling on her mark. Eyes that matched the colour of her jade gown. No accident. As carefully calculated as every other move she made. It was what had kept her alive so far. Although the odds shortened with each day that passed.

She glided to the bar, making sure every eye was on her. Especially his. She gave it four minutes. Maybe five. He started to stumble her way in three. She turned her back on him as he approached, waiting until he was beside her. Only then did she turn and smile, scarlet lips stretching back from perfect teeth, the light playing now across her hair. Platinum blonde. Of course. As lethal as the pistol strapped to her thigh.

He was looking at her just as she knew he would, his eyes widening as he took in every curve. Even from here, she could see his pupils were dilated, his movements unsteady. Good.

The drugs were kicking in. Pretty soon now, he'd be singing like a canary.

They all sang, in the end. Some more than others. This one was going to be tough though. She knew that already. Josef Kieffer, head of the Nazi Secret Police here in Paris and no stupid brute. His methods were subtler than most, his results impressive. But then, so were hers. And she had more to gain. If she managed to crack Kieffer, they could get to the bottom of who was betraying the Paris network. So far, the Germans had arrested nearly three hundred of their agents. They couldn't afford to lose another.

She leaned forward slightly, letting out her breath so that her breasts swelled, magnificent. Let him goggle at the sight. That was exactly how she wanted him. Mesmerised. Made stupid by lust, like all of them. The longer his brain was clouded, the better. It gave her more of a chance. The stakes might be high, but the risks were higher. Get this wrong and she'd be looking at Kieffer from inside one of his cells. Or worse, staring down the barrel of a Mauser. A swifter death than transportation to a camp.

Not that she feared death. She danced with it every day, in one way or another. At night, too, when she dreamed, hearing that splash of water once more, seeing the slow ripples spreading across the river as he sank, the chains weighing him down. But that was another time, another place. Another man. Right here, right now, she had work to do. A war to win. A man to enslave so she could save others.

Kieffer's eyes were curiously opaque as he leered at her.

'Champagne for the lady.'

She glanced at him, arching an eyebrow. 'How do you know I even like champagne?'

'I thought all ladies liked champagne. Have we met before?'

She smiled, the light casting a halo around her.

'I don't think I've had that pleasure,' she breathed. 'My name is Christine.'

ONE

OCTOBER 1943, PARIS, FRANCE

'Bitch.'

I smiled as I stared into his eyes. 'Oh, come now, is that really necessary?'

It was a risk. A calculated one. Allow him to talk to me like that now and the game was over before it had begun. This one liked to be dominated. I'd read the dossier on him from cover to cover. Eugene Schumann, industrialist and Abwehr agent who counted Coco Chanel and her Abwehr spy lover among his friends. A man who was only too happy to employ those incarcerated in concentration camps as slave labour, literally working them to death. But as much as he liked to inflict pain, he also enjoyed receiving it. He blinked. Drew back, sitting straighter in his chair, remembering himself. Remembering where we were. 'My apologies.'

A collective exhale around the table accompanied by titters and glances. I reached across, gathering up my cards and my winnings, glancing over to see Suzanne standing behind him, the merest nod indicating we were on.

I let out a tinkling laugh. 'Beginner's luck.'

Gracious smiles from one or two, although Schumann looked unconvinced.

I kept my smile in place and my eyes on him. 'I think this calls for champagne.'

The temperature around the table rose a fraction. 'Yes, yes of course,' he said, signalling to the sommelier. Taittinger. *Naturellement.* I raised my glass to him.

'To victory,' I cooed.

'Victory,' the table echoed.

Suzanne and I were, of course, wishing for another kind of victory altogether, one in which the Nazis were defeated and driven from France. But for everyone else around the table, it was business as usual. A very lucrative business. Sales of Taittinger had soared since the Germans had roared into Paris, along with profits for those who consorted with the enemy. Schumann could afford to lose a few francs to me. It might even teach him a lesson or two.

I glanced at Suzanne again. It was time.

'Excuse me, ladies and gentlemen.'

I rose from the table, making sure to pause long enough, dusting imaginary crumbs from my satin gown, so he had time to admire the way it clung to every curve. Then, and only then, I looked at him through my lashes, feigning a certain decorum mixed with promise. It was a combination that never failed. As I sashayed from the room, I could sense him rise too. I emerged from the ladies' room to find him pretending to admire the paintings that adorned the club vestibule.

'You're interested in art?'

He turned from the landscape he was apparently studying with rapt attention. 'I'm interested in beauty.'

Bingo.

I dimpled, tilting my head at just the right angle to appear coquettish. 'Are you now?'

'Very much.'

Strange how such an ordinary-looking little man could entertain the thoughts he did. But then, he wasn't alone.

'Champagne?'

He was holding two glasses. Confident. Or, more likely, arrogant, as were most of his ilk. I took the one he was offering me, sipping from it while I looked up at him again, feeling the kick of triumph as that glint lit up his eyes behind his little round glasses. He had me – or so he believed.

They all thought they were irresistible, even if they resembled a bullfrog. Especially if they resembled a bullfrog. But then, power was an aphrodisiac, at least to some. And working for the Abwehr gave him a special sheen, at least in the eyes of some. The military intelligence service considered themselves a cut above the Gestapo, staffed as they were by officers and men like Schumann, while the secret police were of a different class.

'I don't believe we've been properly introduced.'

I let another teasing smile play around my lips. He executed a little bow.

'Eugene Schumann at your service.'

His swaggering tone implied the exact opposite.

'My name is Christine. It's a pleasure to meet you.'

'Just Christine?'

'Just Christine.'

'Then the pleasure is all mine.'

We understood one another. Apparently. I raised my glass and touched it to his, hearing the expensive ring of crystal on crystal. 'To pleasure.'

His expression was priceless. 'T-To pleasure,' he stammered, taking far too generous a gulp of his champagne. I waited until his choking coughs had subsided, watching as he pulled out his handkerchief to cover his mouth and pat away his spittle. He might be a heartless bastard and gauche when it came to women, but he had impeccable manners. All of which would come in handy.

'We have an even finer collection of paintings upstairs,' I purred. 'I chose many of them myself.'

A total lie, but it served my persona as well as my purpose.

He pocketed his handkerchief. 'You did?'

'Don't look so surprised.'

'I'm not. I can imagine you would have fine taste in art.'

'I have fine taste in many things.'

I let that dangle in the air between us.

'Perhaps you'd be gracious enough to let me see your collection sometime.'

I bit back a laugh. This was almost too easy. 'I'd love to. How about now?'

'Now?'

'Yes. Unless you'd rather stay for another game of baccarat?'

'No, no. To be honest, I don't much care for cards.'

'Just art?'

'Art. And other things.'

A clumsy attempt at flirtation. This was going better and better.

'Other things?'

I watched the colour rise in his flaccid cheeks. If I hadn't known better, I would have assumed this man was a virgin. But I did know better. I also knew of his predilection for being tied up and whipped within an inch of his life, another thing that would come in handy.

'Well then,' I said, 'you can tell me about these other things while we peruse my paintings.'

Ten minutes for the pictures. Another twenty for chit-chat. He wouldn't know what had hit him, and I would get everything I wanted – including, I hoped, the names we needed to start tightening the net. Too many of our agents were dead or in custody. We had to find whoever was betraying them before the entire Paris network was destroyed. Schumann might just hold the key. If he didn't, I'd keep going until we'd plugged that leak with whatever it took. Otherwise, this could cost us the war. And there was no way on earth I was going to let that happen.

TWO

I watched the smoke curl across his body. Not quite a perfect ring. I puckered my lips and blew another. Perfect. From here, he appeared dead, although I knew he was just unconscious. At least, I hoped he was. He sighed, a soft rasp that stirred the sheet half-covering him. Alive. Good. At least for now.

Another sigh echoed across the years. More of a death rasp. My stepfather lying in the gutter, his lips parted as bubbles of blood escaped them, foaming at the corners of his mouth, meeting and melding into the spittle that had gathered there as he made a last, desperate lunge for me.

Crack.

The pan coming down on his head again. He never saw it coming. Never thought I might have had the presence of mind to grab it when I ran from the house. It was a heavy bastard, that pan, slowing me down as I staggered towards the alleyway. Cast iron, if I remembered right. Of course I remembered right. I'd never forget the look on his face as he died. It still made me grimace.

I was smiling grimly as I stubbed out my cigarette, snapping back to the present. A good memory, but it was time to leave.

Schumann was well and truly under, in more ways than one. I'd reeled him in slowly, as I always did, extracting what we needed.

I glanced at the piece of paper on the cabinet beside the bed, where I'd noted down the scraps of information he'd already given me. Not a lot but, with any luck, there'd be more to come. In the meantime, he'd wake in a few hours with a fuzzy head and no more, wondering what exactly had happened. Whatever it was, they never guessed what I was really up to. After all, how on earth could the woman who made them feel like the greatest lover on earth have done anything nefarious?

Easily.

Too easily.

Sometimes I wondered if ice had formed around my heart, or if it was simply a shell. That girl in the alleyway, she'd had a soft underbelly. But my stepdad had made sure that hardened, so I shrunk from life, from love, from anything that could ever get through my shell, retreating behind the carapace that was the platinum-blonde hair, the lipsticked smile, the Christine persona.

Chrissie. That was what my mum had called me. Him too. Hissing it in my ear. No one ever called me Chrissie again after that. Not since Tom gave me a hug and shoved a few bob into my hand.

'Take it, sis.'

'It's all you've got,' I'd protested.

'You need it more than me.'

He was right. One final hug and then the train door had slammed shut. I'd pulled down the window and stuck my head out, seeing him and the platform at Victoria recede as we chugged towards Dover and Paris beyond. They said war was coming. And they were right. But everything I learned in Paris equipped me for what I was doing now. If I'd never come here,

I'd never have met Suzanne. I wouldn't be who I was or what I'd become.

I threw on a robe and perched in front of the dressing mirror, smoothing my hair down, reapplying my lipstick then parting my lips to make sure there was none on my teeth. Then I looked in my own eyes. They glittered, some said like emeralds.

'Wankers,' I said aloud. 'They're all wankers.'

The woman in the mirror stared back at me. A face full of secrets, my eyes dark with them. Not so much emeralds as glass, bottling up all that lay behind them. The loneliness. The pain. The anger that still simmered. Maybe that was what drove me. Who knew? I liked to think it was patriotism too. Or perhaps just a need to make sure that no other innocents ever suffered in the way I had. It was why I targeted men like him, the brute lying in the bed, his mouth hanging open, slack. As slack as his morals, never mind his soul.

I scooped my clothes up from the floor and left him to it without so much as an *au revoir*.

Outside, in the corridor, Suzanne was waiting.

'Everything alright?'

'As good as it can be.'

The look that passed between us said it all. I reached into the pocket of my robe, curling my fingers around the scrap of paper. I'd scrutinise the notes I'd made later, although he hadn't given us much. What we really needed were the high-ranking members of the Abwehr and the Gestapo, the ones responsible for making decisions, not recruits like Schumann. But they didn't frequent our establishment. Too canny. Or maybe too busy casting their evil nets.

Right now, I needed a bath so I could scrub myself from head to toe. Another ritual I liked to follow. It made me feel just that bit cleaner although, truth be told, I would never feel clean again. Sullied. That's what I was, even though they always passed out before anything really happened. But still, their very presence disgusted me.

No, Christine. Remember who you are. What you do.

I tilted my chin a fraction higher. I might not be pristine, but I was doing my damnedest for the war effort and that meant something.

I could feel their eyes on me as I strode once more through the club in a fresh outfit, cleansed as much as I ever could be, automatically swaying my hips, falling into the strut that always got their attention. Let them stare. I was proud of who I was and what I did. I didn't need anyone. I was me, Christine, not that girl from the East End. Chrissie. She was dead, at least in my heart. The heart encased in its shell. Too right. Nothing and no one was ever going to hurt me again.

THREE

It was pitch-black in the field, the moon obscured by a thick layer of cloud.

'How long until the drop?'

Jacques peered at his watch. 'Ten minutes, provided they make it on time.'

All I could hear was our breathing, synchronised now as we waited, straining for the sound of the plane approaching. Funny how that happened, two people who hardly knew each other inhaling and exhaling as one. The night air seeped through my jacket, chilling me to the core as we crouched, hidden among the trees that bordered the airfield. Autumn was giving way to winter. I hoped the incoming agents were well wrapped up against the cold.

'When I say, flash your torch to spell out the letter "N",' Jacques murmured in my ear. 'If the pilot responds with the same letter, I'll turn mine on too to guide him in.'

'And if he doesn't respond with the same letter?'

'We abort.'

'Got it.'

He pointed to our left where I could just about make out the swathe of flat grass that served as a drop zone. God knows how these pilots managed to fly low enough so that the agents could land safely, under the German radar.

It helped when there was a well-trained reception committee rather than just the two of us. At least Jacques knew the score. I'd never done this before and it showed, but needs must. There was no one else now that his network was all but destroyed; Suzanne and I operated very much on our own, outside of it. No wonder he needed new agents. I could only hope they'd survive longer than the last lot. The Germans seemed to have an uncanny knack of tracking them down – although none of us were under any illusion that was due to luck. Despite all my efforts, we were still no nearer to finding out how.

I unfurled the fingers digging into my palms. *Patience, Christine.*

I thought I could hear something now – the distant whine of a plane perhaps. Beside me, Jacques was as still as a dog scenting the air, head cocked to one side, eyes darting as he tried to pinpoint where it was coming from.

Then the clouds parted. In the sky to our right, I could make out the grey shape of a plane silhouetted against the full moon, coming closer, its landing light flashing in response to mine. Dash. Dot. The letter 'N'.

Jacques's torch began to blaze now too, and I held mine steady, guiding the plane in. As it flew lower, three shapes dropped from it, drifting down, their parachutes open, two landing diagonally opposite to where we were hiding, the third in the field beyond.

At almost the exact moment they touched the ground, lights blared from the opposite side of the field, far brighter than our torches, a row of them glaring at us as they swept forward like the eyes of a predator in the dark, then flashes of tracer fire from anti-aircraft guns. *Shit.* The blasted Boches. Had they followed us?

I stared at their jeeps racing towards the spot where two of the agents had landed while I could see the tail lights of another heading across the next field.

'Run,' Jacques snarled in my ear.

I already had my gun in my hand, raising it to take a shot.

'Don't be stupid. We're completely outnumbered. They'll just take us down as well.'

He was right. They were on the two agents now, machine guns pointing at them, the lights from their jeeps illuminating the entire scene in ghastly detail. Doubtless they would catch the third too, although there was still a chance he or she had got away. A chance I was willing to take.

'Stop.'

Too late. I wriggled out of Jacques's grasp and was running at a crouch through the trees, working my way round to the side bordering the next field. Ahead of me, across the hedge, I could see torches sweeping from side to side. Good. That meant they were still searching.

I pressed myself against a tree trunk, doing my best to blend into it, all the while trying to get eyes on the missing agent. Then I froze, the hairs on the back of my neck rising as one, a sick, crawling feeling clutching my scalp. Behind me, I could hear someone breathing, so close I could practically feel it.

I shut my eyes as if that would somehow render me invisible. *Idiot. You're not a kid, Christine.* I forced them open, turning at the same time, gun once more raised, finger on the trigger.

'It's me,' hissed Jacques.

I wrenched my finger off the trigger just in time.

'For fuck's sake. I nearly shot you.'

'I wish I'd shot you.'

'Nice.'

We faced each other down in the darkness, breath coming in short pants. 'Come on,' I whispered. 'We can get through this way.'

I dropped to my belly and crawled across the ground to the gap in the hedge I'd spotted. If he followed me, great. If not, I'd still have a go.

I could hear him behind me, rustling his way through, rising to his haunches beside me as we side-shuffled to the tree cover this side, backs to the hedge, weapons at the ready. Luckily, the Germans in this field were busy searching the end furthest from us. Behind us, I could hear vehicles starting up, engines roaring as they sped off with their prize cargo. Two more agents down, damn it. Two agents who were supposed to replace the ones we'd already lost. And now just one stood between the Nazis and a full house. I wanted to roar in rage. Instead, I concentrated on the woods and the undergrowth, treading as softly as I could while my gaze raked both.

Nothing. Not a peep. Where the hell could the other agent be? Surely they hadn't got through the woods and to the other side already. God, I hoped so. I really hoped so. Maybe this time luck would be on our side. On their side, whoever they were.

At that moment, a figure burst from the trees not fifty yards ahead of me and sprinted across the field, making for the road beyond. By the size and shape of her, I could see it was a woman. A small woman at that.

No, no, I screamed in my head. *Not that way.*

She kept running, and for one glorious second I thought she might even make it. Then a yell as a German soldier spotted her, the shouts growing into a chorus, a pack of baying hounds as they began to charge after her, guns raised.

Run! Keep going.

I was digging my fingers into my palm, praying with all my might, my gun trained on the Germans as they kept coming.

More shouts and then a volley of gunfire, a guttural moan escaping my lips in tandem with their bullets, my knees sagging as she fell to hers and then forward, arms spread, jerking just once before she lay still.

FOUR

Jacques grabbed my arm. 'Come on.'

Now we were also running for our lives, sprinting in the opposite direction, back to where the truck sat hidden among the trees on the other side of the wood, the one I'd prayed she would head for instead of straight into the arms of the enemy.

Thank God it was still there, undisturbed, left unlocked for a quick getaway.

Jacques wrenched open the driver's door. 'Get in.'

I was still panting as he stuck the key in the ignition, pausing to listen out before he turned it and fired up the engine, reversing back to the road the way we'd come, lights off, driving as carefully as he could until we'd left the drop zone well behind us. It was only then that I allowed myself to sob, just the once – a raw, harsh gasp that tore at my throat, tearing out my heart with it.

'Those bastards shot her in cold blood.'

'*Nacht und Nebel*,' muttered Jacques.

Night and fog. Hitler's declaration that he wouldn't stick to the normal rules of war but execute enemy agents without mercy, ensuring they disappeared without trace.

She was still wearing her flying suit. Didn't even have time to unzip and bury it along with her parachute. They'd probably bury her in it, in a grave we'd never find, along with all the others they'd executed. She was an enemy agent carrying out an act of espionage on foreign soil. Soil the Germans considered now belonged to them, along with her life. I wanted to rip out my eyeballs, to unsee what I'd just seen. Instead, I stared out of the car window, numb and blind to the Paris suburbs flashing past as we re-entered the city.

Jacques dropped me several streets from my apartment. 'Go the long way round. Check that no one is following you.'

'What about you?'

A bleak smile. 'I'll be fine. I need to find out where they've taken the other two. Although I could make a good guess.'

To 84 Avenue Foch of course. The Sicherheitsdienst headquarters where the Gestapo were based. As the intelligence arm of the SS, the SD claimed first rights to captured agents and *résistants*. They took them there before depositing them in Fresnes Prison, tortured to within an inch of their lives and sometimes beyond that. Almost the entire Paris network was now in Fresnes, a concentration camp or dead, along with a sizeable number of their Resistance contacts. It was why I'd gone with Jacques tonight. There was no one else left to do it.

My hands were still shaking as I inserted my key in the lock and opened the door of my fourth-floor apartment, sweeping the place thoroughly before I was satisfied it was safe.

Through the balcony windows, I could see the streets of Montparnasse below, lights twinkling from restaurants and bars, especially those favoured by the Germans.

Keeping my lights off, I stepped out onto the balcony, breathing in the cold, clear air, filling up my lungs with the sounds and smells of Paris, of what was the closest I now had to home. From here, sounds drifted up, bursts of laughter, a snatch of a song. How dare they laugh and carouse when agents were out there dying? My fingers itched for my pistol. I wanted to fire into the air, to scare them into silence, or, if they were German, to shoot them in the back just as they had her.

She'd looked like a deer as she ran. Or maybe a gazelle. Such a slight figure, graceful even when she was running for her life. I wondered who she was. Who she'd been. Whoever she was, I would never forget her, although I'd probably never know her real name. She was just one more agent, one of the many who'd already died for the cause. As I might die too, if my time came.

When my time came.

The odds weren't good but then, when had that ever stopped me? I was here now. Alive. Fighting the good fight. I'd keep on fighting too, for as long as it took or as long as I could. To win this war, yes. But right now, to find out how the hell the Germans were finding our agents every single time, almost before we knew they were there. It was a fight I intended to win, whatever the cost.

FIVE

'I have a special case for you.'

'Aren't they all special?'

I smiled at Suzanne and crossed my legs, swinging my foot and catching sight of my new shoes. Leather, thanks to our oh-so-generous clientele. Unlike the ugly wooden clogs most Parisians were now forced to wear. Maybe my next target should be the producers who ensured all the leather got sent to Germany, to make those jackboots that were trampling across Europe, the sound of them resonating through every street here.

Three and a half years since the Germans had marched into Paris and things were becoming more intolerable by the day. The bread queues were enormous, the people standing in them near-starving. If they were lucky, they got to barter or spend what little extra they had on the black market to boost their meagre rations while mountains of French produce were sent to Germany to feed the people there. As many a Parisian would mutter, '*Ils nous prennent tout.*' *They're taking everything we have.* Everything except the city's soul.

'I think you'll find this one is very special indeed.'

I stopped swinging my foot. There was a note in Suzanne's

voice that had caught my attention – a note I rarely heard. She only spoke like that when we were dealing with something so secret it demanded the utmost discretion.

'How so?'

She handed me a dossier, sitting back in her chair to give me time to read it. This office was our safe place, tucked away behind a storeroom door in the cellars of the townhouse that housed Le Chat Noir, the club we operated as a front. The other one upstairs was the one the Nazis knew about, next to the salon where we entertained them every night. That one was furnished with a handsome desk and Louis XV chairs offsetting the stern portraits of the French aristocrats who'd once owned this house, gazing down at the debauched antics of the invaders.

Here, the desk was more workmanlike, papers spread out on it when necessary but otherwise locked away in the concealed safe along with the other files. All the intelligence we'd gathered and shared encoded with London. Names, places, dates. All except the names we needed. The ones we were still trying to hunt down. It was one of the reasons Suzanne and I worked alone, leaving the tasks of sabotage and subversion to the Paris network. Or what remained of it. Whatever was in this file wouldn't go beyond these walls. Secrets were currency when it came to the Germans, and neither of us intended to pay the ultimate price.

There was a photograph on the first page of the dossier. A handsome man. American uniform. American teeth, come to that. Clean-cut, the requisite strong jawline lending strength to what was otherwise a sensitive face, the quirk of his mouth hinting at an irreverent nature. But it was his eyes that arrested me. They had a spark in them of something I recognised. Something I saw in the mirror every day. This was a man who nurtured secrets too, who'd suffered in a way that had marked him. Of course, you could say that about everyone caught up in this ghastly war, but still...

Beneath the photograph, his name, neatly typed: Charles Russell III. A Harvard graduate no less. Now a first lieutenant with the Office of Strategic Services.

I looked up at Suzanne. 'What do we want from him?'

'Everything.'

I flicked the pages. An impeccable record. 'There doesn't seem to be much here.'

'That's the point. They're lining him up for an important mission. Perhaps the most important so far. One which the OSS is carrying out with London's blessing. All he has to do is pass the final test and it's his.'

'And the final test is...?'

'You.'

Of course it was. That was my job after all. Or it used to be.

'I thought I was done testing agents?'

'You are, but as I said, this is a special case. And the mission is urgent.'

'Does this have anything to do with our little problem with the Paris network?'

She nodded.

'In that case, I'll do it. When are we on?'

'You'll be introduced to him over lunch tomorrow. We have a table reserved at La Rotonde for you and Marcel. The American is already undercover and working his story so just smile and nod at whatever he says.'

La Rotonde was one of our safe havens, run by staunch supporters of the Resistance. Marcel was our fisherman, baiting the hook with me. The fish were usually the Nazis and their collaborators in the joints they favoured, such as Maxim's. It would make a welcome change to deal with one of our own, and an American at that. Especially one that looked like this.

I studied the photograph, feeling it again. A tug. Almost as if I recognised him. Except I didn't. I never forgot a face, and I was certain I'd never seen this man before. And yet it felt as if I knew him.

Ridiculous. *Focus on the job, Christine.*

'How fast do you want me to move?'

'Fast. You know how urgent this is.'

I glanced at his picture again. 'I know, but I'm not sure I can rush this one. He looks like a tough nut to crack. I can see it in his eyes. This is a man who doesn't give anything away. And he's American. I've never tested one before. I'm not sure how he'll react.'

Suzanne arched an eyebrow. 'I'm sure he'll react like any other man to your charms, possibly with even more enthusiasm.'

'That kind of enthusiasm is precisely what we don't want.'

'Indeed. Hopefully, he'll show restraint. He is OSS after all. Not some GI.'

'Spies can be the worst.'

'Do your best.'

'Don't I always?'

I snapped the dossier shut and tucked it into my handbag.

'Christine...'

'Yes?'

'Are you alright?'

'Never better.'

'It's just you seem... distracted.'

'I'm fine. Really. Now I must be going. I have homework to do.'

Very attractive homework. But it wasn't his good looks that disturbed me. It was that essence of something else. Something I knew all too well. My job was to get to know this man as intimately as I could, to ferret out his secrets, but for the first time ever, I could feel my stomach shrinking at the prospect. I wasn't sure I wanted to know. Or perhaps I did – far too much.

SIX

I felt rather than saw them enter the dining room, a waft of Marcel's cologne drifting across to me as they passed by my table, deliberately close.

I glanced up and feigned surprise. 'Marcel! How lovely to see you.'

'I could say the same for you. It's been far too long.'

He bent and dropped two kisses on each of my cheeks, Parisian style, before straightening as if he remembered the man beside him.

'Christine, may I introduce my good friend Charles Ryan?'

Ryan. So that was his cover name. Charles Russell III had a new role, and he was playing it with panache, the picture of a European businessman in a double-breasted suit with a continental cut. I half-smiled and inclined my head. *Don't give him too much.* '*Enchanté.*'

His smile was more generous, his French impeccable as he replied, 'The pleasure is all mine.'

Of course it was. It always was. I hated what I did and loved it in equal measure, but at least we got results.

Marcel waved at the table he'd reserved, a couple away from mine. 'Why don't you join us? Can't have you eating lunch on your own.'

'Oh, I wouldn't want to disturb you. It looks as if you gentlemen have important things to discuss.'

'Not at all. I've simply been asked to help Charles get to know Paris. Show him around. Introduce him to people. And who better than you, my dear? After all, you know absolutely everybody worth knowing.'

Marcel's face was as open as ever, his charm deployed with such skill it disarmed everyone. He was the epitome of the convivial host and friend. He was also one of our deadliest weapons in the fight against the Nazis, as well as one of the few survivors of the network that had recently been broken wide open. Marcel was almost the last man standing, and only because he was so smart. The Nazis trusted him implicitly, believing he was one of their own. By eating here with Charles in full view of anyone who might be watching, he was sending a message that they should trust him too.

'Well, in that case, I would be delighted to join you.'

Marcel signalled to the waiter, who'd already been primed, as ever. The staff of La Rotonde did what they could to help, including turning a blind eye to meetings like this and alerting us to any infiltrators or spies. Luckily for us all, the Nazis didn't favour the place. It was no doubt too bohemian for their tastes.

A waiter whisked away my glass of wine and placed it on their table, holding out a chair for me. As I sank into it, I glanced at Charles. His gaze was frank, penetrating and focused directly on me.

'Have you been to Paris before, Monsieur Ryan?'

'No, ma'am. Just London and Madrid on business. And please – it's Charles.'

'Business?'

That part was probably true. I already knew that his family owned several newspapers in the US, thanks to the stepfather his mother had married when Charles was ten. Lucky him. No doubt Charles was being trained up to inherit them. All I'd inherited was guilt.

I also knew that was a lie about Paris. His dossier recorded three previous visits, one only a month ago. Well, good for him. What else was he going to try to keep from me? He was an only child, the son and heir, the stepfather having no natural children. Charles could have used that as an excuse to stay away from the front line, but he'd joined up the moment the US entered the war. That either made him brave or stupid. I was about to find out which.

He studied me for a moment, a quizzical smile on his face, before answering my question. 'Yes.'

I almost applauded. A man of few words. I liked that. So far, he was passing the test. But it was early days. We'd see how he got on when the pressure was really applied.

'Christine is a journalist,' said Marcel. 'I understand you have some connection with newspapers, Charles?'

He nodded. 'I do, through my family.'

Better and better. Just enough truth, but not too much. I hid a smile as I took a sip of my wine.

The waiter was hovering, waiting to take our orders. Now for the second act.

Right on cue, the maître d' appeared and addressed Marcel. '*Monsieur*, there is a telephone call for you. I understand the matter is urgent.'

'Would you excuse me?'

Unruffled as ever, Marcel followed the maître d' out into the reception area, leaving me alone with Charles.

I flicked him a look from under my lashes as I leaned forward. That look. The one Madame Joey had taught me.

'*Mais, vous parlez français, Charles. Couramment. Comment ça ce fait?*' I murmured.

He returned my gaze, a barely detectible smile tugging at the corners of his mouth as he, too, leaned across the table, our heads so close they almost touched, keeping his voice low. Anyone watching would think we were already lovers. Anyone trying to listen in wouldn't catch a word. 'I do speak French, yes. Very astute of you. I learned it at school.'

He thought I was French. Good.

'Except that it's not really your language, is it?' he whispered.

Bad. He was better than I thought. Only a native or an expert would know that there was something additional in my voice, an underlay from London. I thought the years spent in Paris learning my trade, if you could call it that, had buried all traces of the East End. Obviously not.

I glanced up to make doubly sure no one was close enough to hear anything. The table nearest us was empty. Still, I kept my voice low. 'I'm British, although I've lived in Paris for a while now.'

No need to mention the time I'd spent back in England honing my craft. The craft that complemented the one I'd learned here.

He sat back a fraction and took a sip from his glass. 'What brought you here?'

'I came here to study.'

'I see.'

His eyes were grey, a darker ring around the edge offsetting the colour even as it changed, his pupils dilating as he held my gaze. Not fair. This was my role. He was my mark, not the other way round.

'Fashion. I came here to study fashion.'

For God's sake, Christine, you're babbling. Get a hold of yourself.

'And you wear it so well.'

That was a definite glint now as his eyes travelled down my dress, taking in the décolletage, the fitted bodice, lingering there. I was grateful the rest was hidden under the table.

'My apologies.'

Marcel reappeared at just the right moment, apparently flustered.

'Is everything alright?'

He shrugged in that Gallic way that no one could learn, not even me. You had to be born with it. 'I am so sorry, but I must go. My wife needs me. But please, you stay and get acquainted. Lunch is on me.'

Perfectly played.

I creased my forehead in concern. 'Is there anything I can do to help?'

'No, no. It's a personal matter. Now please, enjoy. Order whatever you wish. It's the least I can do.'

And then he was hurrying out, the picture of a harried husband which was even more impressive considering Marcel had no wife. He was a homosexual with a longstanding lover of many years, a fact he kept well hidden from the Nazis. It served him well, though, when visiting the *pissotières*, the street urinals where men conducted their illicit assignations, and where the Resistance met too, to pass on vital information. It also meant there was never any tension between us. I could be myself with Marcel, as I could with Suzanne, and he knew it. He also knew I would pick up the reins and get to work on Charles. Although I had a sneaky feeling Charles was about to do the same to me.

I waited a beat and then gave him a knowing smile. 'I expect his wife has found out about one of his dalliances again.'

'I thought Parisians were sophisticated about that kind of thing?'

'It depends on what you mean by sophisticated. No one

likes to be publicly humiliated, and Marcel isn't exactly discreet.'

This time, Charles shifted forward in his seat, taking my hand in his and caressing it with his thumb while he murmured in my ear, his breath tickling the back of my neck. To the casual observer, it looked as if we were about to take this assignation a stage further. Which, of course, we were. 'Really? I would have thought he was the soul of discretion. I would also bet my life he's not that interested in women.'

Jesus. This man was something else. I feigned indifference, removing my hand from his and cupping it under my chin. 'Who really knows anyone? Now tell me about you.'

The easy smile was still in place. I'd hate to play him at poker. Actually, I'd hate to play him full stop. I had a feeling he'd be a fearsome opponent.

'What do you want to know?'

'What really brings you here?'

'The same thing that brings all of us. War work.'

Another good answer. They'd trained him well. 'You can't tell me any more than that?'

'You know I can't, beautiful as you undoubtedly are.'

All at once, I was back there in that alleyway, trapped. Only this time it wasn't by a vicious, sweating stepfather but by the cool, intelligent gaze of this American officer, pinning me down. And I had absolutely no idea what he wanted.

'Thank you. For the compliment.'

'You're welcome.'

This was some dance we were involved in, and I had no idea of the next step. What on earth was happening to me? *Come on, Christine. He's just a man. Just another man.*

I looked him straight in those eyes of his, answering the question in them with one of my own. 'You know what? I'm not really hungry.'

'Me neither.'

'A coffee perhaps? Or a drink?'

He crumpled his napkin and dropped it on the table.

'Let's get out of here.'

I smiled. 'Let's do that.'

SEVEN

'Can I get you a drink?'

I rose from the sofa and undulated over to the drinks trolley. He turned from where he was standing in front of my bookshelves, apparently more interested in them than in me.

'Thank you. Do you have any whisky?'

I uncorked a fifteen-year-old single malt and poured him a generous double, conscious he was watching me like a hawk. No chance to slip anything into it then. Not that I intended to. Just straight alcohol for our test cases. Far better to assess them when they were fully in charge of their faculties, as they should be in the field. Although extra marks to him for suspecting I might.

'Water?'

'Thanks, but I take it neat.'

'Of course you do. Why don't you sit down?'

I kicked off my shoes and pulled my stockinged legs beneath me as I curled up alongside him on the sofa, a fraction closer this time, nursing my own drink.

'Do you read a lot?' I asked.

'When I have the time.'

'You don't have time now?'

'Who does? There's a war on.'

Polite but guarded. Just as I expected.

He looked around the room. 'Nice place you have here.'

'Thank you.'

'Are those your ancestors?'

He was studying the portraits on the wall now, one of a man with a contemptuous little smile that annoyed me whenever I looked at it, the other of a woman who annoyed me equally with her simper.

'They came with the apartment.'

'I didn't really think you were related.'

I borrowed some of portrait man's hauteur to stare at him. 'How so?'

'You have a sense of mischief. They most definitely don't. And you didn't really come here to study, did you?'

A moue of surprise as I played for time. He changed gears fast. 'But of course I did. I attended the Sorbonne.'

My legend was watertight, in spite of my earlier stumble.

'I didn't know they taught fashion at the Sorbonne.'

Sharp too.

'I studied literature there and fashion by simply walking the streets, absorbing the style. The women here have such style, don't you think? The men too.'

'So I see.'

His eyes wouldn't let go of mine as he swilled the amber liquid around in its tumbler.

'And you? Where did you go to school?'

I held back on touching him again. This was one difficult fish to land. Best play him out on his line, letting him think he had the upper hand, before reeling him in.

'Harvard, and then Dartmouth.'

Full marks again for sticking close to the truth. So far, so predictable.

'Was that where you really learned to speak French?'

He laughed. '*Touché*. I learned here, in the south of France. My mother moved to Nice after my parents divorced.'

'I'm sorry.'

'Don't be. They fought like cat and dog. It was a relief when my dad went off with his latest mistress. Of course, he soon replaced her with another one. *Plus ça change*, as they say.'

'They do. So you grew up in Nice? Any brothers or sisters?'

He shook his head. 'Nope. Although I now have two half-brothers. My dad married again, two more times. He's a writer, you see. Thinks everything is research.'

'Even marriage?'

'Especially that.'

'What about you? Are you married?'

He laughed, more heartily this time. 'Hell no. Not after what my dad put us through. Although my mom is now happily remarried, which makes me happy too.'

'You like your stepfather?'

'Very much. He's a kind, decent man who treats her well. He's more of a father to me than my own dad ever was or will be.'

If only my stepfather had been like that. But then, if he had, I wouldn't be sitting here with Charles. Loath though I was to admit it, I was enjoying his company, perhaps a little too much. I was here to do a job after all. It was important to remember that.

I leaned forward to place my glass on the occasional table, my blouse falling open a well-judged fraction.

'How do you know Marcel?' I asked.

Not too wide with the eyes. Just enough to invite confidence. Although I suspected this manoeuvre, too, would have little effect on him. Maybe he simply didn't find me attractive. Or perhaps he was one step ahead of me.

'I don't.' He took another sip of his whisky. 'My boss in

London asked him to show me around when I got here. Marcel kindly obliged. I met him for the first time today.'

'I guess it's a day of first meetings.'

I let the silence play out, watching the firelight flicker, throwing long shadows on the walls and the blackout blinds. I cast a sideways glance at him. He was staring into the embers, apparently lost in thought. 'Shall I put on another log?'

'Allow me.'

He rose, stirring the fire back into life before placing a couple more logs on it while I stared at his long legs, which moved with lupine grace. I rarely wanted them, my marks. Make that never. But this one stirred something in me that I scarcely remembered. He had an aloof dignity that set him apart, but there was more. A fire that burned as low as the one in the grate but threw out far more heat. I recognised in him what I knew in myself: an animal instinct for survival along with a primal allure.

Come on now, Christine. He's a target, nothing more.

He turned then, and I saw something in his expression that hadn't been there before. Something that glittered like ice on the pavement, hinting at danger even as it sparkled.

'Shall we?' he said, holding out his hand.

In spite of myself, I took it and let him pull me up, off the sofa and through the door to the room beyond, all the while wondering exactly who the target was here. So far, he'd passed all the tests; I had no doubt he would pass this next one too. I just wasn't so sure about me.

EIGHT

The bedroom door shut behind him. I stood by the foot of the bed, feeling an unfamiliar flutter in the pit of my stomach. Nerves. This man made me nervous. As if I was the one being tested. I sucked in my breath, standing taller, steadying myself.

'You're very beautiful,' he said, brushing the back of his hand down my cheek, leaving a trail of fire in its wake. 'Very beautiful and very dangerous.'

Pull yourself together, Christine. Remember, he's just flesh and blood like all the rest.

'You think?'

Unspoken questions stretched between us like a silken string, pulling tighter and tighter even as it glistened with promise.

'I do.'

His face was inches from mine. If I moved just a fraction, our lips would meet. I stayed where I was, waiting, a slow pulse beating in my belly, its rhythm telling me that something was off here. He wanted me too. I knew that much for certain. But there was something else. Something that held him back. Maybe he'd rumbled me. If so, good on him.

He leaned back, slackening the tension between us. His eyes were gentle, appreciative. The gleam of lust was gone.

'I must go now,' he said. 'Thank you for a lovely afternoon, Christine.'

I felt a lurch of disappointment. Fought to sound indifferent. 'Must you, Charles?'

'Yes. And hey, it's Charlie. All my friends call me that.'

'Charlie. Right. Well, that's too bad.'

'I know.'

Another small, regretful smile and then he leaned forward and kissed me on my forehead. I felt my heart twist into a tight, coiled knot before it plummeted in freefall. We weren't friends. Probably never would be. But oh, how I wished we were.

'Look after yourself,' he said.

'You too.'

The click of the door closing felt like a stab in the gut. I reached up without thinking and stroked that spot on my forehead with my fingertips. Had I dreamed it? No. That wrench inside me was all too real, along with the sickening sense of disappointment. I'd wanted him so badly. I could have sworn he felt the same. And not just his body. I wanted his mind. His heart. But then he'd turned and walked out the door as if it were nothing, as if he couldn't feel what had shimmered between us, the tangible longing that was so much more than lust.

Dear God. This wasn't in the manual. I wasn't supposed to fall for my targets, and yet I had, hard and fast. In an afternoon. Without him so much as laying a finger on me.

To be honest, that was probably why. The fact he hadn't fallen for it. And yet something deep inside told me that wasn't the reason. It was the inexplicable connection. An instant recognition. The one I knew, to my very bones, he felt too. The electricity that wasn't so much a spark as a current. One that was at once as old as time and irresistibly brand new, as if I was finally alive. Or had woken from a long sleep.

'Good luck,' I murmured to his departed shadow.

Something of him still lingered in the room, a faint masculine scent along with his energy.

I shook my head. Ridiculous. He was just another man. Except that he wasn't, and he never would be.

My fingers drifted to that spot on my forehead again, the exact place where he'd dropped a kiss. Perhaps we'd meet down the road. Perhaps. I wasn't even sure I wanted that. To feel that current burst into flames. We'd burn one another out.

I had no idea what lay ahead for him. He could even now be heading into the arms of the enemy. No good falling for someone I might never see again. It was best he remained a wonderful memory. A glimpse of what might have been.

Then again, I'd never done what was best for myself and I wasn't about to start now.

NINE

'He passed?'

'With flying colours.'

The coffee in front of her was cold; I could tell that without tasting it. Suzanne always let the coffee go cold, too busy thinking of other things. So was I today. Things like Charlie.

Forget him, Christine. The man was a mirage. A dream from the night before. One that could swiftly turn into a nightmare if I didn't get a grip of myself.

'Good.'

Suzanne leaned back a fraction in her chair. As if on cue, the telephone on her desk rang. The secure line. This must be important.

'*Allô?*'

She listened hard, saying nothing, nodding all the while.

'Thank you.'

She replaced the receiver with a decisive click before fixing me in her sights once more, her lips in a grim line. 'That was Marcel. They've got Jacques. The Gestapo arrested him at an apartment in the eleventh. Apparently he'd gone there to meet what he thought was a fellow operative.'

'Oh God, no. Not him too.'

Jacques. We'd been together on that failed op only a couple of weeks before. Such a brave man and a brilliant agent. He was always so careful. It didn't make sense.

Another thought struck me. He was also one of the very few who knew about us and our operation at Le Chat Noir. This wasn't looking good.

'I'm afraid so. From what I understand, the fellow operative was, in fact, a member of the Gestapo masquerading as an agent.'

Bastards. Yet another successful sting.

'Why did he go alone? What happened to the other chap who was working with him, the wireless operator who came from Limoges last week?'

'Apparently, they both had their suspicions about the meeting, so they tossed a coin for it. Jacques lost.'

He certainly did. He was no doubt even now being interrogated at Avenue Foch. That made over one hundred arrests since the summer, agents and their Resistance compatriots, all of them connected in some way to the Paris network. And still we had no idea who the hell was betraying us. Not a whisper from anyone who frequented our establishment, never mind the targets in my seductive sights.

'Christ but the Germans moved fast on this one. Do we know where the other chap is now?'

'He's disappeared, which is either very smart of him or highly suspicious.'

He could yet show up here asking for sanctuary. Or with a Gestapo detachment.

'Do you think Jacques will talk?'

We both knew what I meant.

'Who knows? In the meantime, we need to be extra vigilant. None of them have betrayed us so far, but he might be the one who cracks.'

The odds were shortening with each agent captured. Sooner or later, one of them would give us away to the Nazis. It was simply a matter of time. We were an integral part of the network and yet separate from it, operating our own intelligence-gathering mission. One that could be compromised at any moment.

'What's our next move?'

Suzanne flicked a glance at the phone. 'We'll know when that rings again.'

My pulse quickened. 'We're expecting another call?'

'Indeed we are.'

There was no point pushing her to say anything more. Suzanne operated strictly on a need-to-know basis, and evidently I didn't need to know. I swallowed my frustration and waited, allowing the silence to thicken between us. It was a tactic I used on my marks, trapping them with a chasm of silence so that they rushed to fill it, telling me all sorts of things they shouldn't. Worked every time. Except on Suzanne, who'd taught it to me, along with everything else I knew about tradecraft and the very special skills I also deployed.

It was me who broke the silence. 'Can we get Marcel to put out feelers to Avenue Foch? Find out if Jacques is actually there?'

Marcel had contacts everywhere, including the Gestapo headquarters at 84 Avenue Foch. There was a good chance they were already working Jacques over, which gave us forty-eight hours at most. It was also Suzanne who'd taught us the forty-eight-hour rule during interrogation training. I could hear her now, addressing the class back at Beaulieu. 'Forty-eight hours should give your fellow agents enough time to disperse and get to a safe place. Whatever happens, you must try to remain silent for that long, other than giving your field name and rank.'

A voice had piped up from the back of the class. 'What if we don't?'

'The quicker you talk, the quicker they'll transport you. Then you will die, along with your fellow agents. Never forget *Nacht und Nebel*.'

Two years on, I could still remember the face of that student at the back, a young woman with a pert expression and a ready smile. She always struck me as a jolly sort, if a little overconfident. Perhaps too confident. She disappeared six weeks after she was dropped into France, along with her radio set.

Six weeks was the average. Some were gone within days, especially if they were sent to join what remained of the network here in Paris. And still London kept sending them. I wondered if our warnings were even getting through. Not that we had any way of communicating directly with London now that Jacques's radio operator mate had vanished. The telephone line was strictly local, and even that was a risk. We were marooned, cut off until another operator appeared or we found some other way to reach them.

I pulled another cigarette from my packet and offered one to Suzanne, who shook her head.

'Suit yourself.'

I stuck mine between my lips and lit up, taking in a long drag that filled my mouth with the soothing taste of tobacco. I sucked on it hard, pulling it down into my lungs until I felt the ragged edges of my nerves soften.

'In any case, there's no point Marcel calling his contact,' said Suzanne. 'They've transferred him to Vichy. Kieffer has a new assistant.'

'Damn. Although it's really Kieffer we need to cultivate, if only we could. There has to be a way.'

Josef Kieffer, the local head of the SD or intelligence arm of the SS, in charge of hunting down and interrogating captured agents, reported directly to the head of the Gestapo with whom he worked hand in iron glove. Right now, he was one of our chief suspects, although we had nothing that directly tied him to any of the arrests. All we knew for certain was that there was some kind of op going on, one that was decimating our agents and their Resistance colleagues as well as putting our lives at risk. Kieffer might be one of the main cogs in the machine that was behind it, but we still had no idea who was feeding it. If we could just get close to him, we might yet uncover the truth.

'It's a shame Kieffer's not much of a partygoer.'

Suzanne smiled thinly. 'You never know. We may yet find him gracing our establishment. From what I hear, he's not averse to a drink. Even the head of the SD needs some R&R. This is Paris after all.'

She had a point. The Germans had shown such an appreciation for the charms of the city and its women that they'd appropriated twenty-two of the highest-class brothels for their own use, along with that of their French collaborators. Our establishment, Le Chat Noir, numbered among the chosen few, although ours was different, and it wasn't just because we were the only one with a nightclub and gaming room alongside the themed rooms most offered to cater for any predilection. While they were busy providing pleasure in all its many forms, we also gave sanctuary to any agents or downed airmen who needed it, along with the basement field office where we were sitting even now, waiting for the telephone to ring. Of course, the Nazis knew nothing about this.

As if reading my thoughts, the telephone suddenly sprang to life again, letting out one shrill note. Suzanne picked it up with her customary crisp '*Allô.*' I watched her face change as she listened, lips compressing tighter and tighter while the moments ticked past.

Finally, she spoke. Just five words before she replaced the receiver. 'We'll be there. Thank you.'

I looked at her, waiting, knowing from long experience that

it wasn't a good idea to start throwing questions at her when she had that look on her face. The look she directed at me now.

'What?'

'I didn't say anything.'

'Christine, you don't need to say anything. It's written right across your face. We're on.'

'For what?'

'A meeting. In half an hour at Le Dome.'

'With whom?'

'The Americans.'

'What have they got to do with anything?'

'I have no idea, but London wants us to meet with them just as they wanted you to test one. It makes me wonder what they're up to.'

'Me too.'

There was so much we didn't know, and yet we were expected to operate in the dark anyway, carrying on until ordered otherwise. It was sensible in one way as it meant we couldn't say too much if we were caught and tortured, like that poor bastard Jacques – and bloody stupid in the other as it kept us in not-so-blissful ignorance, forever improvising.

I looked down at my outfit, at the gown that clung to every curve, accentuating the décolletage that so mesmerised our clients they would forget themselves and whisper things that could get them shot. Or sent back to Germany to face the wrath of the Führer. It was a work outfit, but I needed a different kind of uniform for this meeting. Suzanne was, as ever, elegantly attired in a chic black dress that lent her the requisite authority to keep those same clients on their best behaviour.

'I'll go and change. See you by the front door in ten minutes.'

I could see the same fire in her eyes that must have been in mine. We were on. Part of a new op, whatever it turned out to be. For once, I could leave the overstuffed bordello behind and get my hands dirty in a different way. A way that might finally lead us to whoever had destroyed the network, taking our friends and fellow agents with it. The same person who might yet destroy us unless we got to them first.

TEN

There were two of them waiting for us at Le Dome, blending in well among the writers and artists who still looked on the café as a home from home even while German jackboots resounded around the city. I wouldn't have known they were American agents, dressed as they were in what looked to be French-cut jackets, their heads bent over their pastis.

The one facing us rose as a waiter led us to their table, dropping kisses on each of our cheeks.

'At your service, ma'am. My name is Jim,' he murmured in perfect French.

'Just Jim?'

'Just Jim.'

Suzanne regarded him coolly. 'I am Suzanne, and this is Christine.'

I duly received my kisses, turning to receive the same from his colleague.

I just managed to stifle a gasp. 'You.'

He smiled. 'Good to see you again too.'

It was him. Charlie. The man from my apartment. From my subsequent dreams, damn him. What the hell was he doing here? Stupid question. I already knew. He was part of it, and I'd been his final test. Well, I'd show him who was in charge around here.

While his colleague summoned the waiter, I stole a side-ways glance at him. His eyes met mine, and I looked away again but not before I caught his smirk.

Two could play at that game. I crossed my legs under the table, 'accidentally' brushing his thigh with mine as I did so, all the while looking serenely at Suzanne.

'I understand you've recently arrived from London,' she said, keeping her voice low so that only those of us at the table could hear. Not that it mattered as far as the waiters – all of whom were involved with the Resistance – were concerned, or the clientele, who were far too busy discussing their latest masterpiece to concern themselves with anything else.

'We have indeed. Just yesterday, in fact.'

Yesterday. If that was true, then I'd been Charlie's first call. Second, if you counted Marcel. Interesting.

Jim's voice was easy, his manner less so. He reminded me of a dog my stepfather had brought home, a sweet-natured spaniel who soon became highly strung in his presence, her eyes constantly darting around the room, on red alert in case he entered. In contrast to his colleague, Charlie appeared completely relaxed. It made me want to shake him. How dare he be so laid-back in my presence after what had passed between us?

Never mind that nothing had actually happened. He must have felt it as much as I did. That invisible spark, the electricity that fizzed. Surely he sensed it too?

I slid him another look. Apparently not. Well, we'd see about that. They all succumbed, sooner or later. Yes, even Charlie. Not that I was sure I even wanted to seduce him. Maybe, for once, I wanted him to come after me.

I felt his hand brush my thigh then, a featherlight stroke that sent shockwaves running through me. The arrogance. I reached for my drink, acting as if nothing had happened but knowing that everything had irrevocably changed.

'We were in London for a few months before we came here,' he said, aiming his disarming smile at Suzanne.

Had I imagined his touch on my thigh? Maybe. Wishful thinking? *Oh come on, girl. You know better than that.*

'Did you like London?' I asked.

'Not as much as I think I'm going to like Paris.'

His voice was deadpan, his eyes less so. Incorrigible or irresistible? I couldn't decide.

Jim glanced at him. 'I think it's time we levelled with you.'

'I think it is,' I replied.

ELEVEN

Suzanne was weighing them both up. I was pretty sure neither passed muster.

Jim's expression was so earnest I was reminded of that spaniel again. 'As you know, London just signed off on us working together.'

'Us?'

He drew three letters on the table with his finger – O, S, S.

I didn't, but suddenly I was all ears. Us working with the OSS? It was a new one on me.

'I'd heard they were about to,' said Suzanne. 'You're saying this is now official?'

The hum of chatter in the room seemed to fade as she stared him down, not so much cool now as glacial.

'Absolutely. If you wish to confirm that with your people, please go right ahead.'

Now I could see exactly why he was the right man for the job. We could have been discussing plans for a picnic for all any observer would know. The OSS had the unfortunate nickname of 'Oh So Social' on account of the society types it liked to recruit. Jim appeared to be a little less polished than the others

I'd come across, but I was beginning to suspect that slight air of gaucheness was his secret weapon. As for Charlie, he was a different kettle of fish altogether. A fish I was no longer sure I wanted to land now that it appeared we'd be working together.

Suzanne's face softened a fraction. 'That won't be necessary. You come with the highest recommendation.'

'Glad to hear it. Especially as what we have to discuss with you is, as you might say, a delicate matter.'

In other words, top secret. 'Delicate?' I asked.

Jim looked at me. I noticed a slight sheen of sweat on his brow. The room was warm, packed as it was with the chattering throng and blasted with heat by the stove against the winter chill. That sweat was a tell. Either he was the sweaty sort or he was apprehensive about our reaction to what he was about to say. My money was on the latter.

'Don't worry, we're not going to double-cross you,' drawled Charlie, dropping us a wink.

Now I was seriously intrigued. Double-Cross – the codename for the double-agent ops being run out of London by the Secret Intelligence Service, aka MI6.

Suzanne glanced at him, poker-faced. 'I should hope not.'

'Look, I'll cut to the chase,' said Jim, wriggling in his seat. Another tell. Either they'd sent the most socially awkward agent on earth or this, too, was all part of his disarming act. I'd seen so many of them do it, stumbling around until they swooped in for the kill. They probably taught them that before they sent them over to pair up with a smoother partner like good old Charlie here.

'We're as concerned as you are by what's happened to the Paris network, especially with this latest arrest.'

The affable mask had slipped at last. No more pretence at chit-chat. Jim's voice was still low, but there was a new authority to it. This was a man who was used to issuing orders and having them obeyed. 'It's got to the point that an operation we're working on may be compromised by the destruction of your network. Which is why we've come up with a plan.'

Never mind the agents and *résistants* who'd been arrested or disappeared. Their precious operation was obviously far more important.

'What operation would that be?'

'Operation Bodyguard.'

The operation designed to deceive the Germans with disinformation about the Allied invasion. And that was about all we knew because they used their double agents to do most of the dirty work.

'So you value the Double-Cross agents more highly than those here in Paris?' I asked, my voice deceptively soft.

'Not at all. We value all our agents, including you. Which is why we want to carry out a joint op so that we can get to the bottom of what's going on and who the heck is betraying the Paris network.'

I couldn't help but snort at his words. 'You don't think we've tried?'

'I know you have, but so far you've come up with nothing. And now things have become, shall we say, a little more complicated.'

Suzanne's shoulders stiffened so imperceptibly that no one else would have noticed. 'How so?'

'We know that the Germans seized radio equipment when they arrested the last radio operator.'

'They arrested him?'

My eyes met Suzanne's. So they'd got him too.

'Yesterday.'

'How do you know?'

'We received a message from the MI6 station chief here in Paris.'

'I see.'

'We think they also got hold of that agent's codes and crystals. That means—'

I cut across him. 'They can send messages pretending to be from the network.'

'Precisely.'

Suzanne narrowed her eyes. 'Are you certain of that?'

'No. But we suspect it, as do some of your friends in London.'

'You know our friends in London?'

Charlie cut in. 'They helped train us. Or at least, those of us in X-2. We're the new counter-intelligence division of the OSS. Now they want us to work with you. That's why they set me up with that final test from you. It seems I passed.'

His eyes flicked to me before sliding away again. I carried on staring at his left cheek, knowing he could feel my glare. So I was just a test to him. Nothing more. I'd imagined that frisson between us. Fine. If that was the way he wanted to play it, it would be strictly business from now on.

'If you suspect the Germans are using our radios, how is it our friends in London have done nothing about it?'

'Good question.'

'Indeed it is,' said Suzanne. 'Which is why I'm wondering what exactly you want us to do? I assume you have some kind of plan?'

'Yes, we do. As for your part in it, we'd like Christine here to go undercover.'

'There's a surprise,' I murmured. 'After all, undercover is my specialty.'

I could see from Jim's expression that my little joke had fallen flat. I could swear, though, I heard Charlie chuckle under his breath.

'Quite so. Actually, we prefer to think of this as deep cover. It's about as dangerous as it gets.'

TWELVE

'Let me get this straight,' said Suzanne. 'You'd like my agent to carry out a deep-cover joint op with one of yours?'

'With my friend here.'

'Right. And what exactly would this op involve?'

'I can answer that,' said Charlie. 'We've had some high-level and totally hush-hush meetings with the Abwehr. The upshot is, they want to run me as an agent. Or at least, it'll look that way. Their ultimate objective is to penetrate the Gestapo, which would help both us and them.'

'Why on earth would the Abwehr want to do that?'

'Simple. They're under threat. There've been too many whispers of betrayal, many of them coming from the Gestapo. They've been dubbed anti-Nazi and, more dangerously, anti-Hitler. All of which is true, but if the Gestapo manage to prove it, it could be the end of them. Literally.'

'I see. So what's the plan?'

'The head of the Abwehr, Admiral Canaris, is meeting the MI6 station chief here in three days' time. He wants to try to broker a peace deal so that we can end this war. Canaris now thinks Hitler is a lunatic, but unfortunately Hitler is on to him.

That's why he needs someone on the inside of the Gestapo, to find out what they're plotting.'

I looked at Charlie. 'I assume that someone is you.'

He nodded. 'My cover story is that I'm an Irishman here on business by the name of Charles Ryan. Ireland, as you know, is neutral so I can move around freely. I import and export materials both the Germans and the Allies desperately need, like copper and rubber. It means I can claim access to Allied military establishments with whom I supposedly do business.'

'And you have the complete legend set up for this?'

'Absolutely. You saw how Marcel introduced me to you. Every piece of paperwork the Nazis could possibly get hold of checks out. I'm also apparently a bit of a player and like to party with other well-connected folk here, most of them collaborators, along with diplomats and high-ranking officials. That's why the Abwehr recruited me. At least, on paper. Only I've grown a little tired of their ineptitude and worry about whether they're going to continue paying me, so I make it clear I'm willing to be recruited by the Gestapo. And then I recruit you, Christine, to work with me.'

I stared at him. 'You want me to spy for Germany?'

'We want you to pretend to spy for Germany while at the same time helping us infiltrate the Gestapo. That won't just enable us to get to the heart of what's really happening to the network; it will also be crucial in the run-up to the Allied invasion. In return, Canaris will give us all he knows to help us track down whoever's betraying our agents and ensure that our disinformation is passed on.'

'You're insane.'

Charlie beamed at me. 'Thank you.'

'It'll never work,' snapped Suzanne. 'Far too many of the Abwehr and Gestapo have already met Christine. Le Chat Noir is popular with both. They won't believe for one moment that she's suddenly spying for Germany.'

'That's exactly why they will believe it. She's an unlikely candidate. So far, they haven't figured out what you're really up to at Le Chat Noir. All they know is that she's great at what she does and can seduce just about anyone. It makes her all the more valuable in their eyes.'

I caught that 'just about'. And stored it away to use later. 'They might not suspect me, but the Gestapo are certainly going to be suspicious of an Irishman who's now working for the Abwehr. Especially when that Irishman doesn't even sound Irish.'

'Not when they find out that the Irishman has huge gambling debts, along with pro-Nazi beliefs. The accent is no problem. My story is that I attended American schools before returning to Dublin. And the fact I'm already working for the Abwehr will help reassure them.'

'How exactly are they going to find out about these debts and Nazi beliefs?'

'You're going to tell them.'

He seriously was insane.

'You want me to just drop in on the Gestapo and let them know there's an Irish businessman with a few personal problems and fascist leanings that might make perfect double-agent material?'

I could tell from Jim's face that sarcasm really didn't go down well with the Americans. 'We'd like you to spread a little indiscreet gossip when you're, shall we say, entertaining your Gestapo clients.'

I cocked my head to one side, studying him. All the fake affability had gone, replaced by a gimlet-eyed gravity. 'I don't know what you think I do when I'm, as you say, "entertaining" our clients, but I can assure you that this is war work, and it is every bit as serious as your own.'

He had the grace to look abashed. 'I apologise, ma'am. I didn't intend to insult you. I realise that what you do is not only serious but invaluable to us. That's why we're asking you to do this. We need to get the Gestapo to trust you enough that they give you access to the information we need. And if they won't give that access, I'm sure you'll figure out a way to get it. By all accounts, you're the best.'

I glanced at Charlie, who was gazing somewhere over my shoulder. 'I do what I can.'

Jim dropped his voice even lower, as if to underline the gravity of his words. 'Listen, we need you on board. We're about to pull the biggest double bluff this world has ever seen, never mind the Germans. We want to penetrate the Gestapo not just to find out what they're up to but to fill them with so much disinformation, Hitler's head will be spinning. But we also want to build a relationship with the Abwehr and especially Canaris.'

'Why the hell would we want to do that?'

He picked up the water carafe and refilled our glasses. 'Because they may be our best chance of getting rid of Hitler once and for all.'

THIRTEEN

'What the hell was he talking about back there?' I muttered, aware that even out here, in the street, anyone could be listening.

We were strolling arm in arm, two Parisian women apparently chatting about this and that. A couple of German soldiers glanced at us as we passed and then away again, satisfied we posed no threat.

Suzanne ignored them. We might as well have been talking about the weather. 'About the Abwehr being our best chance of getting rid of Hitler? It might just be true.'

She tugged at my arm, guiding me into the Jardin du Luxembourg. I could see the Luxembourg Palace in the distance, now occupied by German troops, but out here among the bare flower beds and fountains, we could talk more freely.

'Admiral Canaris has already tried to broker peace once,' she murmured, pausing as if to admire the view. 'He met earlier this year with the heads of the British and American intelligence services in Spain. He told them he'd helped orchestrate a plot to assassinate Hitler. That one failed, but apparently there's another in the works, should his attempt at brokering peace here also fail.'

An assassination plot. Canaris was either a brave man or a stupid one. 'Do you think the Gestapo are aware of this?'

'I hope not, for Canaris's sake. And ours. But the Americans were right. We need to penetrate the Gestapo if only to find out how they're identifying and tracking down our agents so fast.'

I could see the Nazi flags fluttering from the palace across the pond we stood by, the hated black swastika stark against the blood red. Not too far away was the Hotel Lutetia, which the Abwehr had requisitioned while the rest of the German invaders inhabited most of the other great hotels, their troops treating Paris as their personal playground. For most Parisians, however, there was no play. The gardens looked bleak in the November light, with only the odd figure visible in the distance, scurrying along the paths, keeping well away from the palace.

If I could somehow magic my way back to before the occupation, the park would have been busy with people flocking like winter birds, braving the chill to escape their apartments and entertain their children. Now, it echoed with the ghosts of happiness. Laughter was a scarce commodity these days for the ordinary citizen. Our new overlords had seen to that, although there was plenty of laughter in the five-star restaurants they frequented, gorging while the people starved, and in establishments such as ours.

'I'll do my best.'

Suzanne squeezed my arm. 'I know you will. I also want you to keep a close eye on our American friends. They might be on our side, but it pays to be careful. I'd like to know what they're up to as well.'

'Oh don't worry.' I smiled. 'I think I have the measure of Lieutenant Russell. It's going to be fun keeping one step ahead of him.'

'Just make sure it's not too much fun.'

A single rose adorned the shrub in front of us, blazing scarlet in defiance of the grey all around. I reached out to pluck it. 'Ouch.'

A drop of blood welled from where a thorn had stabbed through my flesh. I put my finger in my mouth and sucked it, almost enjoying the pain. Maybe I did need to be more careful. If I believed in omens, I might have thought twice about my mission, but I didn't believe in anything except serving my country and helping to end this war. Nothing else mattered. It hadn't since the day I'd left England, my heart shrivelled into a tight, cold ball.

I'd sworn that no one would ever hurt me again, and I'd kept my word to myself. I was impervious to love in all its forms. Alright, so I'd momentarily faltered when it came to Charlie, but never again, especially not now I was working with him. If anyone was going to draw first blood, it would be me.

I reached out and plucked the rose, this time avoiding the thorns and handing it to Suzanne.

'Do you know why we think of the red rose as a symbol of love? It's because of Adonis and Aphrodite. According to the myth, he was gored by a wild boar on a hunting trip and died in her arms, his blood staining the nearby white roses so they turned red.'

'I didn't know that. Or that you were a student of the classics.'

'You'd be surprised at what I know.'

'I'm sure I would. Now come on.' Suzanne tucked the rose into her buttonhole and linked her arm through mine once more. 'We have work to do.'

I thought of Adonis as we strolled from the park, of his blood spreading out to stain those petals. He died while Aphrodite lived.

Somewhere behind us, a crow cawed, sending an involuntary shiver through me. Crows. The harbingers of death.

Don't be ridiculous, Christine.

I could still hear its cries as we walked faster now, heading north, towards the Hotel Lutetia, the home of German military intelligence, also known as the Abwehr.

FOURTEEN

NOVEMBER 1938, PARIS, FRANCE

There was nobody to meet me off the train at the Gare du Nord. I waited for an hour then gave up. There was nothing for it but to tramp the nearby streets until I found a cheap hotel. A sleazy little man leered at me from behind the reception desk, his hair slicked down with something that looked suspiciously like engine grease.

The price he quoted was more than I could afford, but it was cheaper than the others I'd tried and my feet were killing me. I took the keys off him as smartly as I could, but he still managed to stroke my hand with his thumb as he handed them over.

The moment I got into the room, I scrubbed my palm with the hard little bar of soap left by the cracked basin until it felt close to clean. Then I shoved the chair under the door handle, jammed the key in the lock, ate the last of the sandwiches Tom had made for me and settled down for the night in a bed that seemed to be crawling with insects.

It felt as if I'd only been asleep for a few minutes when I was woken by the sound of the chair creaking as someone tried the door. I waited, holding my breath.

There it was again. I could see the handle moving.

I grabbed the lamp from the bedside table, pulling it from the wall, and tiptoed over, standing by the lintel, listening hard. I could have sworn I heard him breathing as he worked at the door, trying to push a key in, only to meet resistance from the key I'd jammed in the other side. I heard him mutter something then start to work at the lock with what sounded like a knife.

The lock was so flimsy it gave within a couple of minutes, but I was ready for him. As he came sneaking through, the chair crashed to the floor. He froze and I brought the lamp down on his head with all my strength. He dropped without a sound, landing face down on the floor.

It was that pig from behind the reception desk. Of course. His hair didn't look quite so spiffy when it was covered in blood. I could see he was still breathing. Another couple of blows would finish him off for good.

No, Chrissie. You're better than that.

I kicked him with my toe. He moaned but stayed down. Good enough.

I snapped my suitcase shut, picked it up and crept from the room, past the empty reception desk, out into the street, looking behind me just once. There was no one in sight.

I watched the dawn break over Paris from a bench by the River Seine, which snaked wide beneath me, its banks bordered by a low wall to which small boats were tied. Ahead of me, to my right, was a bridge, and behind that I could see the Eiffel Tower poking into the sky. As the sun rose higher, it glinted off the struts that bisected it. I remembered my mother showing me a picture of it in a book when I was still quite small, before she married my stepfather.

'That's the Eiffel Tower in Paris, Chrissie,' she'd told me, pointing to it. 'One day you'll go and see it.'

I remember gazing at the picture and thinking that I would never, ever see it. How could I when I lived in the East End of

London with its stinking streets and overriding pall of poverty? Even so, my mum had made sure we had books in the house. She'd always had books back home in Ireland, same as she always did the crossword every day, just as her mum had. My dad, by all accounts, loved her all the more for it, although he was a man of few words and even less ambition. My mum, though, she'd wanted the best for us. She always believed that I could fly away, far beyond Shadwell, as far as the bright lights and foreign accents of somewhere like Paris. She would whisper as much when she tucked me into bed at night.

'Remember, Chrissie, you can do anything you want. Anything. You can go and see the world. Live abroad. You don't have to settle for this.'

I could hear the regret in her voice, the unfulfilled wishes and broken dreams. I didn't know that's what they were then. All I knew was that my mum sounded so sad that I'd reach up my arms and pull her down for one last cuddle. She was a cuddler, my mum, all sweetness and warmth, bustling around our tiny house, singing to me and Tom until first my dad died and then my stepfather swiftly moved in.

From then on, she grew quieter and quieter, especially after she gave birth to my half-sister, Elsie, and my stepfather roared at her in rage because he wanted a boy. By then, our Tom had moved out so he had a free run. The son she gave birth to next was stillborn. The one after that died before my mum's belly even began to expand. That was when he began to belt her, swaying home from the pub to use her as a punchbag while I stood by helpless, covering my ears with my hands so I couldn't hear her screams.

Now he would never hurt her again. I took some small comfort in that. And I was here, in Paris, just as she'd said. I wished with all my heart I could tell her that, but there was no going back. It was best she forgot all about me.

Stupid. Of course she wouldn't. She wasn't that beaten

down. But it was better she thought I'd run off than that she knew the truth. She might have hated that bastard, but she never said so. I don't think my mum was capable of hate. But I was, and I hated him for her, wishing him dead so many times. I'd got that wish too. Maybe if I made another, that would also come true.

I could see the sun rising higher behind the Eiffel Tower, splashing streaks of gold and orange across the grey sky. I stared hard at that glowing orb, wishing with all my might.

From somewhere across the water, a bird started to sing. At the same time, I heard a splash from the waters beneath me. A fish perhaps. Or a frog. Even as the sun rose, I felt colder and colder. It was him, calling to me from the deep, telling me that my wish could never come true, not after what I'd done. People like me didn't deserve love. I could wish all I liked, but I was forever tainted, cursed to live without the love of a man now that I'd murdered one.

That was fine by me. In fact, it was better that way. Look what had happened to my mum. To so many women I'd seen growing up, old before their time thanks to slogging away looking after their kids, their home, their man... anyone but themselves. Well, I would look after myself. I had to. There was no one else to do it now.

I looked around me, at the empty boats bobbing on the water, at the bridge beyond where I could make out a solitary figure crossing, probably on their way to work. That was what I would do. I'd find a job. A place of my own. A new life. A better life than the one I'd left behind.

Another splash from the river. I watched the ripples spread across the surface. There was no going back now. What was done was done.

I stood up, spied a pebble by the bench and threw it into the water, smiling as ripples spread from that too. Whatever I did, I swore I'd make my own ripples. People would know me for something and I didn't care how I did it. I'd rather die young than get old before my time. And I'd rather live before I died.

I swung my suitcase as I marched into the rising sun. It was a new start. A new day. I was a new woman. The girl Chrissie was gone. In her place, someone who would never let anyone hurt her again. Someone called Christine.

FIFTEEN

NOVEMBER 1943, PARIS, FRANCE

The chapel was lit only by the candles that flickered in front of the statues of Christ and the Virgin. I kneeled in the pew, hands clasped, waiting. A nun rose from her prayers several pews in front of me and glided past, her eyes cast down until she drew level with me. As she did so, she whispered, 'The side chapel,' and then she was gone, a holy vision off to tend the sick in the convent hospital.

I looked around. The place was empty now, the silence enveloping me in a cloak of conspiracy. According to Charlie, Mother Superior allowed the Resistance network run by MI6 to use this as their Paris headquarters while hiding fugitives and Allied soldiers in the convent dispensary. With its high walls, the convent made an ideal refuge as well as a convenient nest for spies. It was thanks to his MI6 contacts that Charlie and I were here to witness this meeting. Except that he was late. Or perhaps I was early.

The candles guttered, catching my eye. A draught from somewhere. The door into the chapel stayed resolutely shut. It had to be from an inner door or the archway leading to this side chapel. God only knew what I would find in there.

I got up off my knees and approached the altar, taking in the vast crucifix hanging above it, the expression of Christ nailed to it, at once tortured and serene.

'I know how you feel,' I muttered as I sidled to the right, in the direction of the archway. What was it about churches that always made me feel like a sinner? Maybe it was the way they were designed, all shadows and whispers with the promise of salvation dangled in the form of a crucifix and a few candles. As if that would help.

He was there, in the side chapel, not kneeling but sitting in a pew contemplating the statue of the Madonna and Child in front of him. I paused in the threshold for a half-second, taking in the infinite tenderness with which she gazed down at the baby in her arms, a look of such pure love that I almost crossed myself. Almost. I could hear my mum's voice in my ear, her Irish lilt always more pronounced whenever we were in church.

'Get on your knees now, child. Pray to the Blessed Mother.'

No amount of prayer to the Blessed Mother had worked for her, so I guessed it wasn't going to work for me either. I crept as silently as I could up behind him.

'Hello, Lieutenant.'

He didn't give me the satisfaction of jumping. Instead, he turned and smiled as if he'd known I was there all along. 'Good to see you.'

'Is it?' I slid into the pew beside him, close enough but not too close. 'Praying for your sins?'

'Just the ones I'm about to commit.'

I wasn't sure how to take that. 'You only get absolution for the ones you confess.'

'Then I guess I'm screwed.' I must have looked mildly shocked because he added, 'If you'll pardon my French. I didn't take you for a good Catholic girl.'

'I'm not. I'm the worst Catholic you'll ever meet.'

He grinned. 'That makes two of us.'

'But here we are, still whispering when we're inside a church.'

His smile vanished, his eyes flicking to the archway. 'Walls have ears. Even these walls.'

Involuntarily, I looked over my shoulder although I knew there was no one there.

Turning back, I caught sight of the Madonna once more. Was it my imagination or was she gazing at me rather than at the Christ child? I blinked. Trick of the light. Her eyes were still cast down, eternally focused on her baby, the one who was supposed to save the world. A bit like us, pitted against the Germans, determined to win this war and save as many lives as we could, especially those of our agents. If I had to do that by infiltrating the Gestapo with Charlie here, then so be it, although I'd far rather have been working on my own.

'When is Admiral Canaris supposed to be here?' I muttered.

He glanced at his watch, a basic Swiss timepiece that blended with the rest of his outfit. 'Colonel Olivier, the MI6 station chief, should be here in a few minutes. Once he's in position, they're going to bring Canaris in blindfolded so he has no idea where he is, just in case it turns out to be a trap. He'll also have no idea that we're listening in. Insurance, if you like.'

I raised an eyebrow. 'Is this meant to convince me that Canaris is on our side?'

'That too.'

'I'll believe it when I see it. And hear it. I've witnessed too much of what the Germans can do to put my faith in any of them.'

He turned towards me so that he could look me full in the face. 'Canaris is different. He used to be a committed Nazi and even a fan of Hitler. Then he saw what was happening in Poland. He was an eyewitness when the SS locked two hundred Jews in a synagogue and set it on fire. He even saved seven Jews from a concentration camp by personally intervening with Himmler and then smuggling them out of Germany. He passes information to us and aids the Resistance. All of this because he now genuinely believes that his beloved Germany is in the hands of a madman.'

There was an intensity in his voice I hadn't heard before – one which resonated. 'It is.'

Our eyes held for a fraction of a second too long, then his slid away momentarily before he held his finger to his lips. From the main church beyond came the sound of footsteps moving closer as they proceeded up the aisle. Two sets. Both wearing hard shoes. Then a low murmuring and the creak of the pew as one of them sat, followed by the echo of one set of shoes on the flagstones as the other person departed.

Almost immediately, I heard the sound of someone else approaching, this time from inside the church. At a guess, from behind the altar. Naturally, an MI6 man would have his own route into the building.

When he spoke, it was in French. 'Admiral Canaris.'

'Colonel Olivier, I assume?'

SIXTEEN

Canaris's accent was flawless, as was his command of the language. He had the confident, well-modulated tones of a born leader. An educated man.

'At your service. I apologise but I must insist you remain blindfolded. I'm sure you understand.'

Canaris made a sound of assent which exploded into a bout of coughing. I seized the opportunity and rose as quietly as I could, peering around the archway and into the main church. They were sitting a couple of feet apart in the front pew, silhouetted against the light, one with a neatly combed head of white hair and the bearing of an officer, the other observing his every detail. The blindfold covered Canaris's eyes and half his cheeks, but I could still make out his proud, straight nose and the mouth beneath it, at once generous and secretive. An intriguing man. And a dangerous one.

'Excuse me,' said Canaris. 'I have a slight cold.'

He wasn't young or especially well built, and the chill in the chapel penetrated to the bone. Canaris was dressed in civilian clothes, a scarf wrapped around his neck over a thick, well-cut coat. His appearance was immaculate apart from the blindfold.

I suspected that was designed to humiliate him as much as it was to hide his surroundings, but he held his head proudly, refusing to be cowed.

'Let us keep this brief,' he said. 'I have a question I want you to convey to Churchill.'

Olivier remained perfectly still, a spider observing his prey. Except that these two were both spiders, two men at the heart of complex webs of spies. 'Which is?'

'I want to know his terms for peace if Germany gets rid of Hitler.'

'That's it?'

'Yes. Once I know what those are, we can negotiate.'

'Very well. I will make sure that is put to the Prime Minister. I'll let you know when I receive a response.'

I thought I detected a ghost of a smile beneath the blindfold.

'Thank you. If that is all, I'd like to take a moment alone here. To pray.'

Olivier hesitated, clearly taken aback. A spymaster wrong-footed. My instincts about Canaris appeared to be correct. 'I— Yes of course. I'll withdraw. Let me know when you're done and I'll send for your escort.'

With that, Olivier rose and disappeared through the door at the side of the altar from which he'd emerged. Canaris waited for a moment or two after his footsteps had receded and the door had clicked shut. I wondered if he would attempt to raise the blindfold or even remove it, but he simply reached forward with his hands to feel the edge of the pew before he sank to his knees on the cassock in front of him, bowing his head to his folded hands, his lips moving soundlessly as he prayed.

I gazed at him, mesmerised by the evident depth of his piety. It was so unexpected and yet strangely moving. I felt a wash of shame. Here I was spying on a man in such an intimate moment. And yet I had no doubt he would have done the same to me.

He was the head of the Abwehr after all. Responsible for counter-intelligence along with all his other activities and a Nazi to boot. Yet, from what I now knew of him, he aided the Resistance and Jews, along with actively attempting to assassinate Hitler. Perhaps a clue lay in his humility before God. I had no idea what he was praying for, but I suspected forgiveness might be in there somewhere.

At last, he raised his head from his hands.

'I'm ready,' he called out.

I felt Charlie pull at my arm as the door beside the altar reopened and Olivier emerged, his eyes darting towards the side chapel just as I slid back behind the archway. Knowing we were here was one thing, but I suspected he wouldn't be too pleased to have eyes on him as well as ears. I stayed stock-still as the two men marched back down the aisle, only exhaling when I heard the outer door bang shut, sending a blast of air all the way back up to the altar. Or maybe that was my gasp at what I'd just witnessed.

'Well that was quite something,' I said. 'OK, I believe you. Now what?'

He stood, automatically checking to make sure we were still alone and unobserved. 'Not here. Walk with me.'

SEVENTEEN

I followed him out of yet another door behind the statue of mother and child, stepping through into the cloisters that ran around the edge of a central courtyard, half-expecting to see a nun gliding towards us although there was nobody about. I matched Charlie step for step as he began to talk, his voice still low in spite of the lack of company. Wise. Bitter experience had taught us all that nothing and nobody could ever be completely trusted.

'As I told you, before I came over here, I was in London,' he said. 'Being trained by some of your people as well as MI6. They want to set up a joint counter-espionage operation in Paris with us working alongside you Brits. We're the advance party, me and Jim, although our guy in London is in charge.'

'In charge of what?'

'Of us and ultimately you if you agree to do this.'

'I can't agree to anything until I know exactly what it is I'm getting into.'

He paused, leaning back against a pillar, studying me with the deep-set eyes that had first struck me at my apartment. They were the kind of eyes that missed nothing. 'Smart cookie. Your boss said you were nobody's fool.'

'I'm nobody's anything. Unlike other agents, I work alone. I assume Suzanne also told you that?'

'She did, although it doesn't surprise me. Given what you do.'

'What exactly is it you think I do? You see, Lieutenant, I don't think we're so very different. In fact, I'd bet my life we do pretty much the same thing. We seduce people in one way or another so that they'll give up their secrets. You just happen to do it in that little-boy-lost way.'

His eyes crinkled at the corners. 'That's a serious bet.'

'It is. And if I agree to work with you, I might well have to pay out on it.'

His face sobered. 'You might, but I sincerely hope not. We only act on extremely good intelligence gathered by you Brits. Have you heard of Ultra?'

I shook my head. 'We operate on a need-to-know basis with London. As I'm sure you do.'

'Well, you do need to know this. Ultra is the codename for the intel we, or rather you, get from German communications. The Krauts think that the Enigma machine they use to send encrypted messages is uncrackable, but in fact your boys at Bletchley cracked it some time ago.'

'Girls and boys. And we refer to it as Station X out here in the field.'

'My apologies. You're right on both counts.'

It was even colder among the cloisters, but I felt a rush of warmth as his words sank in. We'd cracked their code. Which put us ahead of the game. We were winning, at least on that score. I couldn't help the broad smile that broke across my face. 'They really cracked it?'

'They really did.'

He looked so much younger when he smiled. Almost

boyish. But then, it wasn't so long ago that we were both children. War made you grow up fast. And we had to keep fighting
if we were to win it. 'I assume your presence here is a result of
this intelligence?'

'Like I said, you're a smart cookie. Thanks to Ultra, we
know that there are a number of German double agents positioned around the Normandy coast as well as here in Paris.
Agents ultimately controlled by Canaris. Those agents pose a
threat to the planned invasion of France as well as to the
network here in Paris.'

There had been murmurs of an invasion, but that was all
they amounted to – rumours. We were as much in the dark as
the Germans on that score. 'Any idea when this invasion will
actually take place?'

'That's the whole point. We have to keep the Germans
guessing, although, unofficially, I can tell you it'll probably be
early summer. In Normandy.'

'And officially?'

'Officially we want them to think it's a lot sooner, in the
spring. We also want them to think that the truth is actually the
bluff and that the landings will take place near Calais, which is,
if you think about it, the most logical place. The deal with
Canaris is that he helps us feed disinformation to his agents,
who will in turn feed it back to Berlin. In return, we'll infiltrate
the Gestapo and find out their plans for the Abwehr as well as
Canaris himself.'

'And by infiltrating the Gestapo, we can discover who's
been betraying the network.'

'Exactly.'

'So we feed them the story that the landings will take place
at Calais a lot sooner while tracking down the traitors.' Jacques's
face swam before me. A brave man and yet another who'd been
betrayed and was now facing execution. 'I love it.'

'I thought you might.'

'Does this mean you think Canaris's peace plan isn't going to work?'

He shook his head. 'He's right about one thing: Hitler is a madman. But he's also not stupid, and he's survived every assassination attempt so far. That's why we need to go in the minute Canaris agrees to our plan. This is the big one, Christine. If we get it right and the Germans are looking in the wrong direction, it will turn the war around.'

The passion in his voice pinned me to the spot. His words were whirling around my mind, but there was something in my gut that screamed even louder. I could see Jacques beside me in that field, the young woman running for her life. The life that had ended right there, in a hail of German bullets. But they still had the others who'd been dropped with her. And Jacques. 'What about our agents – the ones they've already taken? Isn't it just as important to try to save them?'

I saw the shutters come down over his eyes. 'There's nothing we can do about the ones they've already got. We have to concentrate on those who are still operational and alive. We need to keep them that way, and the best way to do that is by infiltrating the Gestapo so we can find out how the hell they keep tracking them down and arresting them.'

I held him with my stare, daring him to look away much less lie to me. But I didn't think he was lying. My gut told me that too. And if there was something I trusted far more than my heart, it was my gut, the instinct that had kept me alive so far. 'Alright. I'm in.'

His smile could have lit up the entire chapel as well as these cloisters. 'You are? Fantastic.' He looked as if he was about to fling his arms around me and then, catching the look on my face, thought better of it. Instead, he stuck out his hand. 'Shake on it?'

I remembered another time, outside Sacré-Cœur – Suzanne offering me her hand for very much the same reason. So much had happened since then. Such a lot of water under several bridges and things I never thought I would see or hear. Yet I wouldn't change a thing, then or now. For the first time in my life, I knew that what I was doing was important. That I was actually saving lives as well as ending a few. If this meant doing more of the same, then I was all for it. What I didn't bargain on was Charlie Russell.

The moment our palms touched, I felt it again. Not so much an electric shock as a current that ran through us both, forming its own circuit, one that felt right, as if I were reconnecting with a part of me. I could see he felt it too.

I snatched my hand away. 'Great. What's our first step?'

'Getting the Gestapo to take me on as an agent.'

'Just like that?'

'Just like that. Once you've laid the ground.'

'Ah yes. Something about gambling debts and pro-Nazi principles, as I recall. Along with your disappointment with the Abwehr and your fears that they won't be able to keep paying you much longer.'

'That's about it.'

'So where do you expect me to lay this ground?'

He hesitated for a fraction of a second, his face more serious now, all traces of charm dissolving. 'At your establishment. To a particular Gestapo officer.'

My stomach lurched. All of a sudden, this wasn't sounding so good. 'At Le Chat Noir? What exactly are you asking me to do?'

'Not that.'

'Good. Because I don't do that. Just so we're clear.'

I could have sworn he was blushing. 'Absolutely. Totally understood. We just want you to get talking to him, you know, chat him up. Flirt. Get him a bit tipsy if you can. Act all impressed and then let slip about this Irish businessman who also works for the Abwehr.'

'An Irish businessman who might consider working for the Gestapo too?'

'Got it in one.'

'Who is this Gestapo officer?'

'Kieffer.'

I half-choked on my gulp of astonishment. 'Josef Kieffer? The head of the SD?'

'The very same.'

'The problem is that I've never seen Kieffer at Le Chat Noir. I'm not sure it's his thing at all.'

'We know that, which is why we've arranged something special. It's his birthday soon, so we're organising a little party for him.'

A party? For Kieffer? It was the Americans who were the lunatics. 'At Le Chat Noir?'

'At Maxim's, where his good friend Marcel will encourage him and his fellow officers to carry on the party at your establishment.'

I shook my head. 'I'm not sure Kieffer will fall for it. He's notoriously smart.'

'Which is why Marcel will be spiking his drinks earlier in the evening.'

'I assume you want us to carry on doctoring them at Le Chat Noir? With perhaps something a little more potent?'

'We do.'

As crazy as it sounded, it might just work. The colourless, odourless concoction we used left no trace of a hangover, while the mix of scopolamine and Indian hemp in it loosened tongues. Months of testing it on our unsuspecting clientele had given us what we considered the optimum mixture. We could make it strong enough to knock someone out entirely or merely to relax them so that they would talk. It still wasn't perfect, but it worked. And our subjects were none the wiser, many of them embarrassed that they'd apparently fallen asleep on the job but with no memory of what had actually happened.

I smiled. 'It's going to be quite some birthday party.'

There it was again, that boyish grin catching me in its blinding glare, his eyes alight with adventure. 'It certainly is. One he'll never forget.'

I suspected he might not be the only one.

He handed me a slip of paper on which an address was scrawled. 'Memorise that. You can send a message there if you need me.'

I read the address twice then pulled out my lighter and touched it to the edge of the paper, watching it burst into a ball of flame, a curl of smoke rising from it as it spiralled down to the flagstones, a pile of ash and burned scraps which I ground underfoot until nothing remained.

'Good enough?'

His eyes as he looked back at me were unreadable, but whatever was in them reverberated right through my body. 'Perfect.'

A shaft of sunlight filtered its way through the cloisters, gilding the planes and hollows of Charlie's face with its pale winter gold. A golden boy of the OSS. Or was it fool's gold? I would find out, one way or another. My guess was that Charlie Russell was the real thing, but only time would tell. Time that was ticking by too fast for our agents rotting in Nazi cells. And the only way to stop more ending up there was this mission with this man. I just hoped he didn't turn out to have feet of clay – or, more terrifyingly, a heart that would prove irresistible.

EIGHTEEN

NOVEMBER 1938, PARIS, FRANCE

I eased off a shoe under the café table. Eight hours tramping the streets of Paris looking for work and my feet were killing me. I stared down at the café au lait I was eking out, stirring it with the tiny teaspoon provided, watching it swirl in the cup just as those waters had swirled. *Stop it, Christine.* Time to move on. Especially today of all days.

'More coffee?'

I looked up to see the young woman who'd served me holding a steaming jug. I did a quick calculation. I had exactly forty-eight francs left out of the money Tom had given me.

I returned her smile, embarrassed, and mumbled in halting French. '*Non merci.*'

'It's free.'

'You speak English?'

Her smile broadened as she refilled my cup. 'I do. Here you go, on the house. You look as if you need it.'

Come to think of it, she didn't look typically French, if there was a type. Her hair was reddish gold, and she was taller than average, her buxom figure filling the pretty blue dress she was wearing. Most Parisian women seemed to be built like sparrows, but she glowed with the kind of health you normally see in the countryside.

The café was pretty too, blue-and-white china lining the shelves behind the counter on which cakes and pastries were set out, so perfect that it would almost be a shame to eat them.

At that thought, my stomach growled. I hadn't eaten since the previous evening, trying as I was to make my money last long enough for another night in the even more flea-ridden hotel I'd found. After that, I had no idea what I would do. Find a park bench perhaps.

'Here you go.' She set a plate in front of me on which a couple of pastries sat, one gleaming with dark and sticky caramel beneath which slices of apple nestled, the other an open sandwich topped with cheese and ham. 'This one is tarte Tatin, and that's a tartine. I'm sorry I can't offer you anything more, but that's all we have left.'

I gaped at her then at the plate. It took all my self-control not to snatch up the sandwich and shove it in my mouth. 'There must be some mistake. I didn't order this.'

'No mistake. I know you didn't order it but, again, you look as if you need it.'

I touched my hair, swiping a stray strand behind my ear, trying surreptitiously to swipe my finger under my eyes as well in case they, too, spoke of my lack of sleep and hours fruitlessly walking the streets.

'I-I don't know what to say except thank you.'

'You're welcome. We close in half an hour, but you can stay as long as you wish.'

I shook my head as if to clear my ears in case I was hearing things. The movement seemed to dislodge the tears that had been lurking, or maybe it was the kindness in her voice and eyes. 'I've been walking around all day trying to find work,' I blurted, wiping my cheek with my sleeve. 'But there are no jobs to be had. It doesn't help that I barely speak French. Or that I'm English, I suppose.'

'Nonsense. People from all over the world live here, in Paris. It's a difficult time. There isn't much work for anyone, but it just so happens I need someone to help me here.'

I stared at her, unable to believe my ears. 'You could give me a job?'

'Starting tomorrow, if you like. This is my mother's café, but she's not well and so now I have to run it alone. It may not look like it at the moment, but we are very busy in the mornings. I would need you to help me serve and clear up, as well as take the orders and clean at the end of the day. I can't pay a lot, but it will be fair. Does that interest you?'

Interest me? I would bite her arm off for the opportunity. 'That all sounds... fantastic. What time would you like me to start?'

'We open the doors at 7 a.m. sharp, and I need you here an hour before that.'

'I'm used to early starts. I worked at a factory in London before I came here.'

'You're from London?'

Damn. Me and my big mouth. I would have to learn to hold my tongue. 'No. Yes. I mean, I'm not from there, but I came to work there. There are a lot of new factories what with all the talk of war.'

'Ah yes. People talk here too, but I won't believe it until I see a German soldier walking through that door. Life goes on – that's what my mother says. You just have to keep going. That's why we came here, so we could carry on with our business.'

'Where did you come from?'

A tiny pause. 'Berlin. My mother and I, we're Jewish. My parents moved there from Paris for my father's work, but it was no longer safe to stay after the Nazis took over in 1933. My father opposed their regime and was taken to Dachau just before we left. After that, we knew there was no future for us in Germany. The Nazis, they never forget.'

'What's Dachau?'

I could see her fighting back the tears now. 'It's a concentration camp. The Nazis send people they want to silence there, including socialists like my father.'

'Do you know how he's doing? Is he alright?'

She shook her head. 'We haven't heard from him since he was taken. The Nazis hate anyone who tries to oppose them. They would have come for us too if we hadn't left. Now I hear that they're sending people to Dachau simply because they're Jewish. Which means they have even more reason to hate my father, if he's still alive.'

I remembered Cable Street and those fascists screaming for blood. The blood of Jews. 'Do you feel safe here?'

Her smile reappeared. 'I do. We do.' She wiped her hand on her apron then held it out to shake mine. 'I'm Amalie, by the way.'

'Christine.'

I looked at her, at her sweet, open face, and hoped with all my heart that the talk of war would come to nothing, that the gas masks, the arms factories and digging for victory would not, in the end, be necessary and, most of all, that no harm would come to her or her mother or the millions of us facing the Nazi threat. But somehow, I already knew her faith was misplaced. It was going to be far worse than she could ever imagine.

NINETEEN

'The Germans have crossed the Seine.'

The café fell silent, heads turning to look at Amalie who was crouched by the radio set in the corner. I heard a clatter as a cup hit the floor, but other than that, a deep hush had fallen over the room, everyone straining to hear more.

'Turn it up,' someone called out.

She twiddled the knob. 'It's as high as it will go.'

I held my breath as I listened to the announcer's voice crackling over the airwaves, asking people to remain calm.

'Calm? How can we stay calm when the premier and the entire government have abandoned us?' wailed one woman, dabbing at her eyes with her napkin.

'They've only gone as far as Tours,' I said. 'That was what they told us the other day.'

Tours was far enough. And it wasn't only the government that had left. Trains were leaving the Gare d'Austerlitz every day packed with people, while the roads out of the capital were choked with cars, most of them from the wealthier districts. For the past couple of days, we'd been hearing the sound of artillery fire in the distance, drawing closer all the time. Then there were the bombs they'd dropped a week ago, killing hundreds of people, including schoolchildren. The newspapers had screamed that the government was staying in the city no matter what to protect its people. Now they were gone, leaving us to our fate.

The radio carried on crackling, but the hubbub in the café was rising, a note of panic permeating the voices, some sanguine, others on the verge of hysteria. I gathered up some empty plates and took them into the back kitchen where Amalie had retreated.

'Are you alright?'

Her face, normally rosy with health and happiness, looked grey, her eyes dazed in shock.

'I can't believe it,' she muttered. 'They've broken through so fast. They'll be in Paris at any moment.'

It was true. The German advance had moved far quicker than anyone could imagine, sweeping aside everything in their path. Once they'd evacuated the Allied troops from Dunkirk, it was inevitable that France would fall. Amalie and I had stood and wept as we listened to the accounts of the boats, big and small, crossing the Channel to save those soldiers. Now it seemed it was all for nothing. I could see a solitary tear snaking down her face now, trembling on the edge of her chin, which was still raised, defiant.

'Amalie, you and your mother should go too. Head for the south and try to get to Spain. I can look after this place. It's not safe for you if the Germans take Paris.'

Not if but when. We both knew that.

'No. We're not running. We already had to leave everything we had in Berlin. I'm not doing that again. Besides, we left instructions for Papa with our old neighbours that we'd gone to Paris. If we leave, he won't be able to find us.'

I wanted to shake her, to tell her that her papa was never coming home. Instead, I took a breath and tried to speak as gently as I could. 'You've heard what they're doing to your people in Germany. They're making their lives hell. Think of your mother, Amalie. She's not well.'

As far as I knew, she barely left their apartment. I'd never actually met the woman in the eighteen months I'd been working in the café, but from what Amalie said, she spent most days in her bedroom, in the dark, barely touching the meals her daughter brought to her on a tray. I wondered if it wasn't so much a physical ailment as despair brought on by the loss of her husband along with everything they'd ever owned. Amalie worked hard, but some days the café barely broke even, although she always paid me on time and in full. Then there were the meetings that took place when the café was shut – communists coming to mutter about what would happen if the Germans invaded France while drinking her coffee and eating her food without paying her a penny.

'It's for the cause,' she would say. 'My father was a socialist. These people aren't so different.'

I'd look around at the Gauloise-puffing crew, gobbling up everything put in front of them. She was right. They weren't so different from any other bunch of scavenging bastards. As for their talk of fighting off the Germans, it was as substantial as the smoke rings they blew into the air. Now here we were, the Germans on our doorstep. The time for talking was over.

'Amalie, listen to me. Whatever the Germans did to the Jews in Germany, they will do here too. Worse, probably, now that they're winning. I've seen fascists at work and, believe me, it's not pretty.'

Bullies, the lot of them. I remembered their faces twisted with hate in Cable Street, eyes bulging as they roared and spat at the Jewish people who lived there and the neighbours who stood alongside them, refusing to back down. There was a lot to be said for bravery, but this was neither the time nor the place.

I took Amalie's coat from its peg and handed it to her.

'Here. Get along home and check on your mother. She listens to the radio too, remember.'

According to Amalie, she had it on day and night, blasting through their tiny apartment, listening in case there was any news of her husband. Of course, there never was. But the knowledge that the Germans were advancing on Paris might tip her over the edge. And then what would Amalie do? She'd been so kind to me. Literally saved my life. The least I could do was return the favour.

Amalie took the coat from me reluctantly, her hand trembling. 'Yes, perhaps I should do that.'

'You should, and you should also pack a few things. Get your mother and yourself out of Paris, if only for a few days. Do you have somewhere you can go?'

She shrugged. 'I have a distant relative in Orleans. But what's the point? If they take Paris, they'll take the whole of France. As for going to Spain, my mother can't travel that far. It would finish her.'

We looked at one another, knowing that she had no choice. Either way, they were in danger, although we had no idea yet how much. 'It's up to you, Amalie. Whatever you decide, I'll support you. Just, please, think about it. Those German bastards will stop at nothing.'

'And what about you? Aren't you afraid of what they might do to you?'

I laughed, a harsh bark that sounded hollow even to my ears. 'They can't do anything worse to me than my stepdad did, I'll tell you that for free.'

A pause as my words hung, laden with hate, in the air. Then she took my hand between hers. They felt cool in spite of the warmth of the day and the heat here in the kitchen. 'Whatever he did, I'm sorry.'

I gulped back a sob, steadying myself for both our sakes. 'I'm afraid those Germans could do something just as terrible to you and to me. To all of us. But there's no going back for me, so I guess we'll just have to ride this one out together.'

She pressed my hand to her lips. 'We can do that, my friend. All of us, together. And we'll fight them any way we can.'

Even as she said it, I knew we were making a terrible mistake.

TWENTY

AUGUST 1940, PARIS, FRANCE

She was tiny, the size and shape of a ballerina. Or maybe it was the way she held her head like a swan, regal and poised. She was watching me from the corner table. I could feel it even before I turned.

'Can I help you?'

She didn't smile but rather looked me up and down. 'I believe you can.'

I took out my pad and pen. She was making me feel uncomfortable. 'What can I get you? I'm afraid we only have a limited selection of pastries today. Rationing, you know.'

'A coffee. And then I would like to talk to you, but not here.'

She was gazing out at the street through the café windows. I stared studiously at my pad. This could be a trap. 'I'll get your coffee.'

'Be careful of that woman at the corner table,' I muttered to Amalie as I made her coffee. 'She's a strange one.'

'I noticed her when she came in. She keeps looking at you.'

'She could be an informer. Or worse.'

On the surface, the occupation was civilised at first, but life was becoming harder. Rationing had already begun, which, on the one hand, brought in more people desperate to get hold of bread or pastries and, on the other, meant we ran out early in the day. But it was the growing sense that Paris had become a part of Germany that made us more and more uneasy. The Nazi flag flew over every major building, while the street signs were now in German, some of the shops reserved purely for our conquerors. Even the clocks had been changed to German time. I glanced at ours, still not used to the difference. Eleven o'clock. In the old days, the counter would have been piled high with croissants and brioches at this hour. Now just two remained, sitting forlornly on a plate.

'Your coffee, madame.'

'Thank you.'

She tapped the newspaper she'd spread in front of her with her pen, and I instinctively looked down. There was something written above the newsprint, a few words in blue ink: 'Sacré-Cœur. Twenty minutes.'

She picked up her coffee and took a sip. I hovered, unsure what to do. If she was an informer, it was best to play it safe. 'Will that be all, madame?'

'There is one more thing. I wondered if you could help me with my crossword.'

I gaped at her. 'Your crossword?'

'Yes. See here, this clue: Walk through East End with a weapon.'

I froze, looking again at the newspaper. It was in English. Why the hell hadn't I spotted that before? Maybe because it seemed normal, even after all this time in Paris. But she spoke perfect French. Her accent was Parisian. Why was she reading an English newspaper? Above it all, my mind was working, just as it had when my mum got me to help her with the crossword.

'I – uh – crossbow. Cross Bow. Get it?'

She smiled. 'I do.'

It felt as if I'd passed some kind of test, even though I had no idea what was going on.

She tapped the newspaper again, close to those words she'd written. 'And do you get this?'

Sacré-Cœur. Twenty minutes. I flicked a look around the café, taking in the regulars, Amalie behind the counter. Nothing out of the ordinary. At least, nothing I could see. Except this woman.

'Yes, madame.'

She left five minutes later, folding her newspaper carefully and tucking it into her bag before she walked out without a second glance. I went to clear her coffee cup. There was a five-thousand-franc note under it. An extremely generous tip. Ludicrous, in fact. Or was it a bribe? Hard to tell. My hand hovered for a second before I snatched it up, tucking it away in my apron pocket. Either way, I would share it with Amalie. This was enough to keep us going for a couple more months at least.

'I'm just popping out,' I murmured to Amalie, untying my apron. The café was quiet, the street outside empty. It would take me around eight minutes to get to Sacré-Cœur. I knew because I'd done it many times, wandering around the great white church with its dome that loomed over Montparnasse, seeking the peace that still evaded me no matter how hard I tried. Well, perhaps I would find it there today. Or at least a way towards it.

As I walked up the hill, head down, I could feel a stirring in my soul. I had no idea who this woman was or what she wanted from me. All I knew was that my life was about to change again, perhaps this time for good.

TWENTY-ONE

She appeared as if from nowhere, falling in beside me as I was halfway up the steps, the great white basilica rising above us like a beacon of hope.

'Keep walking,' she murmured as she matched me stride for stride. Three hundred steps and she took each one with ease. I heard a vehicle pull up and looked over my shoulder to see a truck full of German soldiers roar into the square below us.

'Eyes front, Christine. We don't want to attract attention.'

'How do you know my name?' I spluttered.

'The same way I know that you're British, that you come from the East End of London – Shadwell to be precise – and that you needed to leave there in a hurry.'

I felt a hot lump of panic rise from my stomach and lodge in my throat. She knew. She knew all about me. Who'd told her? My mum? Tom? Surely not. 'Are you the police?'

'No. I'm with a different department, one that needs your talents.'

That lump of panic was rapidly dissolving into rivulets of alarm running through my veins. 'I have no idea what you mean. I don't have any talents.'

'Oh, I think you do, but let me spell them out for you. First and foremost, you speak fluent French and your accent is almost flawless. Secondly, you know Paris well. Thirdly, you've demonstrated that you'll do what it takes to survive. Those are the exact qualities we need to help us win this war.'

Relief flooded through me, washing away that roiling surge of fear. 'So you're not here to arrest me?'

'I'm here to extend an invitation. One you should consider carefully. I work for a new department in London, one that will carry out clandestine operations across Europe. Winston Churchill has given it his blessing. I believe his exact phrase was that we are "to set Europe ablaze".'

'Clandestine? You mean spying?'

'Espionage and sabotage as well as aiding the Resistance here. It's how we fight the Germans on all fronts. And we need people like you, Christine, no matter what you might have done in the past.'

We were directly beneath the entrance now, its arches reflecting the three domes above. The shadows were deeper here, but her eyes still shone with the same kind of fervour I saw on the faces of some *résistants*. 'Are you threatening me?'

'Not at all. If you say no, I shall leave and your life will carry on as before.'

I thought of that tip she'd left. Definitely a bribe. 'Except it won't, will it? Because the Germans are making life more difficult every day. And if I say yes, what then?'

'Then you'll come back with me to England where we'll train you in all the arts you need to become an agent. Once you pass the training, we'll deploy you back to France, possibly even here, to Paris.'

An agent. It had a certain glamorous ring to it.

'We'll also ensure that any unfortunate incidents from your past are erased from all records.'

I stared at her. 'What records?'

'Christine, you haven't been convicted of any crime. There are no records as such, just witness statements. We'll make sure that those disappear, along with any trace of your name attached to a missing persons case in Shadwell.'

I gulped. Someone had dobbed me in. Or, worse, had actually seen something. But she could make it go away. Or so she said. 'Can I have that in writing?'

She laughed. 'I knew you'd be perfect for us. Of course.'

'But what about the café? Amalie's been so good to me. I don't want to leave her in the lurch.'

'We can make arrangements for your friend and her mother to get to England, where they'll be safe. It's a miracle they've managed to survive this long, especially now the Nazis are rounding up Jews here and transporting them.'

'Amalie has been very careful to conceal their faith. They changed their surname when they first came here, and very few people know that they're Jewish. Those that do try to protect them.'

She opened her handbag, extracting a packet of Gitanes. I noted the pistol tucked in there too. I had the feeling she meant me to see it.

'Not careful enough. Yes, some people might protect them now, but a few banknotes waved at them by the Germans might change all that. People are desperate. They could be betrayed at any moment.'

I took the cigarette she was offering me, squinting as she lit it from hers, the smoke drifting between us. 'And you say you can get them to England?'

'Yes.'

'Then I accept on that condition. You give me your word that you'll help Amalie and her mother, and I give you my word that I'll join your organisation.'

She smiled at me as if she'd known that would be my decision. To be honest, I had little choice.

'I'm delighted to hear it. Shall we shake on it? Although my word is as good as my handshake, I assure you. I don't believe I introduced myself properly. My name is Suzanne.'

Maybe it was the way she said it or even the way she presented her hand, but something struck me then that I hadn't noticed before. Her accent was perfect. Too perfect. 'You're French. How come you're working for the British?'

'I'm half-French, but I grew up here, in Paris. I went to London just before war broke out. I'm not so much working for the British as working to win this war so we can all live in peace.'

Peace. I scarcely knew what that felt like. Maybe years ago, when I was a child and my dad was still alive, I'd known peace, but once my stepdad entered our lives, it was shattered forever. Now this, this war. And here I was, caught up in it.

'I'll go for that,' I said. 'Peace.'

'I thought you might. Although it's going to be a bit of a fight before we attain it.'

'I'm not afraid of a fight.'

She stood as still as a statue, her head cocked to one side, studying me. 'I can see that. I have a feeling you're going to be one of our finest agents, Christine.'

'You think so? Really?'

'I know so.' She slid her arm through mine, turning so that we began to descend the steps, towards the truck full of German soldiers. All of a sudden, they didn't seem so terrifying.

'I'd like to blow up their stupid truck here and now, and them with it,' I murmured.

'They're not your target. We have much bigger fish for you to catch.'

'I'm good at fishing. My brother taught me, off the docks.'

A squeeze of my arm. 'I'm sure you are. But I think you'll find this is fishing of a different kind.'

Of course it was. And I had a nagging sense I might turn out to be the bait.

TWENTY-TWO

NOVEMBER 1941, SOE 'FINISHING SCHOOL', BEAULIEU, ENGLAND

I clocked her as soon as I entered the interrogation training room. Her eyes widened when she saw me, but, true to form, she didn't say a word. What the hell was she doing here? Stupid question. One to which I already knew the answer. She'd signed up, like all the rest, determined to do her bit. Except that for Amalie, it was doubly dangerous. She wasn't just joining SOE; she was Jewish. Half of me wanted her to fail there and then so she wouldn't have to face that danger. The other half was full of admiration for her courage and determination in getting this far. The courage I knew all too well.

'Good morning, ladies and gentlemen,' said Suzanne. 'Welcome to Beaulieu. Today we'll be introducing you to the art of interrogation, but first I want to go over the results of your provocation tests.'

I scanned the room, trying not to focus too hard on Amalie. One or two, I knew, also recognised me from their provocation tests. That they were still here meant they'd passed, managing not to break or blab in spite of the carrots I dangled in front of them. The stocky, ruddy-cheeked young man in the front row had been particularly reticent, scarpering as quickly as he could from our encounter in a Liverpool bar, while further along was a slightly older, more studious-looking fellow who'd professed that he preferred poetry to women. Something told me he might be Bletchley bound.

Even at this stage, they could fail the provocation test. One wrong word from them now and they'd be out the door. To their credit, all of them kept their eyes on Suzanne as she opened her file of reports, each of them detailing how individual students had done.

'One of the most vital things you'll learn as an agent is how to maintain your cover story or legend. The ability to do so means the difference between life and death. That's why we test you regularly and in different ways. I have here the reports on your latest tests, during which you were subjected to provocation in one way or another. You all passed, otherwise you wouldn't still be here, but I have a number of comments to make.'

I could see Amalie out of the corner of my eye and wondered who'd tested her and how. With the men, we used the weapons of drink and flirtation, but women were trickier, often already wary of both as a matter of course. Good student that she was, she kept a straight face, eyes front, not even acknowledging my presence as Suzanne ran through her comments, focusing on the usual minor gaffes, though even the tiniest slip could prove fatal.

'You must live your new role, thinking and acting as that person would at all times. We've already had one agent whose cover was blown because he went into a French café and asked for a *café noir* when everyone there knows that milk is rationed, so all coffee is black by default. It's retaining and using details like that which could save your life.'

I could feel the students listening intently, especially

Amalie. When it came to my reports, I watched one or two squirm.

'If someone of the opposite sex flirts with you, always ask yourself why. I realise you might consider yourself devastatingly attractive, but they could have an ulterior motive. Thankfully, none of you went so far as to give anything away, even in those circumstances, and for that, I commend you.'

The stocky young man glanced at me and just as quickly looked away again. I'd deployed every trick in my book, but he'd remained politely disinterested. A chap at the back with Byronic good looks had proved more susceptible, dropping me a wink before he sadly announced that he had to get back to his cover-story job as a salesman. I'd decided that the wink was in character and gave him an extra mark, although it could have gone either way. Luckily for him, he wasn't winking now but looking rather pale at my presence in the room.

'For the final few minutes, I'll give the floor to my colleague here. Some of you have already made her acquaintance. Others have not had that pleasure.'

I took Suzanne's place in front of the class, including them all in my gaze. 'Congratulations. You've passed this stage of your training, but I don't want you to think that it's over. We can test you at any time while you're here and especially when you least suspect it. I want you to be on your guard at all times, particularly if you come across someone like me.'

There were a couple of muffled guffaws. I glared at the back row. 'Did I say something to amuse you?'

The Byronic recruit looked shamefaced. 'No, ma'am.'

I made a mental note to reassess his report. 'In that case, you're dismissed.'

The class rose as one and marched from the room. I fell in behind them, moving up the line to murmur to Amalie, 'The library,' before making my way there.

Moments later, the door to the library opened, and she

appeared, looking both defiant and delighted to see me. I motioned to her to shut the door.

'It's alright. We're alone.'

She moved forward and engulfed me in a hug. 'Christine, it's been so long. Oh my goodness, your hair! It's so blonde now. You're so glamorous. You look wonderful.'

'Thank you, but please don't mention that I ever looked any different or that you knew me before.'

'Of course I won't. Are you angry with me? Please tell me you're not.'

I gently disentangled myself, taking a step back. 'I'm not angry with you. How could I be? I'm just worried for you, that's all.'

'There's no need to worry. I've done well at my training.'

'So I see. It's not that which worries me. I know you'll make a wonderful agent. But, Amalie...'

'My training name is Annette.'

I smiled at her. 'Thank you. Point taken. But still...'

'I know. I'm Jewish. All the more reason to do this. If those bastards catch me, then at least I'll have done all I can to help win the war. I couldn't just sit back and do nothing, Christine. Not when I speak French and German and know Paris so well.'

She was right. The recruiters must have welcomed her with open arms. She was perfect for the job. A job where the life expectancy of an agent dropped into France was just six weeks. I could fail her to stop her going, but Amalie would just find another way. She was that kind of person. A woman who would do what was right, no matter the personal consequences.

I took her hand. 'You'll be brilliant out there in the field. Just promise me one thing.'

'Anything.'

'Promise me you won't let them take you alive. If it comes to it, use your pill. The one they give you before you leave. It's what it's there for.'

She squeezed my hand. 'Don't you worry. They won't catch me. And if they do, they'll never take me alive.'

I looked at her, at that lovely, open face always so full of warmth and laughter. She wasn't laughing now. Neither of us were. Yet the warmth was still there, still wrapping itself around me even as I felt the cold clutch of fear in my gut.

TWENTY-THREE

Lights blared, eyes blinking, terrified faces staring up at us as we dragged them from sleep, barking out orders.

'Get your flight gear on. Now. You're coming with us.'

The women hastily scrambled into their jump suits, casting fearful glances at the male instructors, while Suzanne and I observed from the shadows, dressed for night reconnaissance in head-to-toe black. I could see Amalie, calmly following orders. *Good girl.* We watched as they were marched down the stairs, bundled into jeeps and driven off into the night.

Suzanne handed me the first aid kit. 'Let's go.'

We leaped into our jeep, following at a discreet distance. Each of the five women would be dropped at a separate location on the treacherous heathland peppered with bogs and hidden ponds. If they stuck to their training, they'd make their way to the rendezvous with their reception committee without succumbing to the terrain or one of the many other hazards we'd set up, including instructors dressed as German soldiers and wielding German weapons, ready to pounce and arrest them in an all-too-realistic manner. If they failed, they'd be dropped from the course. This was too important a test not to pass.

The night air was chilly. It would be even colder in a few weeks, when we dropped them into France. I had no idea where these women were headed, but chances were at least one of them would be sent into the mountainous regions where the Maquis had set up camp. The Resistance fighters had named themselves after the rough terrain in which they hid out, partly to avoid conscription into forced labour in Germany but mostly to conduct guerrilla warfare against the enemy. The agents we sent to work with them had to be as tough as they were. There was no room for weakness, especially not if you were a woman.

A distant yell broke through my thoughts. As one, Suzanne and I leaped out of our parked jeep.

'It came from that direction,' I hissed, mindful that the exercise was still underway. The bone-chilling scream that followed dispelled any idea that we should stick to the programme. We were running now, breaking through the undergrowth, feet pounding over the rough ground.

'Stop!' I flung my arm out just in time. We were teetering on the edge of one of those hidden ponds, its banks all but hidden by the same gorse and bracken we'd been fighting our way through. In the middle of it, I could make out two figures, one with her arm under the other's chin, hauling her out towards the far bank.

More shouts as a couple of the other instructors appeared waving torches, shining them on to the scene unfolding in front of us. I could see the face of the one swimming now, kicking out with all her might as she tried to keep the other one calm.

'Amalie.'

She didn't hear me, concentrating as she was on not letting the other woman pull her under as she thrashed around, taking in gulps of water as she kept trying to scream. Another moment or two and they'd both be under. The water in the middle of the pond was deep and perilously cold, the reeds that lined it treacherous. Amalie was out of her depth and she knew it. It was then that I saw her raise one fist and land a punch square on the other woman, knocking her out. Seconds later, one of the instructors was splashing towards her, taking the now limp woman from her and dragging her onto the bank as Amalie, too, crawled to safety looking utterly spent.

I felt Suzanne's hand on my arm. 'Let the instructors deal with it.'

We were here to observe. I knew that. And yet it took everything I had not to race to Amalie's side and fling my jacket around her. Instead, I watched as the instructor led both women to one of the jeeps.

Just as they reached it, Amalie looked over her shoulder, straight at me. Or so it felt. There was no way she could have seen us. We blended into the darkness, crouching as we were now in the undergrowth, dressed from head to toe in our night fatigues. And yet, somehow, she knew. She was going to be one hell of an asset to us, but oh how I wished she wasn't so damn good at this. She was my Amalie. My friend. But there was absolutely nothing I could do to protect her except hope and pray she'd survive whatever faced her out there.

TWENTY-FOUR

SEPTEMBER 1942, PARIS, FRANCE

She was sitting behind the bar knitting while she kept a weather eye on her girls. The place was still quiet this early in the evening, although there were a couple of Abwehr officers in a booth being plied with champagne by two young ladies who appeared to be hanging on their every word. If only they knew. I clocked them as we approached the bar, which was as elegant as the rest of Le Chat Noir, a polished swathe of wood behind which an unimaginable array of bottles was on display.

I hadn't seen such a variety of whiskies since the start of the war, although it was champagne the Nazis notoriously loved, especially the Abwehr officers. From what I'd heard, they had a regular supply delivered to the Hotel Lutetia where they were stationed in five-star luxury. Although there was nothing five-star about their operations. They might pass the agents they arrested on to the Gestapo for interrogation, but that still meant their hands were as dirty as those of the secret police.

Madame Joey peered at us over her spectacles then went back to her knitting. The bartender greeted us. 'May I help you?'

Suzanne tilted her head regally. 'We have an appointment with Madame. We've just arrived from Baker Street.'

At that, Madame Joey wound her wool around her knitting needles, put them to one side, removed her spectacles and got to her feet. She was of medium height but slender, so she appeared taller, her golden hair teased into artful waves that highlighted her cheekbones, above which cat-like eyes regarded us with interest – especially Suzanne.

'Come with me,' she said, emerging from behind the bar, beckoning us to follow her out of the salon and through a door set discreetly behind a velvet curtain, hung so that it appeared as if there were just another of the floor-to-ceiling windows behind it.

Once through the door, we were in a small but extremely neat office, the desk clear of papers, while behind it a filing cabinet bore alphabetical labels on the drawers. I wondered what was in there. Routine paperwork probably. Along with the records that were rumoured to be there, the ones that were no doubt locked away, apart from the rest.

Madame Joey must have noticed me looking because she waved an elegant hand at the cabinet. 'It's all there. Every single customer who has passed through these doors since we opened them, although we've archived the records from before the occupation.'

I looked at her. 'You have their real names?'

'Mostly. The Germans are proud to come to a famous night-club like ours.'

Not to mention its other delights. Le Chat Noir wasn't just a supremely elegant club set in a four-storey townhouse; it was also a bordello of such repute that the Abwehr, who considered themselves a cut above the Gestapo thugs, favoured it over all the others. The Abwehr might be composed of officers and gentlemen, but when it came to their pleasures, they were as ungentlemanly as the rest.

'What about your other visitors?' asked Suzanne.

Madame Joey didn't blink. 'I'm not sure what you mean.'

'Come now, madame. We know that you harbour British agents and downed airmen, along with Jews. We're grateful to you for that. But I need to know if you've kept any records of them. Records which might lead to them, or others, being compromised.'

She moved like a cat too, sinuous as she sank into her chair and motioned for us to do the same. It was only once she'd lit up the cigarette she inserted into a black lacquer holder that she chose to answer the question. A shrewd operator. But then, she'd have to be to run this place as she did.

'I can assure you that there are no records of any British agents or airmen, let alone Jews, in this establishment. As I said, I really have no idea what you're talking about.'

Suzanne extracted an envelope from her handbag and pushed it across the desk. 'Open it,' she said. 'It may jog your memory.'

Madame Joey's expression didn't change as she slit open the envelope with a paperknife that looked lethally sharp and read the letter inside it. I could make out a stamp or seal on the bottom of it through the paper, but that was all, although I could make a rough guess at the contents. It was how we worked.

'That's very generous of you,' she said as she folded the letter and slid it back into the envelope. I had no doubt it would be filed in the same place as her other secret records. 'But I don't do what I do for money. I do it for the love of my country and because I hate everything the Nazis stand for, especially their treatment of the Jews. Only a couple of months ago, they herded thousands of them into the Velodrome d'Hiver and held them for days without food or water before sending them to Auschwitz. Since then, I have helped hundreds to escape. It's the least I can do.'

'I'm glad to hear it,' said Suzanne. 'I expected nothing less

from you. That's why we chose Le Chat Noir for our operation. The compensation we're offering is to cover any loss of
business or your other expenses while I take your place for a
while.'

The two women exchanged a look which sent my senses
tingling. I wondered if they'd met before. There seemed to be
some kind of compact between them, an unspoken accord. Or
maybe it was my imagination.

Madame Joey emitted a husky sigh. I made a mental note to
add it to my repertoire. 'That's the first problem. People come
here to meet the girls and to party, of course, but they also come
because they know I choose the best. The best girls, the best
champagne, the best food we can find, although the Gestapo
and the Abwehr are very helpful in that regard. It may sound
arrogant, but I am Le Chat Noir. I created this place, and it
wouldn't be the same without me.'

'Indeed, madame, which is why we're making it clear that
this is merely a temporary situation. You will apparently be
taking care of a sick relative in the south while I, your cousin,
come to cover your absence, along with Christine here –
another cousin.'

Madame Joey's feline gaze swept over me. I could almost
see her tail flicking. 'Do you have any relevant experience? I'm
sure you're excellent at what you do, but this requires, shall we
say, quite special skills.'

Suzanne laid a hand on my arm. 'Christine is a highly
trained agent who tests other agents before we let them loose in
the field. She does so by seeing if they'll talk and let slip their
secrets or succumb to her evident charms.'

Madame Joey was assessing those charms now, and I could
see by the look on her face that she felt there was room for
improvement.

'I see,' she murmured, taking another long drag from her
cigarette, her nails as perfectly lacquered as the holder she flour-

ished. Then she jumped to her feet as if she'd made some kind of decision. '*Allons-y.*' *Let's go.*

We followed her up the stairs to another landing, where the walls were lined with fine art. There was a mixture of landscapes, still lifes and portraits, all of them exceptional works. I paused in front of one, the only nude, its rich oil colours offset by a gilded frame, contrasting with the alabaster skin of the young woman who gazed out at me. She looked as if she was barely more than a teenager, her dark hair falling over one shoulder, the eyes that gazed out at me from a heart-shaped face at once defiant and despairing. I knew those eyes.

I could feel Suzanne at my shoulder. 'It's you, isn't it?' I asked.

'Yes.'

I looked from her to Madame Joey. So many secrets. And it was obvious they were keeping this one to themselves.

Madame was already moving on, stopping in front of another painting hung at the far end of the landing, the largest. It was of Notre-Dame at dawn, the light playing softly on the river that flowed around it, reminding me of another dawn I'd seen over Paris – my first.

Madame stepped to the far left of the painting and pressed on a precise spot on the wall there. I watched open-mouthed as the wall swung open to reveal a hidden room beyond.

'I have an excellent carpenter,' she said as we stepped into the room and the wall swung back into place behind us. The room was perhaps three times the size of her office, with four camp beds set up against the far wall and a table and chairs in the centre. Thick carpet covered the floor, deadening our footsteps as we trod across it.

'The working rooms are below this,' said Madame. 'We don't want our clients to hear anything suspicious.'

Another staircase led down from the room, the tiny window next to it the only source of daylight.

'Where does that go?' I asked.

'It leads down to the cellars. The staircase is also hidden. It opens out through what looks like a storeroom to a back door, which provides a perfect escape route. We bring our guests food from the kitchens. They stay here until we can get them out of Paris safely.'

I noticed a discarded toy rabbit on the floor beside one of the beds.

Madame clucked, swooping on it. 'A family was staying here, but they left early this morning. Their little girl must have forgotten this. Poor mite.'

I stared at the rabbit in her hand, a lump lodging in my throat. For some unaccountable reason, I could feel tears pricking my eyeballs. Maybe the rabbit reminded me of my little sister Elsie, or perhaps it was the way these people had to run, leaving almost everything, just as I had. 'Where did they go?'

'It's best I don't tell you.'

'Of course. I suppose they're Jewish?'

'They are, God help them.'

If my experience was anything to go by, He wouldn't. 'I have a great friend who's Jewish. She's safe now, in England, along with her mother. You're saving lives, madame.'

'We do what we can.'

'Indeed you do, madame.'

'How many working rooms do you have?' asked Suzanne.

'Ten. We have two shifts, so we have twenty girls working over twenty-four hours.'

'You operate day and night?'

'Yes, although there are obviously times which are quieter, and then it gets busy again in the evening. I employ two receptionists who are capable of running the place if I'm not here. They are completely trustworthy and utterly discreet.'

'Do they know about everything you do?'

'They do. They know, for instance, that one of my new girls is actually Jewish. Sarah. She looks just like Rita Hayworth – or at least she will once my hairdresser has performed her usual magic. Sarah was desperate to stay here, in Paris, to be close to her grandmother, who's being kept safe by the nuns at the convent. The sisters often pass on their guests to me when they're ready to be moved, but the old lady is too frail to go anywhere.'

Suzanne glanced around once more. 'Who brings your, ah, guests here?'

'A *résistant* called Marcel Aragon. I believe you are already acquainted with him, Suzanne. Marcel knows *le tout* Paris and is very well connected. It means he can socialise with the Germans while at the same time serving the cause.'

'And you trust him? This Marcel?' I asked.

'Implicitly.'

'Then we must meet him,' I said. 'We'll need his help if we're to pull this off.'

'Not just his,' said Madame Joey. 'If we are to do this, then I need to train you. Especially you.'

I drew myself up to my full height, happy to note that I towered over Madame Joey just as I did Suzanne. 'I can assure you I have been thoroughly trained.'

'Not in the arts you need to learn.'

I looked from her to Suzanne. 'I fear you may be mistaken about what it is I actually do. I talk to my subjects, yes. Flirt with them. Maybe even a little kiss. But that's as far as it goes.'

Those cat eyes were narrowed now, a question mark in them. 'Pah. By the time I've finished, you'll be able to seduce anyone with little more than a look and get all their secrets out of them before they realise what's happened. We start tomorrow.'

'Madame is a great teacher. The finest,' said Suzanne. 'I should know. She was the one who taught me.'

TWENTY-FIVE

Madame Joey circled me twice, taking in my new hairstyle and outfit, all the while raking me with her cat-like stare. 'That's better.'

I patted the platinum blonde waves the hairdresser had painstakingly created. Beside me in the salon, a young woman had joked and laughed as she was transformed into a dead ringer for Rita Hayworth, her natural dark-brown locks dyed a flaming red. This had to be Sarah, Madame Joey's new girl. Now here I was too, one of them in training. All I knew was that it would be nothing like any other training I'd gone through, although it might prove even more useful.

'You have a natural allure which is good,' said Madame. 'But you are also too strong, too independent. When these men come here, they want to relax. To feel like a pampered prince. They want to trust that they can talk to you and that you will listen.'

'That's great,' I said. 'The more they talk, the better for us surely?'

'But of course. Although you must always remember that you are no longer testing recruits here. Many of our customers are Abwehr officers. Some are Gestapo. They are master interrogators themselves. Suzanne tells me you are already superb at what you do, but we need to make you even better.'

I glanced at Suzanne hovering behind Madame, wondering yet again just what it was she'd learned from her. The obvious probably. Which made me wonder all the more.

'Do you use anything to loosen their tongues?' asked Suzanne.

'Only alcohol and charm.'

'And your girls, do they extract any information from them that's useful to the Resistance?'

'They make notes of anything they can find out or that the client inadvertently tells them. We can't push them too far or they'll get suspicious. So far, we've only managed to extract the locations of their garrisons in and around Paris, as well as the odd boast about how badly they treat the agents they've taken prisoner. Nothing more than that.'

'We'll need to up the ante. Have you ever considered drugging them?'

'Naturally, but I fear they would realise what we'd done.'

'Not if we do it the right way. We have a division in England that's been working on truth serums and powders. They're still refining them, so they're not yet perfect, but they leave no trace. Even better, the subject has no memory of what's happened.'

Madame Joey clapped her hands. 'Marvellous. That's so clever. I assume you have some with you?'

'I do, and our people in England are delighted that we're testing them out on the Germans. As I said, they're still working on them, so they're eager to hear our results.'

'Perfect. Although you must be careful they don't spot what you're doing. The Germans are an unforgiving lot. I don't want you to disappear as well.'

I saw something pass between them, an affection that was palpable. Suzanne had said nothing more about her former asso-

ciation with Madame Joey, and I hadn't asked, but it was clear
to me that they held one another in high regard. It didn't matter
to me one way or another if Suzanne had worked for her or
what she'd learned. If I was about to learn the same, then it
would only stand me in good stead. She was a remarkable
woman in so many ways.

Madame Joey poked me in the ribs. 'What did I just say?'

It was only then that I realised she'd been speaking to me. 'I
have no idea.'

'Your first lesson is to pay attention at all times. It's the tiny
details that matter. You can pick up a lot of clues from how
these men look at you and treat you. Most are absolute gentlemen, which is bizarre considering what they do. Especially the
Abwehr, who are in a different class to the Gestapo.'

'I'm already adept at reading people,' I said. 'I don't need to
learn how to do that.'

'Really? So you think you can read a German? You know
how differently the Abwehr and the Gestapo think? You understand how to seduce each of them so that they will not just want
you; they'll fall in love with you? That's the secret, you see.
Make a man fall in love with you and he'll tell you anything,
with or without a truth serum.'

I stared at her hands, waving in the air as she spoke,
weaving pictures of their own. She was like a conductor while I
was the soloist who needed to fit in with the orchestra. She was
right. German men marched to a different tune. One that I
needed to be able to play. 'I'm game for that,' I said. 'How do I
make a man fall in love with me?'

'The first rule is to make him want you and only you. You
do that by finding your own inner fire and fuelling it so that you
burn brighter than all the others. Then, just as with a real fire,
men will want to come and warm themselves by you.'

'I can do that. A smile, a flash of a low-cut gown. Always
works.'

Madame shook her finger. 'That's not real fire. That's just a few fireworks.'

Behind her, Suzanne was nodding as if she, too, knew the secret. Come to think of it, Suzanne had a way of making you do anything for her without so much as a smile or a few sweet words. It was how she'd got me talking to her in the first place, a perfect stranger in a Paris café. 'Tell me then – what is real fire?'

'Think about a fire, the flames. They dance. They throw out heat and light. They're lovely to sit by and to look at. But put your finger in them and you'll get burned. That's exactly how you should be. Luminous. Warm. And always slightly out of reach.'

Of course. Now she said it, I could see it. Suddenly the alluring smile and the low-cut gowns seemed like nothing more than cheap tricks.

'It comes from the inside,' Madame Joey went on. 'It starts in here.' She tapped me in the centre of my chest then pointed to my stomach. 'And in there. You must feel with your heart and soul that you are a goddess, a force of nature just like a fire. Men may come and feel your warmth and light, but they never, ever get a part of you.'

Where she'd tapped on my chest, just above my heart, I could feel something melting. The ice I'd wrapped around it perhaps. No, it wasn't that. It was the permafrost that had been there since my father had died. I'd learned about that from books too, the permanently frozen layer that covered parts of the earth. But there were some things you couldn't learn from books. The things I could see in Madame Joey's all-knowing gaze. She saw me, just as she saw everything.

'I understand,' I said, my voice thickened by tears.

'You think you do, but you don't as yet. That's because you haven't yet learned to love yourself. Until you do that, you will always be vulnerable. A vulnerable person is dangerous, especially in our line of work.'

I wasn't sure if she meant spying on the enemy or sleeping with them. The two appeared to be interchangeable, at least here. 'Alright then – teach me how to love myself, if that's what it takes.'

She snorted. 'I can only begin to do that when you drop your defences. You are fighting everyone, Christine. The whole world. When the biggest battle you must win is in here.'

I could feel her hand on my head this time, the heat that came from it seeping through me. She was the fire and I was sitting by her, soaking up everything she said, just as I had sat with my mother when she would read to me. Every now and then, Mum would look up from the page, telling me as much with her gaze as she did with the words she was reading. Madame Joey was doing that to me now. My chest heaved and a sob ripped from my throat, tearing the air between us.

She patted my cheek then handed me her handkerchief. 'There, there, *ma petite*. You're already learning.'

No hug, no taking me in her arms as my mum would have done, and for that I was grateful. Look but don't touch. Madame was right. I longed for that hug, and yet I was afraid of it at the same time. It was an irresistible combination.

'You must always make a man feel that he is privileged merely to be in your presence. Yes, even the Gestapo. Especially them. That way, you're not like the other girls, the common prostitutes they can buy all too easily. You're a courtesan, a woman of stature. Someone they must earn. In your case, by giving away their secrets.'

I gulped. Never once had I had to sleep with one of my test cases to decide whether they passed or not. The truth was, I'd never wanted to, and even if I had, it would have been unprofessional to do so. 'Just how far does a courtesan go?'

Madame and Suzanne exchanged a look. I could feel a band in my chest tightening.

'As far as is necessary,' said Suzanne. 'But no further. I leave that up to your judgement, Christine.'

I plastered on that smile, the one that was already less open. 'Whatever it takes.'

A fire, that's what I was now. Come too close and I'll burn you. Come just close enough and I'll set you alight in a different way. If only I was deploying this on a man I could actually love, a man who would love me back properly instead of the enemy.

Love myself first. Tall order. I wasn't made for love. At least, not a love that ever lasted. I'd loved my dad and he was gone. I'd loved my mum too, but she was also lost to me now, as were Tom and Elsie. Maybe it was better this way. Only one of us got hurt and it wouldn't be me. It would never be me again now that I had a new weapon. I could feel that permafrost melting some more. Set Europe ablaze, Churchill had said. Well I would burn it down in my own way.

TWENTY-SIX

OCTOBER 1942, PARIS, FRANCE

Suzanne crumpled the message and threw it into the hearth, where it caught light. It might only be autumn, but it was bitterly cold. 'SOE is setting up a new network here in Paris.'

I looked up from the dossier I was studying. 'Are they going to work with us?'

'No.'

'Good.'

We smiled at one another across the desk. Madame Joey had finally departed the previous day in a flurry of valises and suitcases. No doubt the Gestapo and the Abwehr were already aware she'd left, which was exactly what we wanted. The night before she left, we'd made an ostentatious public arrival, climbing out of a taxi to be greeted by her and swept into the building along with our luggage.

'When do you think they'll come calling on us?'

'The new network?'

'No. The Gestapo and the Abwehr.'

Suzanne glanced at the bejewelled watch that encircled her wrist. 'I should say sometime this afternoon, once they've had a chance to check us out.'

Our stories were watertight and the paperwork perfect, as it should be. We had new passports, ration and identity cards, along with travel papers issued in the prefecture of Haute-Savoie, to where Madame Joey was supposedly travelling. In fact, she was taking a connection to Marseilles with the help of an agent and a new set of papers which would allow her to reside there in anonymity until it was safe to return.

There was a knock at the door. 'Come,' called out Suzanne.

One of the receptionists poked her head around it. 'There's someone here to see you, madame.'

'Who is it?'

'Monsieur Aragon.'

'Show him in.'

Seconds later, an ebullient figure flung open the door and exclaimed, 'What a vision of loveliness,' taking first Suzanne's hand and then mine and bestowing on each a kiss. 'Marcel Aragon at your service.'

We'd met only a few days before when Madame Joey issued her final instructions, but this posturing was perfect and perfectly timed. Moments later, Pauline reappeared looking a little more flustered. 'Hauptsturmführer Braun to see you.'

Marcel raised an eyebrow at us. 'One of Kieffer's men,' he murmured, turning the full force of his charm on the man who strode briskly into the room, a small white dog under his arm, an apparently permanent sneer on his face.

'Hauptsturmführer Braun, what a pleasure to see you again.'

The German barely glanced at him, moving closer to the desk so that he loomed over us, a tall, pale figure with curiously vacant eyes, clutching his dog, who appeared to be nervous. Small wonder, given the scent of pure evil that wafted from his master. 'Hauptsturmführer Braun. This is a courtesy visit.'

I almost laughed. If there was one thing the SD didn't do, it was courtesy.

Suzanne stayed firmly in her seat. 'Madame Suzanne,' she said, her voice coolly polite.

He turned his watery gaze on me, and I noticed he had a twitch under his left eye, barely perceptible but interesting all the same.

'And this is my cousin, Christine.'

'Your cousin?'

His smile was loaded, the implication unmissable. I wanted to slap him. Instead, I matched him smile for smile. 'We're a close family.'

'Won't you sit down, Hauptsturmführer Braun?' added Suzanne. 'Some coffee perhaps? Pauline, could you bring some water for the dog?'

The poor creature looked as uncomfortable as we felt.

'That will not be necessary,' snapped Braun. 'This is, as I said, just a quick visit to welcome you to Paris. I'm sure I will see you again soon.'

With that, he turned on his heel and marched from the room.

'Well he was a charmer,' I muttered. 'That poor bloody dog.'

Marcel peered out into the corridor, checking the coast was clear before closing the door. 'Interesting that Kieffer sent one of his underlings. Braun hasn't been in Paris long, but he's already proved himself a nasty piece of work.'

'Should we be worried?' asked Suzanne.

'We should always be worried, but I don't think there's any immediate cause for concern. The Gestapo know that this place is popular with their men. They want you to understand that they're still in charge and that it's thanks to them you have champagne and caviar in stock.'

'Champagne and caviar that's consumed by them,' I said. 'While they're being entertained by our ladies.'

Marcel spread his hands in an unmistakably Gallic gesture. 'But of course. And you are, shall we say, the new leading lady?'

I regarded him coolly. 'In name only.'

'Naturally. I didn't mean to imply anything.'

'Christine is an expert,' said Suzanne. 'Madame Joey was good enough to share a few of her secrets with her...'

Marcel nodded in understanding – I'd been trained as a lethal weapon against the Nazis.

It wasn't just her secrets she'd shared. My hair was blonder, my lipstick a brighter shade of red, my attire alluring without being obvious. Best of all, I could now slink in a way that was pure Madame Joey. She wasn't the only one who could move like a cat.

'I'm delighted to hear it,' said Marcel. 'Sadly, I must leave you now too. I have a lunch date. An important one.'

'Oh?'

He tapped his nose. 'All in good time. *A bientôt.*'

Another bow and a wave of his stick as he left. Strangely enough, I hadn't noticed it before. Come to think of it, he had a limp too, one he disguised well but couldn't completely hide.

Suzanne clocked me looking at him. 'Marcel was badly injured when a rescue mission went wrong. He nearly died. It's a miracle he's still here, let alone that he does what he does.'

'What does he do exactly?'

'He knows everyone. Connects the right people. Even the Germans. Everyone needs a Marcel, especially us. He's one of the reasons we're able to establish a network here in Paris. Marcel will liaise between us and them, all the while working for the Resistance.'

'And we're absolutely sure he can be trusted?'

'With our lives if necessary. I know that because it was my life he was saving when he was shot.'

'By the Germans?'

She shook her head. 'By someone working for my father.'

I stared at her. 'Your father? Why? Where?'

'Here in Paris. My father isn't a good man. In fact, he's a

total pig. Marcel helped me escape the day I turned eighteen. It's thanks to him I got to London and that, in a roundabout way, I was able to come back here and do what we're doing. One day I'll deal with my father. Right now, we have a much more important job on our hands.'

For once in my life, I was speechless. Suzanne's story, in some ways, was like my own. Perhaps that was why she understood me so well. Why she'd given me a second chance.

'Promise me something,' I said. 'When the day comes to deal with your father, let me help you.'

She reached across the table and took my hand between hers. 'Thank you. But there are some things in life you must do alone.'

TWENTY-SEVEN

3 DECEMBER 1943, PARIS, FRANCE

'Churchill replied with his terms. Canaris wants to meet with us.'

I glanced around at the other people in the café then back at Charlie. It felt as if the weight of this war sat heavily on our shoulders, or at least what could prove a turning point in it. Ridiculous, I know, when so many others were involved, but they weren't the ones meeting with the chief of the Abwehr, a man who brokered deals with Churchill. 'What did he say?'

'Churchill? I have no idea. All I know is that Canaris wants to go ahead with the plan. We're meeting him at the convent again. Five o'clock sharp.'

Dusk was falling as we made our way through the streets towards the Rue de la Santé, the setting sun gilding the edges of the buildings that housed the empty shops and silent bars where those who hadn't yet been conscripted into forced labour might gather for a swift glass of rough wine before scurrying home to avoid the nine o'clock curfew. These weren't the streets where the German soldiers cavorted or where their officers sought their pleasures in places like Le Chat Noir. This was the occupied Paris of the ordinary citizens, a place where defiance was rarely uttered aloud but instead simmered behind closed doors.

Canaris was already waiting for us when we arrived, sitting in the front pew of the side chapel, eyes fixed on the statue of the Virgin and Child. I wondered if he was deep in prayer or thought, so still was he. As we approached, he at last turned his head, rising from the pew to greet us. In spite of the civilian clothes, he still had the bearing of a naval officer, his English impeccable as he introduced himself.

'Wilhelm Canaris. It is a pleasure to make your acquaintance.'

Charlie shook his hand. 'Likewise, Admiral. Why don't we all take a walk through the cloisters?'

Canaris looked startled for a moment then nodded in understanding. 'I can assure you that I came alone and I am not wearing any recording equipment. You can search me if you wish.'

'That won't be necessary. I think you have more to lose than we do.'

At that, Canaris smiled, a rueful smile that contained at once regret and resolve. He was doing this out of principle and a deep love for his country. I couldn't help but admire him for that even while I hated him for being who he was.

He looked at me. 'You're British?'

'Is it so obvious?'

'Not to my fellow Germans, no. Your French is flawless. But there is something about the way you carry yourself that reminds me of other British agents I have met.'

'It must be something they teach us.'

'Indeed.'

He had the gaze of a seafaring man, ocean-blue eyes looking beyond the horizon until they suddenly focused on me with surprising warmth. 'You remind me of my daughter,' he said.

'I do?'

'Not in the way you look, but there's something about you. I have two daughters. One, unfortunately, is handicapped. You might say that's why I'm here.'

We were heading through the door now, out into the shadowy cloisters, Canaris walking between us, his profile almost noble in the dim light cast from the windows of the convent. He appeared taller than he actually was, the quiet authority he exuded tangible. How a man like this had ended up doing Hitler's bidding was anyone's guess, although I could understand why he now opposed him. I didn't need to look at Charlie to know that we were going to let Canaris do the talking.

'The Nazis don't want people like my daughter,' Canaris went on. 'They think they should be exterminated. That they defile the purity of the race and are a burden on society. It's how they feel about the Jews and anyone else they consider dirty in some way. So they murder them.'

The wind was whipping through the cloisters, snatching at his words. I had to lean closer to hear him. Canaris glanced at me, although I could see his thoughts were far away, possibly with his family back in Germany. This man had hunted down and even murdered some of my fellow agents as the head of the Abwehr, sending his spies into Britain and the United States. The same spies that had been caught and turned by our people so that they were now spreading disinformation back to the Abwehr. I wondered if Canaris knew. Probably. He was a wily old fox, if there ever was one. A fox increasingly on the run from Hitler's hounds.

We stopped at the far end of the cloisters, where there was a bench set to overlook the courtyard at the centre. No doubt it was full of flowers in summer, but right now it was bare, the soil slumbering until spring.

Spring. The time of the supposed invasion. Not even Canaris must know any different. Especially not Canaris. He might want to do a deal with us now, but he was still the enemy. He stood by the bench, once more apparently deep in thought.

'I understand you received a response from Churchill,' said Charlie at length.

'I did.'

'Care to share it with us?'

'The terms of peace are quite clear. Unconditional surrender.'

'Well that's not going to happen, is it?' I blurted out.

Another rueful smile, fleeting this time. 'I'm afraid not. Hitler will never surrender.'

'Then what's the alternative?'

I was pushing, I knew it. And yet I had a feeling that whatever Canaris said next might well alter the course of history, if only his own.

'The alternative is to do to Hitler what he does to the Jews and the disabled and anyone else he hates. Believe me, it is hatred. A completely irrational one. He blames the Jews along with others for Germany's defeat in the Great War. The fact that we surrendered then still traumatises him. That is why I can tell you with absolute certainty that he will never surrender in this war. Which leaves us with no option but to eliminate him.'

The wind had momentarily dropped, his words falling into the stillness that had descended. There was nothing but this place, this time. The three of us standing here, talking about the assassination of the man who'd terrorised Europe for years, murdering millions.

'How do you plan to do that?' I asked.

'It's best you don't know.'

'Fair enough,' said Charlie. 'But what we do need to know is what you expect from us.'

Canaris tilted his head, contemplating the consequences of what he was about to say. 'I want you to infiltrate the Gestapo by acting as agents for them and find out what they know about our plans. The SS has long wanted to take us over. Things have become more complicated since the Gestapo infiltrated an anti-Nazi circle in Berlin in September. They got hold of some incriminating documents which could prove fatal for the Abwehr as well as all those involved with the circle. The people who belonged to it are currently on the run, but I fear the Gestapo will catch up with them any day.'

For a moment, Canaris appeared to shrink in the face of the fate that awaited each and every one of them, looking for all the world like a man in his twilight years, wizened by life and its cruelty. Then he remembered himself, straightening his shoulders under the coat that had briefly appeared to swamp him.

An equal master of strategic silence, Charlie let him stew for a few seconds. 'What do we get in return?'

This was it. All in. Time for Canaris to show his cards. Again, the wily fox chose his words with care. 'I will give you what you want.'

'Which is?'

'Let me speak plainly. We are all playing the same game when it comes to espionage. The British. The Americans. The Germans. You want what I would want, which is to ensure that the right information is passed to Berlin by my agents. Information that serves your cause. I'm sure you would also like to know the identities of those agents, especially those positioned around the coast watching for signs of an invasion.'

There were no flies on Canaris. I would give him that. His dignity was almost painful. Almost.

'The same agents who betrayed my colleagues? Who sent them to their deaths? You're absolutely right, Admiral. I want to know their identities and much more.'

Canaris looked at me as if seeing me for the first time. 'As I said, we are all playing the same game. It is unfortunate that it can have deadly consequences, but this is war. A war that has destroyed too many lives along with a country I no longer recognise as my own.'

I bit my tongue. Canaris might need us, but we needed him too, and he knew it. 'Then let's try to stop this madness sooner rather than later. We'll get what you need out of the Gestapo, one way or another.'

A genuine smile this time, one that lit up his faded eyes, washing them once more with colour. 'I have no doubt you will.'

Somewhere in the chapel behind us, a door slammed. The wind catching it probably. Perhaps the gods sending a warning. We were doing a deal with the devil after all. A thunderclap wouldn't have been out of place. Instead, the echoes of the words the wind had whipped away were being played back to us. Or at least the power that lay behind them. Help Canaris and we could be helping the whole world escape a madman. Get it wrong and not even the heavens would spare us.

TWENTY-EIGHT

4 DECEMBER 1943, PARIS, FRANCE

I saw him almost as soon as I was through the door, sitting at a table with Marcel and his friends as prearranged, just to the right of the bar. Marcel raised his napkin to his lips, patting the left-hand corner to confirm Kieffer was the one sitting to his left, although I recognised him at once.

Josef Kieffer, the head of the SD here in Paris, the birthday boy and my target. I glided forward, leaning one elbow on the bar as I half-turned, presenting him with a mesmerising display of cleavage along with a waft of my favourite perfume. I saw him look and then look again, his eyes glazed, his mouth slack. Good. Marcel had done his work well. He was just drunk enough to be emboldened, but not so much that he would fall into a stupor. At least, not yet.

I turned back to the bar; felt rather than saw him as he stumbled to my side, waving at the bartender. He was a few inches taller than me, thickset and muscular. Even though his eyes were glazed, they were also peculiarly opaque, like pebbles. They were scrutinising me now. 'Champagne for the lady.'

I glanced at him, arching an eyebrow. 'How do you know I even like champagne?'

He stared at me and for half a moment, I thought he might erupt. Then whatever was in his bloodstream took over and he gave me a disarming smile. 'I thought all ladies liked champagne. Have we met before?'

I bestowed a smile upon him in return, not so wide as to encourage him but just gracious enough to appeal. 'I don't think I've had that pleasure. My name is Christine.'

He returned my smile. 'Josef Kieffer.'

The bartender placed a glass of champagne in front of me. I raised it to him before taking a sip. 'Actually, it's my favourite drink. I was just teasing you.'

'I know.'

The friends he'd left at the table were nudging one another at this spectacle. I was pretty sure they'd never seen their boss in quite this kind of state, although he was, by all accounts, no stranger to socialising. Kieffer was famously affable to his victims, preferring to use guile rather than force to extract their secrets, leaving the dirty work to the torturers he employed. I would have to be extra careful when handling him.

I lowered my chin and looked up at him from under my lashes. 'Are you celebrating something?'

'It's my birthday.'

Guffaws and cheers from the table, where someone broke out into a chorus of 'Happy Birthday'. Evidently, they'd all had quite a lot to drink or perhaps Marcel had worked his magic on them wholesale.

'Excuse my men,' said Kieffer. 'We've been celebrating.'

'So I see.'

One of them abruptly pushed his chair back and strode over to plant a kiss on my cheek. Out the corner of my eye, I saw one of our security men twitch. They were here to make sure that the customers behaved respectfully towards the ladies, even the German ones. Although to be honest, it was more often the French clientele who had to be firmly but politely escorted from the premises. It was Madame Joey's golden rule that boorish behaviour was not to be tolerated, no matter from whom. Suzanne stuck to it now that she was in charge, exuding the kind of no-nonsense attitude that reminded grown men of their mammas.

Kieffer snapped a rebuke. 'Please accept my apologies on his behalf,' he said.

The German mumbled an apology in turn and slunk back to the table. Kieffer might be spiked to the eyeballs, but he was still very much in control. It was time to add a little extra spice to his drinks as well as to our conversation.

'More champagne?' I murmured. Little did he know that the barman had been filling my glass with sparkling apple juice.

Kieffer beamed. 'Let's have a bottle.'

Precisely what I hoped he'd say. The bartender duly popped the cork on a bottle of Taittinger and placed it in front of us in an ice bucket, pouring us a glass each. We had the timing down to a fine art. Just as the last drop was poured into Kieffer's glass, I brushed my hand against his, leaning forward so he got an uninterrupted view of my décolletage, while at the same time concealing the barman's sleight of hand as he tipped in the potion.

'I do hope you're having a happy birthday,' I cooed.

He smiled beatifically. 'The best one I've ever had.'

I handed him his glass and clinked mine against it. 'To birthdays.'

'To birthdays.'

He took a long, satisfying gulp.

Over at the table he'd abandoned, his men broke into another chorus of 'Happy Birthday'. I signalled to the maître d' and a gaggle of girls appeared, surrounding them, bearing a birthday cake, all smiles and giggles. I could see Sarah playing her part to perfection, casting coquettish glances our way as she set the cake down, pouting in a way that would have made the real Hayworth proud.

'I believe that's for you,' I said, taking another sip from my glass so that Kieffer mirrored me.

'What?'

He was growing fuzzier around the edges. Pretty soon now he'd be putty in my hands.

'That birthday cake is for you.'

He squinted at the cake in the middle of the table, candles alight.

I whispered into his ear. 'Why don't you blow those out?'

He ogled me, the look on his face unmistakable. 'I would rather do that to you.'

I pretended I hadn't heard him. He was just about ready for the next stage if his current state was anything to go by.

'Come on.' I laughed, taking him by the arm and helping him down from his stool.

He staggered to the table and bent over it, blowing out the candles while his men whooped and cheered. He beamed at them all, delighted with himself, then his gaze settled on Sarah.

His eyes narrowed, taking on a mean glint.

'Are you a Jew?' he snapped.

She took a step back, her eyes darting around, looking for an escape route even as she shook her head.

'You look like one,' Kieffer went on. 'Doesn't she?'

He reached out and grabbed her breast, twisting so she winced, then slapped her face, bringing tears to her eyes. The security man took a step forward, but I signalled to him to stand down. Kieffer's men were all gawping at her, some laughing, others rounding on her like a pack of hounds scenting a kill. Any moment now, they'd be marching her out of here and off to one of their prisons. Or worse, one of their camps.

'I-I'm not...' Sarah stuttered, throwing me a pleading look.

I stepped forward and took her by the arm, steering her

away from the table. 'Come now, gentlemen. Don't you recognise a good Catholic girl when you see one? We attend Mass together, for goodness' sake. This young lady is no more Jewish than I am.'

Kieffer grunted, not entirely convinced. Suzanne swept up to the table along with a waiter bearing an ice bucket. 'More champagne, gentlemen,' she cooed. 'Compliments of the house.'

Out the corner of my eye, I watched her lead Sarah from the room and relaxed slightly. As the waiter popped the cork, Kieffer's men turned their focus back to the task in hand. Drinking themselves into a stupor.

I placed my hand on his arm. 'Why don't we go somewhere quieter?'

He surveyed the scene, seeing his men now glugging back the booze once more as they fondled the other girls. I let my hand linger on his arm a moment longer than necessary. He licked his lips. 'Why not?'

As I guided him from the bar and towards the main staircase, I kept up the small talk, gesturing towards the paintings on the walls. 'We have a fine collection of paintings. Are you interested in art at all?'

'I'm interested in you,' he replied with a leer.

Better and better. The professional Kieffer would have been horrified by his own behaviour, but this wasn't the professional Kieffer. This was the malleable, manipulable version. The one who was going to recruit Charlie and then me by the time I'd finished with him.

'Have you seen the upper floor?' I continued. 'It's where we conduct our more private chats. I have my own rooms up there.'

That seemed to spur him on. He almost galloped up the last few stairs, stumbling over the top one.

He giggled. 'Silly me.'

I inserted my key in the lock. We kept my working rooms locked at all times in case any of our clientele should come snooping. Not that they would find anything. I'd bugged the place myself just to make sure. 'Not at all. Do come in.'

'Beautiful,' he slurred.

I wasn't sure if he meant the salon or me, although it was certainly a lovely room, decorated with the exquisite taste that was the hallmark of Le Chat Noir. It also had perfect acoustics, which meant we captured everything that went on in there all too clearly on our equipment. Kieffer didn't even glance at the lamp or the armchair where the bugs were located. Instead, his eyes were fixed on the bed visible in the room beyond, along with everything it promised.

I made straight for the sofa, where a fresh bottle of Taittinger was already conveniently sitting in its ice bucket on the table in front of it. 'Why don't we sit here and have another drink?'

He was still staring at the bedroom, so I patted the sofa firmly, holding out a glass to him with my best pout. 'What's the matter? You don't want to sit with me?'

His gaze shifted to my chest once more. I suppressed a sigh. They were so obvious, all of them. All except one. He was much harder to read.

I pushed the thought from my mind and focused on the task in hand, who was glugging his champagne now as if it was lemonade. With men like Kieffer, it always boiled down to one thing and that was how quickly and easily they could get what they wanted.

I took the glass from him and smiled sweetly. 'Tell me more about yourself. Do you like it here in Paris?'

He grabbed hold of my thigh, squeezing it so hard I had to stop myself crying out. 'I like you.'

A tinkling laugh, the one I deployed as a delaying tactic. 'You're such a flatterer. You remind me of an Irishman we had in here the other night. He said the sweetest things, but then, he would. He owed us a great deal of money by the time he'd finished at the tables, but that didn't seem to bother him. Apparently there's more where that came from. According to him, he's some kind of spy.'

I thought I saw a spark of interest in Kieffer's eyes. Hard to tell as they were so glazed. I pressed my point home. 'He tried to make me believe he's on a top-secret mission. Something to do with ships and steel. I'm sure it was all a ruse to try to get out of paying his bill. Although I have to say he seemed to be very friendly with some of the Abwehr.'

Kieffer's gaze sharpened, the veil of alcohol and drugs falling away as my words penetrated it. 'Have you seen this man before?'

'No, never. Although he said he'd be back. Said he liked spending time with people who "know how the world should be run". That was after we'd emptied his pockets. I expect he's going to try and win back his money, fool that he is.'

'If you see him,' said Kieffer, extracting a card from his wallet, 'I want you to contact me. This is my direct line.'

It wasn't a request. The cocktail of drink and drugs we'd given him might have temporarily dissolved his inhibitions, but professional Kieffer was back, the consummate Nazi officer.

'Of course,' I murmured, tucking his card into my brassiere. The move wasn't lost on him, but at that moment, there was a perfectly timed knock at the door. I moved to it before Kieffer could protest.

Marcel stood there.

'My deepest apologies, Major,' he said. 'But there's an unfortunate situation involving your men. I'm afraid we need you to intervene.'

Kieffer tried to leap to his feet, staggered and then righted himself. I pretended I hadn't noticed.

'It is I who must apologise,' he said, 'for having to leave you so abruptly.'

I dimpled as he kissed my hand once more. 'It's a great pity, but I do hope we'll see you again soon.'

'I hope so too,' he said, his eyes drifting yet again to my bosom, where I'd made sure to leave a tiny corner of his card poking out. 'And if you need to get in touch with me, you know where to find me.'

'I most certainly do.'

The moment his back was turned, I gave Marcel the thumbs up. We were on. He'd taken our bait. Now we had to keep feeding it to him until both Charlie and I were officially Gestapo agents. In the meantime, we had to get Sarah out of here. It had been a gamble attempting to conceal her among the other girls. And any good gambler knows when the game is up.

I could taste the bile burning the back of my throat. I swallowed hard. We weren't really working for those bastards. It was all a bluff. A huge deception to divert the Nazis away from the real invasion while finding out which bastard was betraying our people. One thing was for certain – once I knew who it was, I was going to finish them myself.

TWENTY-NINE

5 DECEMBER 1943, PARIS, FRANCE

The banging on my door only matched the banging in my head, the two reverberating in chorus as I stumbled to see who it was. I applied my eye to the peephole and saw Charlie raising his fist to rap on the door once more.

'OK, OK,' I said, unlocking first the deadlock then the bolt. 'Keep your hair on.' He looked at me as if I was speaking in tongues.

'It's a British expression. Probably an Irish one as well. You should learn it. In any case, what the hell are you doing here?'

'Great to see you too.'

He closed the door behind him and slumped on to the couch.

'Make yourself at home,' I muttered.

'Thanks. I will.'

'Can I get you a coffee?'

'That would be great. You look as if you could do with one too.'

'Charmed, I'm sure.'

'Not at all. I know you had a late night. How did it go?'

I swiped under my eyes, trying surreptitiously to remove

any traces of make-up that might be smudged there. 'It went well, now that you ask. I mentioned you and your little gambling habit that got you into trouble.'

'And?'

'He bit. Gave me his card and told me to get in touch if I see you. I suppose that means I should give him a call now.'

'Maybe wait until we've had coffee.'

'Milk? Sugar?'

'You actually have some?'

'Of course. The Gestapo keep us well supplied, as do the Abwehr. Although we make sure they don't know that the other is also stocking our shelves.'

'Very wise.'

I thought fast as I waited for the water to boil. Yes, I'd let him into my apartment. That didn't mean I needed to let him into my life. It was already too complicated. I'd seen other agents distracted by love affairs, and it always ended in disaster. Not that this was any kind of love affair, and nor would it become one, no matter how many sparks flew between us. Although, judging by his lack of reaction, he was either oblivious to them or far too used to creating a stir when it came to the ladies. Well we'd see about that. By the time I returned with a tray of coffee, he was already examining the books on my shelves.

'You have eclectic tastes,' he said, taking the tray from me and placing it on the table.

'Thank you, but my delicate little arms could cope. You said before that you like to read. Was that true?'

If he was taken aback at the sharpness of my tone, he didn't show it. 'Yes. Anything I can get my hands on. Always have.'

I couldn't help but smile. 'Me too. My mum insisted we have books in the house. I had a library card from when I was five.'

'Snap. Although we had our own library.'

The moment he said it, he looked embarrassed, as if he'd blurted out something obscene.

'Your own library, eh? You lucky thing.'

I loved the way his cheeks creased when he smiled, although he'd probably hate me for even thinking that. Actually, I hated me for thinking that. *For God's sake, Christine.*

'I was lucky. Am lucky. My family are in publishing, you see, so I've always been fortunate in that regard.'

'My family was usually in trouble, so you're definitely the lucky one.'

He looked at me as if he wasn't quite sure if I was joking. 'Is that why you're here? To escape the trouble?'

I could feel my stomach tightening. 'Something like that.'

He reached for the pot and poured the coffee. 'My mother always said I was attracted to trouble.'

'It's practically my middle name,' I quipped.

'See what I mean?'

His tone was light, his expression anything but. As he handed me my cup, our fingers brushed. The cup rattled in the saucer, slopping coffee over the side. Holding my hand as level as I could, I took a steadying sip and then another. All the while, he was regarding me with devilment in his eyes.

'So tell me: what's our next move?'

For half a second, I wondered if he was talking about our mission or something else. Something altogether more frightening. 'You tell me.'

'I say we go for it. Strike while the iron is hot. I'll drop by the club tonight and pretend to lose another stack of money. It's a Friday so there are sure to be some of Kieffer's men around, wanting to start the weekend as soon as possible.'

'Good idea. I'll make sure I'm in the gaming room so they notice me talking to you. Of course, I'll also let him know that I've seen you again.'

'Great. With any luck, word will get back to him from his men as well.'

I could feel it, that surge of excitement I always got when embarking on a mission. And what a mission. One that could actually help end this war. 'I could even call him from Suzanne's office. Act as if I really want to help him. That way, when he recruits you, it's going to be even easier to suggest bringing me on board.'

'At this rate, he'll be recruiting you first.'

I met his smile with one of my own. 'Would that be such a bad thing?'

He put down his coffee and sat back, his gaze unwavering. 'You love it, don't you? The intrigue, the game.'

'Yes and no. I love that we can spy on the enemy without them realising and that the information we gather is doing a lot of good. I hate the fact I have to even breathe the same air as them, let alone...'

'Let alone what?'

His voice was soft, barely above a whisper, his eyes inviting confidence.

I stared him out. 'You know.'

'I don't. Enlighten me. Just how far do you go? Would you have stopped me that night, or would you have let me go all the way?'

My pulse was quickening now so that I could feel its thrum. 'What do you think?'

'I don't know. That's why I'm asking.'

'I'd have stopped you of course.'

'Really?' He sounded almost disappointed.

'Yes, really.'

'That's a pity.'

'You think?'

'Yes, I do. I really do.'

Definitely disappointed. More than that, regretful. Which

was exactly how I felt too.

All at once, the room was tilting, white noise filling my ears. I was staring into a void, one that terrified me. I tried to swallow. My throat was sandpaper dry, my words scraping out. 'This is my job. An important one. It's what I do.'

'What about when it stops being a job?'

'It doesn't. And for the record, no, I don't. Not with them.'

The void began and ended with his eyes. They were staring at me now, deep pools into which I could fall and drown if I wasn't careful. He reached out and touched my hair, stroking it back from my face, tucking a strand behind my ear. 'You're so damn beautiful,' he said. 'Especially when you're like this.'

I tilted my head. 'Like how?'

'A little mussed up, like you just got out of bed.'

'I just did.'

He threw back his head and laughed. 'I love that. No messing around. You tell it like it is.'

'Only when I'm off duty. Put me to work and it's a different matter.'

I dropped my gaze, staring down into my cup, as much to escape his scrutiny as anything else. The strand he'd tucked behind my ear fell forward.

'That curl's as stubborn as you,' he said. 'And I've seen you at work, remember?'

How could I ever forget?

'That was just a standard test. You passed. No big deal.'

He feigned hurt. 'Oh I get it. You gave me the standard routine. What do I have to do to get the VIP test?'

'You work it out, Russell.'

'Please, it's Charlie.'

'Alright, Charlie. I'll let you know when you qualify. Now if you don't mind, I have some work to do.'

He got to his feet with a regretful smile. 'I'll leave you to it then. In the meantime, I'll be working on my gambler routine. See you tonight.'

It was only once I'd closed the door on him that I caught sight of myself in the hall mirror – hair a tangle, smudges under my eyes. Under all of that, a smile, one I quickly extinguished. So much for beautiful. I had a job to do. A mission to accomplish. Charlie Russell might be a charmer, but he was just a means to an end, a partner in crime. If you could call fighting the Germans a crime. It was sobering to remember that's exactly how they would see it. A crime punishable by death. And there was no way I was dying for anything but the cause.

THIRTY

He was already hunched over the table when I entered the gaming room, watching the turn of the cards with the desperate look of a man on a losing streak. I studied the other men at the table for a moment. A couple of collaborators I recognised. Another man I didn't, although I would bet anything he was an Abwehr officer. There was something about the cut of his dinner jacket, not to mention the haughty tilt of his head.

I glided to the table, and as I did so, someone else entered the room and moved to stand opposite me, observing the play. Braun. Kieffer's sidekick, who liked to carry a dog under his arm, although mercifully he didn't have it with him now. I could feel his eyes on me, so I kept mine on the table, watching Charlie throw hand after hand, playing just badly enough that it appeared ill-judged rather than deliberate. He was good, I would give him that, raking his hair with his fingers and looking increasingly distraught.

I leaned over at an opportune moment and murmured, 'Can I get you a drink?'

It was my job, after all, to encourage the players to keep spending even if that meant they lost their shirts.

'A whisky,' he muttered. 'Make that a double. Scotch. None of your damn Commie rubbish.'

I nodded to the waiter hovering by the door. 'Can I get you anything else?'

He looked up, doing a convincing double take. 'How about a kiss?'

The haughty type I had down as an Abwehr officer gave him a reproving look while one of the Frenchmen sniggered, knowing what was coming.

'Another remark like that and I'll have you thrown out of here,' I said, my words dripping with honey, although there was a sting attached. 'Perhaps you should concentrate on your cards.'

'Aw, macushla, don't be mad. I was just playing.'

And doing it so well. He was the epitome of the annoying drunk, just loud enough that everyone in the room could catch his accent. One or two stiffened, looking at him curiously. The ghoulish Braun remained dead-eyed, although behind them there was a flicker of something.

'Where are you from?' he asked, his voice as flat as his gaze.

'Dublin, not that it's any of your business,' slurred Charlie, a hint of an Irish brogue slipping out.

'You sound American. Not Irish.'

Charlie waggled a playful finger at Braun. 'Don't ever say that to my mother. She'd eat the head off you. Make no mistake. Sure, I went to school in the good old US of A. My father had to take us there for work seeing as there was none in Ireland, but I still bleed green. Want me to prove it?'

Not a flicker crossed Braun's face. 'That will not be necessary.'

'Hey, I'm serious. You want to see if my blood is as green as any other Irishman's? Go ahead. Shoot me.'

'I do not need to shoot you. I can tell you're an Irishman from the way you cannot hold your drink,' jeered Braun.

For half a second, I thought Charlie might overplay it and actually punch him. Then the waiter reappeared, placing his drink on the edge of the table. 'Your whisky, monsieur.'

Charlie ignored it, his attention apparently on the game and his dwindling pile of chips. Finally, he threw in his last chip with a despairing groan, downed his drink in one and rose from the table. 'Thank you, gentlemen. And lady.'

'Can I offer you another drink? On the house?'

He squinted at me. 'A drink? Why the hell not?'

The Abwehr officer tutted.

I offered Charlie my arm. 'If you'd like to come with me, I'm sure we can arrange that.'

He lurched as he took my arm, just enough to indicate that he'd had too much. 'Macushla, I'll go with you anywhere. Especially to bed.'

It was too much for the Abwehr officer, who leaped to his feet. 'Sir, that is no way to behave in front of a lady.'

'A lady, you say? I could have sworn this was a whorehouse.'

An audible gasp from the German. In its wake, a frozen hush fell across the room. Perfect. As was Charlie's next move, attempting a deep bow that ended with him flat on his back, staring up at me. 'Would you look at that? You're gorgeous from this angle too.'

At my signal, the security men stepped forward, scooping him up off the floor between them and dragging him, protesting loudly, from the room.

'My apologies, gentlemen. Please continue.'

Then I, too, made my exit, taking with me the impression of their expressions, especially those of the Abwehr officer and the Gestapo ghoul, Braun. Disapproving on the one hand, detached on the other, although in both I detected a glint of interest. Excellent. That was what we wanted.

Downstairs in Suzanne's office, Charlie was already waiting

for me when I entered. 'Good work,' I said. 'You're on their radar.'

'Well done, both of you,' said Suzanne. 'Now make your call.'

I pulled Kieffer's card from my purse and dialled the number, my heart thudding as I did so. No matter how long I did this, I would never quite get used to dealing directly with the Germans. It felt so wrong. Unnatural. And yet I had to do it. It was my job.

He answered on the first ring. 'Kieffer.'

'It's Christine from Le Chat Noir.'

I didn't have to ask if he remembered me. Of course he did. Kieffer was the kind of man who remembered everything, even when that memory was clouded with drink. 'How can I help you?'

'It's I who can help you. Do you recall me mentioning an Irishman? One who likes to gamble? Well he's here tonight and we're about to remove him from the premises. He got a little too enthusiastic, shall we say, while he was drowning his sorrows. His name is Charles Ryan.'

'I see. I assume he lost?'

'He did. Quite a lot of money. I have his telephone number if you'd like it.'

'I would.'

I read out the number from the slip of paper Charlie handed me. A line set up just for Kieffer, tapped so that our people could listen in.

'Thank you. I'll be in touch. Goodbye.'

I stared at the receiver, stunned. 'He hung up on me.'

'Kieffer's a man of action, not words. Let's wait and see what he does next,' said Suzanne. 'In the meantime, we need to throw you out. My guess is that he has someone on the way even as we speak, so we'd better make sure they have something to see.'

Charlie flashed a rueful grin. 'Great. First I lose. Then I get thrown out, and I don't even get the girl.'

'Yes, but with any luck, you'll get the German.'

'*We'll* get the German. We're a team, remember?'

Our eyes met. 'How could I ever forget?'

THIRTY-ONE

6 DECEMBER 1943, PARIS, FRANCE

He was back the next morning looking disgustingly well for a drunk who'd been thrown out only hours before. The receptionist called down to the office. 'There's a man says he needs to see you. A Monsieur Ryan.'

I looked at Suzanne, poring over the list we were making of all the known agents and Resistance contacts we'd lost from our network. It totalled well over three hundred now. 'I'll go.'

'Give Mr Ryan my regards.'

He was leaning on the bar looking completely unrepentant. 'I believe I left my wallet here.'

I wore my polite but professional smile. 'Mr Ryan. It's good to see you again.'

I looked at the bartender, busy polishing the fresh glasses. He was new. An unknown quantity. All the staff were hand-picked for their loyalty to the Resistance, but you could never be too sure. Especially not now with so many agents in prison or already executed. For all we knew, the Gestapo had managed to insert one of their own in here, although so far everything appeared to be continuing as normal. If you could call hiding fugitives while drugging, seducing and extracting information from our customers in any way normal.

'Philippe, has anyone found a wallet?'

'Unfortunately not, madame. If they had, it would be here, under the bar.'

As he ducked down to take a second look out of courtesy, Charlie leaned towards me and murmured in my ear. 'Kieffer called. He wants to have lunch. Today.'

'That was quick.'

He winked just as the barman resurfaced.

'I'm sorry, sir. If we find it or someone hands it in, we'll let you know.'

'Don't worry about it. I probably left it in my hotel room or somewhere stupid. I'm only concerned because I'm having lunch at Maxim's with a business contact. I'm sure it will be fine. They know me there.'

Maxim's. The Nazi restaurant of choice. And Kieffer's favourite. 'What time is your lunch?'

'One o'clock.'

'If you have any trouble, tell them to call me and I'll vouch for you. You are, after all, one of our best customers.'

A slight exaggeration but the right kind of emollient for this situation.

Charlie bestowed another broad grin on me. 'Why, thank you. That's very kind of you.'

'Not at all. We hope to see you again soon, Mr Ryan.'

As it turned out, very soon indeed. I made sure I was at Maxim's well before one o'clock, seated behind a pillar from which I could peer out without him or his companions seeing me.

Marcel was the first to arrive. Interesting. I hadn't known he was coming. Then Charlie, smartly dressed in a suit as befitted a businessman. I watched as he took his seat, leaning towards Marcel to share a joke, their shoulders shaking in shared laughter. I wondered if they shared secrets too. Marcel was our man, but loyalties could swiftly change. As for Charlie, only time would tell. He was good, I would give him that, rising to greet Kieffer when he appeared at their table, smiling into his eyes just as he'd smiled into mine. Secrets and lies. The currency of a spy.

'How's it going?'

Suzanne slid into the chair beside mine, glancing at the cocktail in front of me then up at the waiter. 'A Dubonnet please.'

Once he was safely out of sight, she murmured, 'Anything to report?'

'Kieffer arrived just before you did. They seem cordial enough.'

The shared jokes had given way to more intense conversation, but I could see from the way Kieffer was sitting, his shoulders relaxed and open, that he didn't suspect there was anything amiss. The other two were playing their parts to perfection, Marcel the smooth French go-between, while Charlie was just the right side of brash businessman. There was another man with Kieffer, one I didn't recognise, nodding at what was said while saying nothing himself.

'The tricky part is going to be convincing the Gestapo that someone like Charlie wants to work for them.'

Suzanne took a sip of her Dubonnet, her eyes never leaving the scene unfolding in front of us. 'Indeed, although they should swallow the part about him being deeply anti-communist and pro-Nazi. They already know about the gambling problem. That was well played.'

The place started to fill up with what felt like half the Wehrmacht, along with the plain clothes ghouls of the Gestapo. Our happy quartet talked on, Charlie listening to Kieffer rather than saying too much, Marcel oiling the wheels, the other man still nodding, unsmiling. I toyed with my food, not wanting to tear my eyes away while at the same time trying not to attract attention. One or two of the Abwehr officers nodded a greeting as they passed our table, although the Gestapo, to a man, pretended we didn't exist.

'He's gone for it,' murmured Suzanne.

I looked up from my plate. They were shaking hands, Kieffer rising now along with his sidekick, indicating he had other things to do. Cordial smiles all round. Charlie and Marcel sinking back into their seats, exchanging more conversation. The waiter pouring the last of the wine into their glasses. Glasses they raised and discreetly clinked together before drinking.

I looked at Suzanne. 'We're on.'

THIRTY-TWO

JANUARY 1944, PARIS, FRANCE

I huddled into my coat as I slipped out of Le Chat Noir and headed down the street. In my head, a list of errands. In my heart, a question. No news for nearly a month. No news was good news. Or so they said. In my book, no news was infuriating.

'Well, fancy seeing you here.'

I was a heartbeat away from bumping into him. Without giving me time to respond, Charlie looped his arm through mine and murmured, 'Walk with me. They're watching.'

'Where the hell have you been?'

'Long story. Now try to look happy to see me.'

I plastered a smile on my face, all the while seething. Almost an entire month without a word. 'I thought we were in this together?' I murmured.

He tightened his grip, returning my smile. 'We are.'

As we reached Café la Rotonde, his footsteps slowed. 'How about a drink?'

It wasn't a question.

Inside, he made for a window table, pulling out my chair for me before the waiter could say anything. 'Two glasses of your finest champagne.'

I bit my tongue. This was evidently all part of the pantomime we were playing, with Charlie directing for the benefit of our audience. I gazed at him rather than out through the café window. If they wanted a good show, they'd get one.

'How have you been?' I simpered. 'It's been so long, I was starting to worry about you.' I couldn't quite hide the vinegar beneath the honey.

He leaned forward and gazed into my eyes. 'I agreed with Kieffer I'd clean up my act if I was going to work for him.'

The waiter placed our glasses of champagne on the table with a flourish. I picked mine up, feeling the crystal stem, cold between my fingers.

'He doesn't mind you drinking then?'

'He doesn't mind what I do so long as I get results. No more losing at the tables though, as according to Kieffer that makes me vulnerable to approaches from other agencies.'

I choked back a laugh. 'What about womanising?'

'Funnily enough, that's why I'm here.'

'I thought it might be.'

'I've spent the last few weeks slowly convincing him that you could be very useful to him in between passing on useless information.'

'Does he know that it's useless?'

'Of course not. But he's very interested in you as a potential agent. That's why he has two of his men watching us from that car parked across the street. The car you're not going to look at because you're busy being in love with me.'

'With you?'

'Absolutely. That's the story Kieffer bought. We already have a bit of a thing going, you see. Something you'd rather your boss didn't find out about because you're forbidden to fraternise with the clientele outside of work.'

'I am?'

'You are. She doesn't want them spending anywhere else besides her club. What's more, you may be a little bit pregnant and need my help to deal with that.'

'What happens when they find out I'm not pregnant?'

'Unfortunately, you'll lose the baby. That will give you time to disappear for a while if necessary. And if this all goes to plan, it will be necessary.'

'I suppose you're the father?'

'I am.'

'Congratulations. That's only the second immaculate conception in history.'

'Told you I was a good Catholic, didn't I?'

'You're not that good.'

He leaned forward and plucked an imaginary speck of dust from my shoulder. 'How do you know?'

Damn him and his touch sending thrills right through me. 'Charlie, you and I aren't ever going to be declared saints.'

He smiled into my eyes. 'Might as well sin together then.'

That clutch at my heart again. My guts. And the rest. *Forget it, Christine. It's just a game.* I took another sip of my champagne. 'How do you suggest we do that?'

'We're going to go from here to the Ritz, where we spend a little fun time together. I've already told Kieffer that's where I'm staying. At some point, Kieffer's men will knock on the door and catch us there in flagrante. I smooth things over, and that's when you agree to work under me, so to speak.'

'You're funny.'

His fingers twined around mine. 'Christine, this is no laughing matter.'

'Believe me, I know.'

'I believe you. Now finish up your drink and let's move this on to the next stage.'

I gulped it back. 'See? I simply can't wait to get my hands on you.'

He threw a bundle of notes on the table. 'There you go. I feel the same.'

As we sauntered out arm in arm, I kept my gaze on Charlie, all too aware of the eyes watching from across the street. 'Have you already booked the hotel room?'

'Officially, no. Unofficially, Jim is already in position in the next room. That way we can record everything that's said so no suspicion falls on either of us later. We can also get pictures of Kieffer's men for our files.'

'Oh great. An audience.'

'I thought you liked an audience?'

'Quite the opposite.'

'Then you're a better actress than I thought.'

If only he knew.

The Ritz was the perfect place to conduct an affair. It always had been, even in wartime, not least because the staff were the souls of discretion. It also helped that they were stalwart supporters of the Resistance on the sly. The receptionist smiled in greeting, having evidently been primed for the purpose.

'Mr Ryan. Good to see you again, sir. Your usual room?'

A handsome tip slid across for the benefit of any watching Gestapo. 'Thank you. You'll ensure we're not disturbed?'

'But of course, sir. Anything else I can do for you?'

I gazed lovingly at Charlie. Might as well make the right impression for Kieffer's benefit. 'That will be all.'

The room was small but still luxurious, the Germans having requisitioned the best rooms and suites for themselves, with Hermann Göring taking the Imperial Suite. Of course. I wondered if he was up there now, planning how to make the lives of Parisians even more miserable while he stole their masterpieces.

The Ritz was a hotbed of Nazis living cheek-by-jowl with the very people they were suppressing. Then there was Coco Chanel, who lived here with her Abwehr lover, her rooms not too far from this one. Above all, this was a place for lovers. I moved to the window, all of a sudden unaccountably shy. This was ludicrous. I'd done this a hundred times before, although never as the supposed target.

'Like a drink?'

A bottle of champagne in a bucket was set out on a tray, along with two glasses.

'Is that a prop?'

'You could say that.'

I heard a tapping noise and looked down to see it was my own fingers dancing nervously on the windowsill in tandem with the butterflies doing a tango around my stomach. Nervous? I didn't do nervous. Except when it came to this man. Somehow, he got under my skin, right down to the raw nerves. The same nerves he sent tingling with a simple touch.

'Come here,' said Charlie, his voice gentle, the look in his eyes anything but. I stayed where I was, staring across the gulf between us, not quite meeting his gaze.

'Christine, I promise I'm not going to hurt you or let anyone else hurt you either. Ever. Now, please trust me. We don't have much time.'

He glanced at the door then back at me. His inference was clear. The Gestapo would be here soon, and they needed to catch us in the act or at least the prelude. Still, my feet seemed to be stuck to the floor. Yes, I'd done this a hundred times at least. But none of those counted. I couldn't remember a single one of their faces, never mind their names. The only face I'd ever seen in my dreams was his. The only man I'd ever really wanted was him. And now that we were here, I had no idea what to do.

Sensing my hesitation, he crossed the room, taking me in his arms and murmuring in my ear. 'It's alright. All you have to do is pretend. Is that so bad?' He eased off my coat, shrugging off his own so that it fell to the floor, his hands as gentle as his voice.

No, it wasn't so bad. Not bad at all. In fact, it was wonderful being there at last, held by him, feeling the heat from his skin inches from mine, inhaling the cologne I remembered, the one that had lingered in my memory long after he left. But he wasn't leaving this time. He was here, with me. And I wanted him so much it hurt, a deep ache of longing for something so much more than just the physical. I wanted him heart and mind, body and soul. All of him. Just as I wanted him to have all of me.

Then he was pulling me down onto the bed, unbuttoning my dress, all the while murmuring softly. The sweetest things. Words of endearment. The very words I'd longed to hear from him. Realisation washed over me, thoughts crashing one against the other. This was it. Love. Trust. Whatever you wanted to call it. And the only way to do it was to let go of the lies and the pretence, the persona we both played. It was just him and me. The two of us. I wanted it so much, and yet it scared the wits out of me.

'The thing is,' I whispered against his lips. 'I don't ever want to pretend. Not with you.'

He buried his face in my neck, dropping butterfly kisses all the way up it and down again until I was begging silently for more.

'Then don't,' he murmured. 'Let's never pretend. At least, not to one another. You're perfect just the way you are, bruises, scars and all. And I don't mean the visible ones.'

I cupped his face in my hands so that I could look straight into his eyes. I had to see what was there, to know if it was real or not.

What I saw sent a long shudder through me, a ripple of relief and acceptance and coming home. He was mine and I was his in that moment. I knew that. I'd always known that. We were so alike, Charlie and I, both scared of the inevitable. We could face down death with fortitude, but love was a different matter. And yet it was there, shining out of his eyes, along with a vulnerability that made me coil tighter around him, wanting to never let go, my body screaming 'at last', my heart whispering the same.

Cutting through the maelstrom of thoughts and feelings, a rapping at the door, growing louder. I groaned aloud. 'They're here already.'

More knocks. Impossible to ignore. 'I'm sorry,' muttered Charlie, tugging my bra down in one swift move before he rolled off the bed and made for the door.

'OK, OK, I'm coming,' he called out.

'Open up.'

Two men burst into the room dressed in plain clothes, one carrying a camera which he immediately began firing, the flash going off as, half-blinded, I played the outraged woman, grabbing the bedclothes to cover my modesty. He took shots of Charlie too, standing in his shorts and nothing else. I glanced at his companion. Jesus. It was Braun, his predatory eyes roaming over me as if I were a creature caught in his snare.

'Who are you? What is the meaning of this?' Charlie demanded as the pair began rifling through my handbag and anything else they could find in the room. I knew there was nothing incriminating, in fact quite the opposite, but it still turned my blood to ice to watch them. One false move, even a suspicion on their part, and we were as good as dead. All I could do was keep breathing as evenly as I could while maintaining that air of injured innocence.

Satisfied he had everything he needed, the one with the camera nodded to Braun, who scoffed, 'Come now, Mr Ryan. I think you know why we're here.'

'I don't know what you're talking about.'

'Ah but I think you do. We like to keep an eye on the people we employ. Especially someone like you.'

I feigned shock and horror. 'What's he talking about, Charlie? Do you know this man?'

Charlie shrugged, the picture of helpless resignation. 'I've been meaning to tell you...'

'Tell me what?'

He reached for a robe and handed it to me. 'You'd better sit down.'

'I'm already sitting, thank you very much.'

Braun pointed to a chair. 'Sit here.'

Wrapping the robe around myself, I flung aside the bedclothes and stalked to the chair, glaring at the two men and then Charlie in turn before sitting as tall as I could, silently hoping they wouldn't notice my legs trembling. Never show fear. My cardinal rule. Whether it was in a dank alleyway or looking down the barrel of a gun. A predator can always smell it, and the only scent I wanted to leave them with was the stench of their own death.

'How can I help you, gentlemen?'

Frost dripped from every word.

'It's not so much how you can help us as how we can help you.'

Braun's French was clumsy, his accent crude. But his tone conveyed everything he needed to say.

I turned my glare on him, my fingers itching to wipe the look of triumph from his face. 'Really?'

He smiled, pulled a packet of cigarettes from his pocket and offered me one. I ignored it. 'We're here on behalf of Sturmbannführer Kieffer. I believe you are acquainted with him.'

'I am acquainted with him, and I'll be sure to tell him of this outrage.'

'I wouldn't bother. He already knows.'

He tucked away his packet of cigarettes and pulled out a pipe instead, taking his time lighting it, enjoying what he thought was my terrified bewilderment. I widened my eyes, acting now for all I was worth. 'What do you mean?'

'I mean that Sturmbannführer Kieffer ordered this, shall we say, meeting. He has a proposal for you.'

'He does? Then he can deliver it to me himself.'

He studied me with the look of a man who was reaching the end of his patience. 'Sturmbannführer Kieffer is a busy man, as am I, so I will make this brief. We know of your situation, madame. It is perhaps fortunate for you that your, ah, friend here is currently in our employ and is therefore in a position to help you.'

I gave him a tinkling laugh. 'You're joking.'

'I'm not.'

A quivering lip now as I turned on Charlie. 'Are you really working for the Gestapo?'

'Yes, I am.'

'So you've been spying on me?'

'Not at all. I merely mentioned that I thought you could be useful to them as well.'

'Useful?'

'Yes, Christine. You're smart. You meet a lot of people through your work, people who could pass on information to you that might prove valuable.'

'I see. It's me you want to turn into a spy. And I thought you loved me.' I threw in a shuddering sob for good measure.

Braun smirked and relit his pipe. The smoke curling from it filled my nostrils, taking me back to our poky parlour in London, my stepdad lighting up his pipe in there, the smell of it soaking into my mum's cushions, my real dad's old armchair. I hated that smell. I still hated it now.

'You will be well rewarded. I understand that you are pregnant. We can take care of that too.'

Time to turn on the outrage. 'You told them that?'

Charlie shrugged. 'I had to.'

I turned my glare back to Braun, one now tinged at the edges with just the right amount of trepidation. 'What if I refuse?'

'Then unfortunately the photographs we have taken will find their way to your employer. From what I understand, she will not look kindly on you fraternising like this.'

'No. Please don't do that. I need my job. I have to send money to my family. My mother, she's not well.'

It wasn't hard to get the tears flowing now. All I had to do was think of my mum and how she'd suffered.

Braun sniggered. 'If you lose your job, I'm sure we can find you another in one of our brothels.'

I wanted to hit him. Hard. The German brothels were notorious for the cruelty with which they treated the women, who were little more than slaves. Rumour had it they even ran brothels in their death camps. Braun's implication was clear. 'Fine. Have it your way.'

'I take it you agree to our offer then?'

I sighed. 'I suppose I have no choice.'

His eyes gleamed, as pitiless as the glacial wastes they resembled. 'You don't. Mr Ryan here will give you your orders. You report directly to Sturmbannführer Kieffer. You will be hearing from us.'

I sat taller in my chair, refusing to be cowed, to back down.

Braun's smile was triumphant.

But mine was deadlier. 'I have no doubt I will.'

THIRTY-THREE

'Kieffer wants to meet with us both.'

Charlie's words echoed around the empty chapel. Two days since the hotel room set-up and I still couldn't get the stink of Braun's pipe out of my nostrils. It reeked of everything that was evil about the Germans, along with the same callous disdain that my stepdad had shown. But then, like the candle burning in front of me, what had passed between Charlie and I shone a light through the darkness. Whatever it was. I still wasn't sure, looking at him. I don't think he was either. There was so much promise and so much to fear.

Even as I gazed at it, the candle guttered and died, sending another scent into the air, hot wax and smoke mingling, over-laying the centuries of incense that had permeated this place. We were quite alone, and yet I felt a presence here. Stupid. Or maybe not. It felt as if someone unseen was trying to send me a warning.

'When?'

'Tomorrow at noon. He'll send a car.'

I looked down at my intertwined fingers that formed a fist,

trying perhaps to fight off that ominous feeling. 'What do you think he wants?'

'He's a cautious man. I think he wants to see for himself how we work together.'

I raised my head, looking him straight in the eye. 'How do you think we work together?'

'I think we do very well.'

A silence so deep I could hear the soft hiss of the other candle flames as they flickered. Or maybe that was my imagination too. I wasn't sure I even trusted my senses anymore, never mind my instincts. It was his fault. This man, sitting alongside me, so close I could once more feel the warmth from his body through my coat. The same body that had covered mine for a few brief, glorious seconds, sending out even more heat. The mouth that had uttered those words. Words I would hold in my heart forever.

'Why are you smiling?'

'Am I?'

'Yes.'

'I was just thinking.'

'About?'

'It doesn't matter.'

But it did. It very much did. At least, to me.

He tilted my chin with one hand, the other sliding around me, setting every nerve alight. I felt it again as our lips met, that sense of coming home. Charlie was my safe haven, and I was his, even as we teetered on the edge of a precipice together. Finally, reluctantly, we drew apart, Charlie tracing my mouth with his finger one last time, his eyes full of regret.

'We have to go.'

'I know.'

'Right then. I'll let you leave first. I'm meeting Jim in a half hour.'

'Did he get some good photographs?'

'They're already on file. Nothing too revealing of you, I promise. Like I said, this is to protect you as much as it is to add to the intel we have on the Abwehr.'

'I believe you.'

'I hope you do. Truly. We have to trust one another, Christine. It's the only way this will work.'

He wasn't just talking about the mission. I knew that. But trust wasn't a word I knew too well. Once upon a time maybe, but no longer. And yet back there, in that hotel room, I had felt myself yielding to him, opening up the part of me that longed to let go, to trust. To give myself to another human being and receive them in return.

I did up my coat buttons. 'I'll see you tomorrow then.'

A swish of my skirt as I slipped out into the aisle, raising my eyes to the crucifix dangling above the altar, blood dripping from the wound in Christ's side. He'd trusted his disciples and look where that got him.

I turned and walked down the aisle, hearing the candles sigh again as I passed them. For half a second, I fancied it was Charlie sighing my name.

THIRTY-FOUR

I was barely through the door of Le Chat Noir the next morning when Suzanne summoned me to the office.

'They're dropping in a new team for the Paris network. An organiser, a wireless operator and a new courier.'

I stared at her. 'That's utter madness. Look what happened last time.'

I could still see that young woman running for her life, the bullets slamming into her, cutting it short. As for the other two, we had no idea where they were, although it was safe to assume they were either dead or in the same place as Jacques.

'I know, but there's nothing I can do. There wasn't even a BBC broadcast. Marcel just sent word. London is adamant. They insist we need to replace the agents we've lost here, come what may.'

'Then they're sending more people to their deaths.'

'I agree, but the only thing we can do is try to keep them safe.'

'How can we do that when we couldn't keep the others safe? Especially now that they have Jacques.'

God help him. I tried not to think of what Kieffer and his

men could be doing to him even now. It was better not to dwell on it. All I could do was hope and pray he didn't break, for all our sakes.

'We have to try. We need a network here in Paris. It would take longer to set up a new one from scratch than to use what remains of the old one.'

'You and I are what remains of the network, along with Marcel, and none of us were ever really part of it. We did our thing, and the network did theirs.'

'It worked until these arrests started. The new team can try to resurrect what we had.'

I stared at my hands. I could have cheerfully used them to wring the necks of whoever in London thought this was a good idea. 'When is this drop?'

'Tonight.'

'You're joking.'

'I wish I was, but I only got the message this morning. It just shows how much we need a wireless operator and a courier, loath though I am to admit it.'

'We should be there to meet them. We can't let them drop blind. Either the Germans got lucky with the last lot, or someone must have given away the time and place.'

We looked at one another. The same someone we were trying so hard to track down with absolutely no success. Whoever it was, they had access to top-secret information, the kind of details that were only ever sent encrypted or passed on by word of mouth. My money was on the first.

Suzanne sighed. 'The problem is that we may be trying to track down a ghost, or rather a radio set that used to belong to one of the operators.'

The operators who were now banged up in Fresnes Prison or on a transport to some unspeakable camp in Germany if they weren't already there.

A memory stirred. Amalie telling me about Dachau,

where her father had been taken. Back then, I'd been so inno-
cent. Now I knew the ghastly truth, thanks to the reports that
had filtered out, carried by brave escapees. These were places
of death, centres of mass extermination where the inmates
were treated worse than animals, the Nazis reserving their
harshest treatment for those they despised most, such as the
Jews. Jews like Amalie's father. I wondered if he was even still
alive. As awful as it was to think so, it might be a blessing if he
wasn't.

'Can London help?'

Suzanne rubbed her temples, a gesture that told me the
thoughts were crowding in thick and fast but still not adding up.
'They maintain that everything appears normal with the
messages they decrypted.'

'Except that we know they're not. Somehow the Germans
have access to them. I thought we were the ones who'd cracked
their code, not the other way round.'

'I don't think it's so much a code they've cracked as at least
one agent.'

I nodded slowly. 'Possibly several now that both the Abwehr
and the Gestapo have had a go at them.'

'I wouldn't blame them. They are only human after all.'

We looked at one another, remembering. 'Nor would I. As
we both know, there's only so much you can do to train someone
to hold out against torture. After that, it's down to sheer grit,
and even then, the Nazis know how to break almost anyone.'

None of our training, not the mock interrogations or being
hauled out of bed in the middle of the night, sleep-deprived, to
be alternately screamed at or tripped up with a series of clever
questions, could prepare you for the real thing. The Nazis were
relentless, as I knew all too well.

'What time is the drop tonight?' I asked.

'Just after midnight. They're dropping them near a village
called Saintville. It's not far from Chartres.'

Chartres was a good hour's drive away, south-west of Paris. 'Are we going alone?'

'You're going alone. I have to stay and run this place, and Marcel is busy with a function tonight at which an important German general will be present.'

'What about the Americans?'

Suzanne took another long sip of her coffee then nodded. 'We don't really have much choice.'

'I'll go and ask Charlie if they can help. I have his address. His apartment isn't too far from here.'

'Is that wise? I have no doubt the Gestapo are watching him and probably following him too.'

'You know me – I'm careful. There's no other way to get hold of him or that other chap, Jim. We don't have much time. It's going to take us at least an hour to get to the drop zone.'

Suzanne pursed her lips, thinking hard, then nodded. 'Very well. But make sure you get back here by three o'clock, or I'll come looking for you.'

'As if that won't set the Gestapo alarm bells ringing.'

'Three o'clock. I'll see you back here.'

That gave me around forty minutes to get to Charlie's and back again. I was on my feet and out the door before she could change her mind. One of the reasons Suzanne was so brilliant at what she did was that she never took unnecessary risks. One of the reasons I had so nearly failed my training was that I took them all the time. I liked to think it was how we worked together so well, balancing one another out. I wasn't so sure Suzanne felt the same.

THIRTY-FIVE

I gave myself a final once-over in the mirror, tugging my dark wig more securely into place then covering the whole with a hat I pulled low before wrapping a scarf around my throat. Good. Now my face was barely visible. Next, I shrugged on a baggy coat and sensible shoes that wouldn't have looked out of place on a Parisian matron. It was freezing cold outside so no one would give me a second glance.

One final thing – I had to change my walk. A few moments' practice replacing my customary sashay with a far more muted shuffle and I was satisfied. If there was one thing I excelled at, it was being a chameleon. It was why they'd picked me out of training to be an *agente provocatrice*. Although I often thought it was why Suzanne had picked me for my role long before that, perhaps even as far back as that first time she met me in the café where I was already busy shedding my past en route to the woman I would become. The woman I'd just buried under a disguise.

Taking one last look at myself in the mirror, I almost curt-seyed. In another life, I might have joined the theatre. Instead, here I was in the theatre of war.

I slipped out of the back door and in among the other Parisians scurrying along the pavement, going about their daily tasks while trying to attract as little attention as possible. It was safer that way. The Germans tended to pick on anyone who stood out. Blending in was what kept you alive, whether that was in a bordello or out here, with the ordinary citizens who were simply trying to stay under the radar so they could get through each day unscathed.

I recited the address in my head as I trudged along, head bowed, shoulders hunched. The apartment was a few streets from Avenue Foch. Trust the Americans to choose a safe house in the 16th. No slumming it in Pigalle for them.

I stopped to light a cigarette in a doorway opposite the building, looking back down the street to check I'd not been followed and across at the apartment block itself to make sure there was nothing out of the ordinary. Only when I was satisfied there were no German agents watching did I cross the street and press the bell for the concierge.

The concierge looked me up and down, a knowing expression on her face. I wondered how many women came calling at apartment eight. It seemed from her expression I was most certainly not the first. As if to confirm my suspicions, a woman answered the door when I knocked.

'Hello. I'm looking for Mr Ryan.'

If she didn't know his codename, I'd make my excuses and leave.

A moment as she studied me with clear hazel eyes, her dark hair swept behind her ears, displaying a pair of small, gold hoop earrings. She was startlingly pretty in a very French way. A bolt of something I scarcely recognised shot through me.

'Your name?'

'Christine.'

'A moment.'

The door shut once more, and I could hear low voices – hers

and that of a man. When the door opened again, Charlie stood there. 'Christine. This is a surprise.'

'Evidently.'

'Come on in.'

He looked as if he'd just got up, shirt open, his hair standing on end, a day's growth of stubble adorning his chin. That pang again, twisting my stomach. Surely to God I wasn't jealous? Charlie was just a man after all. And before that, my mark. *Who are you kidding, Christine?* Myself obviously.

'Sleep well?' I asked, instantly wishing I could have bitten my tongue.

'I didn't, thanks, as it happens.'

'I must be going,' said the woman. '*Au revoir*. I will see you soon.' She offered me her hand. 'It was good to meet you. I've heard a lot about you.'

'Good to meet you too, and I wish I could say the same.'

I stared after her as the door shut, a faint scent lingering in the air, one that tickled my memory. Not her fragrance but Charlie's, standing just behind me, his face unreadable. I remembered the scent now. It was the same one I'd smelled that night in my apartment and again just a few nights ago at the Ritz. That musky, lemony mixture of cologne and pure male. Or rather, not so pure. *Focus, Christine.* You have a job to do.

'We need your help,' I said. 'There's a drop tonight. They're flying in a new team to run the Paris network. The problem is, there's no one to meet them now that the Gestapo and the Abwehr have arrested the entire network between them. I can't ask what remains of the Resistance in case they're compromised too, and I don't want them to be dropped blind. Can you come with me?'

'Of course.'

I blinked. I hadn't expected it to be this easy. 'Great. What about your friend?'

'Jeannette? She's otherwise occupied.'

'I meant your friend Jim.'

'Ah, right. He's busy too on the same op as Jeannette.'

'So she's X-2 as well?'

'She's part of something different we're running with you Brits.'

'And you can't tell me about it?'

'Afraid not.'

'I see.' A pause. 'Well, I'd better be getting along too.'

'Are you OK?'

'Never better.'

He didn't look convinced. 'Good. In that case, I'll see you later. What time and where?'

'I'll pick you up outside the Gare Montparnasse at ten thirty sharp. That should give us plenty of time to get to the drop zone. Come out of the station as if you've just got off a train. That way we have a ready excuse if anyone stops us. I'll be your loving girlfriend picking you up in a black Hispano-Suiza.'

'No acting required then?'

'You're funny.'

'I'm not kidding.'

I had no idea if he was or not. 'Right, well I'll be off. Remember: ten thirty sharp.'

He was still grinning as I closed the door. Bastard. So long as he was there on time, that was what counted. Charlie might like to think he had the upper hand. If so, he had a shock coming to him.

THIRTY-SIX

True to his word, he was there bang on time. I pulled up to the station at 10.29 p.m. precisely. One minute later, he strode out, hat pulled over his face, and jumped into the car, planting a resounding kiss on my lips, one that lingered far longer than it needed to.

'Nice outfit. Better than the last one. Nice car too.'

I glanced down at my black slacks and boots. Serviceable, unlike the car, which was not just sleekly beautiful but fast. 'It's Madame Joey's. She left it for us to use.'

'So your little ruse was just to get a kiss from me?'

'You wish.'

'No harm in wishing.'

I snorted as I thrust the car into gear. We drove in comfortable silence out through the Paris suburbs and towards the drop zone. So much remained unspoken. Or perhaps nothing at all. I thought I was good at reading people. It was what kept me alive after all. And made me good at my job. When it came to Charlie, though, I was flummoxed. I couldn't tell if he was playing or serious or even testing me too.

'Saintville's that way,' he said, breaking the silence. 'We just passed a sign.'

'How did you know we were heading for Saintville?'

A beat, long enough for my heart to start thudding in time with his, getting faster every second.

He let out his breath on a long, slow exhale. 'OK, I'll level with you. We have our own separate communications system in X-2. We got the message about this drop at around the same time you did.'

So that was why he'd agreed so readily to come along. He was already prepared. 'When exactly were you going to tell me about that?'

'I wasn't, but I'm dog-tired so it just slipped out.'

Had it? Yes, he was new to the field. Or at least, new to X-2. I'd been his final test after all. His passing-out parade. Although he'd never once been stupid enough to fall for that. Or me. Until now.

'Maybe you should get more sleep then.'

'I would love to, but I had to stay up all night on that other op.'

'Look, if you're involved in something else here, don't you think it's only common decency to tell me what it involves? It's my life at stake too, remember. If you're so damn tired, you might just make a fatal slip.'

He stared out through the windscreen. For a man who said so little, he managed to speak volumes with his silence.

'OK,' he said at length. 'You're right. Again. We've been running this op with you Brits since the summer, inserting small teams of local operatives in the countryside around Paris ahead of the invasion to report on German troop positions and movements.'

'If you've been running this op with us, how come I don't know anything about it? I'm sure Suzanne doesn't either, or she would have told me.'

'That's because we're running it with the Free French and SIS.'

Secret Intelligence Services. MI6. Who, of course, hadn't felt the need to inform us. 'What's this op called?'

'Operation Sussex. I'm sorry no one told you about it, but it's not up to me.'

He rubbed his eyes, lapsing back into silence.

'If you're not up to this, just say and I'll do it on my own.'

'I'm totally up for this, and there's no way I'd let you do it on your own.'

'I don't need your permission to do anything, Lieutenant Russell.'

A brush of his hand on my knee, different to the time before. This was meant to reassure, not send my pulse racing. 'Hey, I'm on your side, remember?'

I jerked my knee. A reflex reaction. 'Are you?'

'What do you mean by that?'

'Nothing.'

Which, of course, meant everything.

'If you don't trust me, why the hell did you bring me along?'

'I honestly have no idea.'

'Fine. You're absolutely right. You're better off doing this on your own. Pull over and I'll get out here. I'll make my own way back to the city.'

'You know I can't do that.'

'Because you need me?'

'Loath though I am to admit it, yes.'

Another shimmering silence.

When he spoke this time, it was without a trace of the banter that normally passed between us. 'Maybe that's why I annoy you so much.'

I glanced at him in surprise. 'You don't annoy me.'

'Keep your eyes on the road, and yes, I do. Thing is, Christine, if you and I are to work together, we need to get along as a team. I know you're used to doing things alone, but right now you have a partner, and that partner is me.'

I bit back a retort.

'But you know, maybe that's the real issue here. We do get along, in a different way. We get along so well it scares us both.'

I took my eyes off the road for a second. 'What do you mean?'

'You know what I mean.'

Of course I did. That inexorable pull between us. The same dizzying feeling I got when I looked over a cliff and the waters beckoned, siren-like far below.

Another sign flashed up through the windscreen. Saved by the bell. 'We're here.'

THIRTY-SEVEN

I slowed the car to a crawl, steering down a farm track, cutting the engine and turning off the lights before pulling the map from the concealed compartment under my seat. A handy precaution Madame Joey had installed in case she was ever stopped and searched.

'The drop zone is there,' I said, stabbing at the map. 'From my approximation, we're here. There's a copse to the left of the zone, but otherwise the only cover appears to be these hedges running alongside the field.'

Charlie leaned over, studying the map intently. 'I took the liberty of contacting one of our teams out here. Their mission is to find drop zones and safe houses for incoming agents. They told me there's a barn not too distant from this drop zone. A sympathetic farmer owns it. They've used it for other drops. They also said they'd be happy to beef up the reception committee.'

I didn't know whether to hug him or hit him. What mattered most, after all, was the safety of our agents. 'That was very kind of you.'

'Not at all. We're all on the same team.'

Ah yes. The team thing. 'Do you know where this barn is on the map?'

He pointed to an area just behind what looked to be a line of trees separating it from the drop zone. 'About here, according to the coordinates they gave me. Luckily, as you can see, it's not marked on the map, which means our German friends have no idea it exists.'

Lucky indeed. And with a bit more luck, the Germans wouldn't stumble across it either. 'Perfect. We can hole up there.'

'That's what I thought. It's only a hundred yards or so from the actual drop zone as the crow flies.'

He was right, although those hundred yards ran across a stream and through another wooded area. Even more cover.

'That's settled then. Let's go.'

We made our way back to the main road and turned down another track towards the barn, bumping over ruts and potholes until, finally, it appeared, the track running on from it to the farmhouse that sat low in the lee of the hill. There was no light on in any of the windows, but still, we sat in the car for a good five minutes, watching.

'If we've used this field successfully before, chances are it's safe,' I murmured.

'I'm not so keen on chance.'

'Me neither, but it's all we've got. Where are we meeting your people?'

'They said they'd find us.'

'Impressive.'

I opened the car door and slid out, carefully secreting the key on the right-hand front wheel. Good for a quick getaway and far better than tucking it in my pocket for the Germans to find if I got caught.

The barn was vast, its arched entrance leading into a cavern stuffed full of wagons, tools, bales of hay and, on closer inspection, anything else the farmer could hide away, including a few barrels of wine and what looked like some hams hanging from the rafters, all of it visible as dim, grey shapes in the moonlight that filtered through the broken windows. This far from Paris, there was nothing to bomb, and I doubted many patrols came out here, but still, he was taking a risk.

I moved to one of the windows, looking out at the fields beyond, more grey oblongs punctuated by the silhouettes of trees and blurred by hedges.

'It's just before midnight,' I said. 'That's the drop zone there.'

Charlie came up behind me, looking over my shoulder to where I was pointing. I could feel his breath on the back of my neck, a strangely comforting sensation.

I stared out at the fields again, seeing that young woman sprinting across the field, delicate and yet so determined, a hunted creature running for her life, a life that had ended in a burst of bullets, her face landing in the dirt. It would be different this time. It had to be.

I scanned the horizon, the trees, looking for anything that might indicate the presence of the enemy. Nothing. 'Where are you, you bastards?' I murmured. 'Are you out there?'

'No one followed us,' said Charlie. 'I'm absolutely sure of that.'

'They didn't last time. They got there ahead of us.'

'There's no way they can know about this drop. Our lines are secure. You heard about it from a trusted source rather than a radio message.'

I turned away from the window, staring at him, his face stark in the moonlight, its crevices and hollows more pronounced. Hollows that held secrets, as did his soul. 'As far as I'm concerned, no one is a completely trusted source. Not even you, Charlie. Or your people, come to that.'

'Smart.'

'Maybe.'

I glanced at my watch again, listening hard all the while. No sound of a plane. No noise at all except that of our breathing and what I would swear was Charlie's heart beating, although it could have been my own filling my ears.

There was another sound above it, the soft tread of footsteps. I whirled to see the woman from his apartment, Jeannette, along with a couple of men, all three of them dressed entirely in black, the torches in their hands switched off.

'We checked the field. All clear. What time is your plane due?'

I checked my watch again. 'Twenty minutes from now.'

'We should move out. Get in position.'

'I realise that. We were waiting for you.'

Her teeth flashed in the dim light. 'Well we're here now.'

'Thank you for coming.' I turned to Charlie. 'You have your torch?'

'I do.'

'I don't know how you conduct your drops, but here's how we do it. I'll flash the letter signal. The pilot will respond. Then, and only if he gets it right, you all flash yours in formation.'

'Roger that,' said Charlie. The others nodded.

'The ground is too hard to bury the chutes and their flying suits, so we can bring them back here and burn them.'

One of the men piped up. 'What if someone sees the smoke?'

'If we do it inside this barn, we should be able to contain it.'

He looked doubtful. 'OK.'

'I have a better idea,' said Jeannette. 'There's a slurry pit on the other side of this barn. We can throw them in there.'

Charlie threw her a smile. 'Good thinking.'

I suppressed a surge of irritation. She was only trying to help. Even so, I was in charge here. And I didn't appreciate that smile. 'Fine. We'll do that. Should anything go wrong or we get separated, we rendezvous back here.'

With that, I headed for the door, feeling rather than hearing Charlie fall in beside me.

'If it does go wrong, I want you to know one thing,' he murmured.

'What's that?'

I would never know what he was about to say, because at that moment I heard it. The distant whine of a plane.

THIRTY-EIGHT

We were in place with seconds to spare, crouching in the ditch behind the hedge that bordered the field. I flashed the letter signal. The pilot flashed back with his landing lights – dash, dot, dash, dot. C for Charlie.

'OK,' I whispered.

Everyone moved into position, forming a wide arc, torch beams turned skywards to guide the pilot in. The plane was descending, figures falling from it, parachutes opening only a few hundred feet above the ground, the air currents catching them so that all but one landed in the next field.

'Shit. We need to get to them.'

I was rising off my haunches and about to sprint across when Charlie grabbed my arm. There were lights in the distance, beyond the neighbouring field in which they'd landed. Lights which were moving at such speed they could only belong to vehicles. In a few more seconds, they'd reach the spot where two of the agents had landed. I could see the other one staggering around in our field, trying to disentangle themselves from their parachute.

'Let go of me,' I hissed. 'We need to help them.'

'It's too dangerous. Those look like German jeep lights. Do you want to get caught too?'

'No, but what else can we do? We can't leave them there like sitting ducks.'

'She's right,' whispered Jeannette. 'We can distract the Germans while you extract your people.'

I looked from her to Charlie. 'How the hell are you going to do that?'

'I have an idea,' muttered Charlie. 'You two come with me.'

With that, he was running back to the barn, keeping low, taking Jeanette and one of the men with him while the other stayed with me.

'Come on then,' I murmured, getting to my feet and racing in the opposite direction, towards the agents, all the while seeing the lights draw closer and closer, keeping low, my eyes raking the field for the one who'd landed closest, gesturing to the Frenchman with me to head towards the others.

'Over here,' I hissed as loudly as I dared, seeing them break free at last from their chute. As I moved closer, I could see it was a man, although he looked barely out of his teens. 'Go that way, through the hedge and keep going until you reach a barn. It's hidden behind the trees. Wait for me there.'

He gaped at me.

'Go on,' I urged. 'Hurry. I'm going to get the others.'

'You're English.'

'Yes. Now hurry. The Germans will be on us any second.'

He needed no further encouragement, gathering up his parachute as he'd been taught and stumbling past me. I kept going, trying to outrun those lights, vaulting the hedge at its lowest point, tearing my clothes free as they caught and snagged, forcing myself onwards to where I could see three figures now running towards me. Behind them, the lights were much bigger and brighter now, sweeping across the adjacent field. Shit. Those were definitely German jeeps. Who else would be racing across a French field like that at dead of night?

All at once, another pair of lights raced across, weaving between them, circling round and round as the German vehicles spun in turn, unable to keep up with the faster car.

'You mad bastard,' I muttered. It had to be Charlie. In my car. If he totalled the Hispano-Suiza, I'd kill him.

I could hear shots now, but whether they were from Charlie or the Germans, I couldn't tell. Then another noise, the roar of a tractor lumbering towards the lights too, picking up speed. We had surprise on our side, but we were still hopelessly outnumbered. There must have been four jeeps in that field and God knows how many German troops. Kieffer really was determined to get his hands on our agents, dead or alive.

'Run,' I snapped at the agents and my helper, beckoning to them to follow me. 'Come on.'

As I sprinted back across the fields, I didn't dare look back. It was only when I got to the edge of the woodland that shielded the barn from the open ground that I halted, gasping for breath. They were right behind me, parachutes abandoned. No point in hiding them. The Germans had seen everything. All we could do now was try to disappear.

As they reached me, they pulled off their headgear and I gasped.

'Amalie.'

THIRTY-NINE

I held my breath as we crept into the barn. Still empty. For now. I pushed the door to, urging them forward, forcing myself not to look at Amalie. Of all people. Here. Into the heart of a network that was doomed. I knew it. London knew it. What the hell were they thinking? Right now, the best I could do was try to keep them out of German hands and alive. No easy task with Kieffer's men snapping at our heels.

'No talking,' I ordered. 'Everyone move to the back of the barn, behind those hay bales. I'm going back to try to find the others so we can get you out of here.'

They were all staring at me, or rather past me, over my shoulder. I turned. A man stood there, rifle at the ready. He looked at me and then at the agents still in their flying suits, sizing up the situation, holding a finger to his lips before beckoning to us to follow him.

The Frenchman with us moved forward, shaking his hand vigorously while murmuring, 'Salut, mon ami.'

This must be their sympathetic farmer friend. Good. Still, I held my gun close to my side, ready and willing to use it. He glanced at it as he ushered us along the track and into the farm kitchen, where his wife stood waiting, a pot of hot coffee on the stove. The farmer closed and bolted the door behind us before fastening the shutters across the windows then motioning to us to sit.

I tried not to stare at Amalie as she took her cup of coffee from the farmer's wife with a whispered, '*Merci*,' the stove casting enough light for me to be able to see the weariness on her face along with that of the others.

They must have been travelling since dawn, driving down from London to Tangmere before all their clothes and other items were checked over to make sure they bore no indication they were from England. After that, the long, tense wait until their flight was given the go-ahead followed by final instructions that included the offer of a suicide pill. Most took it, sewing it into their cuffs in case of necessity. I remembered when I was offered mine, staring at it in horror.

'It's that or the worst the Jerries can do to you,' said the sergeant in charge. 'Believe me, even the best break and then they take their mates with them.'

The pill was no longer sewn into my cuff. Instead, it was hidden under the stone of the ring I wore constantly on my right hand, a gift from a Gestapo admirer. I'd figured I might as well put it to good use, and how better than outwitting the Nazi torturers?

I glanced again at Amalie, remembering what I'd told her back at Beaulieu. I wondered if she'd listened. If she had her own pill sewn into her cuff or hidden elsewhere.

Our eyes met. I looked away again. The less I knew, the better. Especially when it came to someone like Amalie.

We must have sat in that farmhouse kitchen for an hour or more, silent apart from the sound of the coffee bubbling on the stove and the occasional sniff from the farmer, when there was a tap at the door.

Instantly, everyone froze, eyes sliding towards the door. The farmer shook his head, waving towards the next room. His wife quietly extinguished the flame under the coffee pot, took Amalie by the hand and led us all through into the salon.

A moment later, I heard the farmer call out, '*Qui est là?*' *Who's there?*

Another voice, too low for me to make out, although it sounded male. I was so tense I could feel my stomach aching, my shoulders rigid against whatever was coming next. The sound of the door opening. A scraping noise as the farmer bolted it again. Then footsteps. More than one set. My finger was curled around the trigger when he strode through into the salon where we were clustered, holding his finger to his lips as he had when he'd led us from the barn. On his tail, Charlie, along with his two companions. I wanted to slap him, the stupid, brave idiot.

'What the hell did you think you were doing?' I hissed.

'Saving your ass and everyone else's,' he retorted.

'Where's my car?'

'It's safe.'

The farmer made a slitting motion across his throat, pointing to the windows and the door. I got the message.

'We waited to make sure we weren't followed,' whispered Jeannette.

I was warming towards her. She had a cool head on those shoulders and a streak in her I recognised, one that didn't conform for anyone.

Ten long minutes later, the farmer led us back into the kitchen where his wife immediately began fussing round, bringing out hams and cheese from the larder, along with hunks of corn bread, pressing all of us to eat.

I cast a surreptitious glance at Charlie as I bit into the bread and slurped my coffee, which wasn't coffee at all but that strange chicory mixture that was all many people could get. At least out here in the countryside they could raise their own meat and grow vegetables, along with the corn that was turned into flour, the Germans taking the wheat for themselves. He wasn't eating or drinking anything. Instead, he kept glancing at the door and the windows, as if he expected the Germans to break through them at any minute.

'Here,' I said, handing him a piece of bread along with a slice of ham. 'You need to eat something.'

He barely looked at it. 'We need to get out of here.'

I stared at him. 'Why? Shouldn't we stay put until we're sure the Germans have left?'

My words were obliterated by the sound of an explosion. The farmer rushed to the window, pulling aside the shutters so we could see flames shooting from the barn at the end of the track.

Another huge explosion followed by a crash as part of the roof gave way, caving in and collapsing as the fire took hold. Silhouetted against the inferno, two jeeps along with soldiers, weapons raised, obviously intending to cut down anyone who burst from the burning barn.

He slammed the shutters across again. 'This way.'

As one, we rose from the kitchen table and followed him to the back door. He opened it, pointing out into the darkness at the fields beyond. To our right, woodland offered cover.

'The car?' I whispered to Charlie.

He pointed to the right.

I headed in that direction, stepping out of the door first, leading the way. This was my op, and I was determined to see it through without any casualties if I could possibly help it. No time to think about how much some of these people meant to me. Each was equally important right now. It was up to me to keep them alive, whatever it took.

FORTY

The car was hidden in a derelict piggery, its bodywork riddled with bullet holes, two tyres completely blown out.

'I thought you said it was safe?' I hissed at Charlie.

'It is.'

'You can't drive it in any case,' said Jeannette. 'Every German patrol between here and Paris will be on the lookout for a car with bullet holes. Fortunately for you, it was dark and the car was moving so fast I doubt they got a good look at the make and model. We have a man locally who can repair it. If anyone asks, you can just say it's in the garage.'

She was right. Which left me with a new dilemma. 'Do you have any other transport we can use?'

'You're better off going back to Paris by train,' said one of the men. 'But you need to split up. They know three of you parachuted in, although they don't know how many of us there are. We kept confusing them as much as we could to give you time to get away.'

'What about the farmer?' I asked. 'Will he talk?'

Jeannette shook her head. 'He's loyal to a fault. We can only hope they believe he knew nothing about it, that some bunch of Resistance rabble stole his tractors and were using his fields without permission.'

We both knew it didn't matter what the Germans believed. They'd beat the life out of him anyway without needing an excuse. That poor man and his wife, plying us with food they could barely afford to share.

'I want you to check on them once we're on our way,' I said. 'Find out if there's anything we can do to help. At the very least, we can try to compensate them for their tractor. I assume it's in the same state as this car?'

'Worse. Don't worry, we'll see to it. Right now, we must get you all to a safe house.'

I glanced at the car again, then at the agents huddled behind Charlie, Amalie calm and resolute in spite of our situation. If it meant holing up in a safe house until we could get back to Paris, then so be it. 'Lead on,' I muttered. 'Let's get out of here.'

What felt like hours of silent trudging across fields and along empty lanes later, we hit a hamlet where the houses sat lifeless in the dark, their windows blank and shuttered, although I had the feeling someone out there was watching.

Jeannette led us to one that sat on its own, some distance from the others. She knocked on the door twice, waited, then knocked three times in quick succession. A scrawny man opened it, squinting at us.

'Alain, we have some guests,' whispered Jeannette, ushering us in as he opened the door wider.

'I was expecting you. They've already been here looking.'

That was fast. 'Did they say who they were looking for? How many?'

'Three English people. That's what they said.'

I looked at Charlie. 'Tomorrow morning, we split up. Jeanette, can you get us travel permits?'

'Yes, but not by tomorrow morning. It will take a day at least.'

A day.

I drew Charlie aside. 'We're supposed to be meeting Kieffer at noon. We can't miss that meeting. There's too much at stake.'

'You're right. We can't give him any reason to get suspicious. Especially as it was no doubt Kieffer who ordered this ambush tonight, seeing as he's in charge of counter-espionage.' He turned back to the group. 'We need to be in Paris by midday. It's important. Is there any other way we can get there? One that doesn't involve travel permits?'

'My brother has a truck he uses to deliver produce to a café in Paris where he sells it on the black market,' said Jeannette, indicating Alain. 'Or that's what the Germans think. We use that same café as a post box, so he also carries messages backward and forward, hidden in the cheese. People, too, sometimes. The Germans turn a blind eye because they take their share.'

The black market, or *marché noir*. The only way many Parisians could get anything above and beyond their meagre rations. Everyone loathed the black marketeers, especially as outlets were run by criminal gangs while, at the same time, people could not do without them. At least they weren't the *bureaux d'achats*, the central buying offices set up as a racket by the German authorities, which bought up local goods cheap and sold them on at a vast profit back home in Germany.

'Would he lend us that?' asked Charlie.

'Of course, but it's a big risk. The Germans will be stopping and searching every vehicle on the roads around here, looking for anyone who might be an agent or Resistance. We'd need to disguise you well and say that he's indisposed. Normally he takes someone with him to help unload, but if there are three of you, they might suspect something.'

'It could work,' I said. 'To be honest, it's about our only chance.'

Charlie nodded soberly. 'It's worth a shot. If they catch us, we'll just have to try and talk our way out of it. The one thing we can't do is miss that meeting with Kieffer.'

'Agreed. And we only have a few hours to get there. It's nearly 5 a.m. We need to be on the road by 8 a.m. at the latest. So come on – where's this truck?'

As it turned out, the truck in question was almost in worse shape than the Hispano-Suiza, being so riddled with rust it was hard to imagine how it held together, never mind how it covered the miles between here and Paris without falling apart.

'That's the idea,' explained Jeannette's brother. 'The Germans take one look and they either laugh or they wave it through. They can't imagine such a wreck could be used for anything nefarious.'

He handed Charlie the keys. 'You need to deliver everything to the Café Louisette in Saint-Germain as usual so no one suspects anything.'

I snatched them out of his grasp. 'I'll drive,' I said. 'I've seen what you can do.'

Charlie simply pulled the cap he'd borrowed further down over his forehead. It went with the filthy old overalls he sported, which matched mine for sheer squalor along with the woollen hat that covered my hair. We looked like the perfect pair of country bumpkins. Or at least I hoped we did. Our papers were borrowed, the photographs in them hastily replaced with our own. With any luck, they would also stand up to German scrutiny, although I was banking on the fact we smelled so ripe that any self-respecting soldier would simply stand back and allow us to pass.

The truck was already loaded with the eggs, meat and cheese destined for Paris. Jeannette's brother tapped one of the cheeses. 'These ones here with the rind, they're the ones that contain messages. We put the rind on afterwards to conceal where we've sliced them. You deliver those along with the rest but make sure you hand them directly to the café owner, Andre. He'll make sure they get sent on to the right Resistance cells.'

Before we clambered in, I shook Jeannette's hand. 'Thank you for everything.'

'Don't worry. We'll get your people to Paris. I'll see you there.'

'I hope so.'

I looked at Amalie. '*Sois sage,*' I whispered. *Be careful.*

She gave me the same smile she'd given me at Beaulieu and before that in her little café. 'You too.'

Then we were off, driving towards Paris, guns tucked into our belts, a heap of moving rust all that stood between us and the Germans. Dawn was breaking across an angry sky, orange and purple slashing through black clouds. It matched the feeling in my heart, the rage that never quite left me. At times it boiled over, but mostly it simmered, flowing like hot lava when necessary. Or, as it did now, sparking something else.

I focused on the road ahead stretching in a winding ribbon, constantly alert to the sudden appearance of a German vehicle or a roadblock ahead. I could feel Charlie beside me doing the same. 'What was it you were going to say to me back there?'

'When?'

'Back at the barn. You said you wanted me to know one thing.'

'Oh yes. So I did.'

'So what was it? The thing?'

We rounded the corner to see lights blaring at us. Two German trucks and a jeep pulled across the road, soldiers at the ready. I slowed to a halt.

'Papers,' snapped the soldier who approached.

I handed them out through the window.

A long moment as he studied them.

Another soldier joined him, one with stripes on his arm, looking at the papers then at us before raising his gun. 'Get out of the truck.'

FORTY-ONE

I stood as still as I could, trying not to attract attention as the Germans systematically went over the truck. One jabbed Charlie in the side with his machine gun. 'Open it,' he commanded, marching him round to the rear doors. I stayed where I was, keeping an eye on the cab. Concealed in the false bottom of the glove compartment, under a stinking pile of old cheesecloth, were the guns we'd stashed there, along with spare ammunition.

Out the corner of my eye, I could see a German poking around near the dashboard. An excited yelp and then he held up a bottle of what looked to be rough wine. If only he knew it was, in fact, a Molotov cocktail, ready for a rag to be stuffed in it and hurled, lit, at the appropriate target. If he asked, I would pass it off as spare gasoline, but he didn't. Instead, he threw it to one of his mates, who fumbled and almost dropped it. I held my breath. Too close for comfort.

As was the soldier now circling me, snapping out rapid-fire questions. 'What's your name? Where are you from? What are you doing with this truck?'

I kept my eyes down. 'You have our papers. We come in

every week to deliver our produce. Why is there suddenly a problem?'

I could have bitten my tongue. He pushed his face into mine, so close I could smell the beer on his breath. Not only stupid but drunk. Just my luck. 'Problem? What problem? You say there is a problem?'

'No. There's no problem.'

He jerked his gun up and tore my hat off with it. I could feel my hair tumbling around my face. He was staring at me now, his eyes moving across my face, down my body until my flesh started to crawl.

'Hey, look at this one. She's not so bad for a farm pig.'

I held my breath, hoping he would get bored, that the lure of the free food in the truck would prove greater. I could hear Charlie giving monosyllabic answers as another soldier shouted questions at him. *That's it*, I thought. *Let them think you're a dumb peasant.* The soldier was still staring. I could see his brain cells starting to kick in. Any moment now, he might even put two and two together.

More shouts as the soldier with Charlie started calling to his comrades to get over there and help with the looting. The one with me grabbed me by the arm. 'You come with me.'

They were piling into the back of the truck, grabbing whatever they fancied. I saw one reach for the cheese with the rind on it. The cheese with the messages secreted inside. Then his greedy eyes fell on the large brie in the next box and he grabbed that instead, crowing in delight.

All at once, I felt something touch my leg. I looked down to see a dog, its eyes looking up at me, pleading. The poor creature appeared half-starved, so scrawny its ribs were sticking out. The next moment, it was leaping into the back of the truck too, sinking its teeth into a ham. I saw one of the soldiers kick at it then raise his gun.

'Don't you dare,' I screamed at the top of my lungs. 'Leave the poor dog alone.'

The soldier glowered, turning his pistol on me. 'You want to die like a dog instead?'

I caught the look on Charlie's face, but I didn't care. 'Go ahead. Shoot me. Prove just what a coward you are.'

For a long moment, I thought he might, then his eyes shifted, widening as someone behind me roared in German. 'What is the meaning of this? What is going on here?'

'A stop and search, sir. These people say this is a weekly delivery.'

The officer glanced at us then at the truck. 'Their papers are in order?'

'Yes, sir.'

'Then let these people get on with their business and get back to your stations. You are soldiers, not common thieves.'

The men slunk away, still bearing their booty. The officer gave me a longer look. 'Well, what are you waiting for? Make your delivery.'

I didn't need to be told twice, slamming the back door of the truck and jumping into the cab while Charlie scrambled into the passenger seat.

At the last second, the dog jumped in beside me. I put my foot down, and we roared off in the direction of Saint-Germain before the German officer could change his mind. The dog hopped up on the seat between us and licked Charlie's face.

'You stink,' he said, rubbing his head. 'Which means you'll fit right in around here.'

I burst out laughing, a mix of relief, hysteria and something else. That thing I didn't want to name. 'Hold on tight,' I said. 'We've only got half an hour to drop this lot off and make it to Maxim's.'

Charlie threw an arm over the dog. 'You heard her, Scruff.

Believe me, this lady doesn't mess around. It's one of the things I love about her.'

The screech of the engine in my ears, the truck rattling and groaning. Street corners flashing past, signs a blur. And all the while, a word resounding in my head. Love. A big word. Just a casual remark. Maybe. He loves me. He loves me not. On and on I drove, never once taking my foot off the accelerator, trying to hide the stupid smile on my face.

FORTY-TWO

Kieffer's smile was so thin you could have cut cheese with it. 'I like my people to be punctual.'

He'd obviously been sitting at the table for some time. The breadbasket was all but empty, a pile of crumbs on his side plate. I took the chair that the waiter was holding out for me, opposite Kieffer, while Charlie slid in beside me. We'd barely had time to change, never mind take a shower. Kieffer's nose wrinkled as if he'd caught a whiff of something pungent, but he was too punctilious to say anything.

In a way, it was thanks to him we were late. The damn German patrol had held us up for a good twenty minutes helping themselves to what they fancied, no doubt selling some of it on the black market which the Gestapo helped run. We'd made it to the café and then to Charlie's apartment via my place by the skin of our teeth, leaving the dog there with a large hunk of ham and a bowl of water. Now here we were, still mud-streaked under our clothes, lunching in Maxim's.

'It's my fault,' I said. 'I had to go and see my doctor.'

That had the effect I intended. Kieffer steepled his fingers, scrutinising me from behind them. 'Are you unwell?'

'No – I... It's delicate.'

Kieffer shifted his gaze, sensing perhaps what was coming.

Charlie placed a hand on my arm. 'Christine is no longer in the family way.'

'I see.' Kieffer cleared his throat. 'Well that is no doubt for the best.'

It certainly was. It was also the perfect time to spin that particular yarn to get us out of a potentially tight spot. Kieffer was a stickler for etiquette except, perhaps, when it came to extracting what he wanted from the enemy. That he was staring at two enemy agents right now was something he must never guess, although it would surely have crossed his mind. Best then to keep that mind focused on the idea that we were loyal to his purse, if nothing else. I'd no doubt he'd be hearing about a certain incident at Saintville soon enough.

I pulled out my handkerchief and dabbed at my eyes, noting his discomfiture and milking it for what it was worth. 'I'm sorry,' I whispered. 'Please excuse me. I'm fine.'

He signalled for a waiter and, when one appeared, growled, 'A glass of water for madame, please.'

I sipped at it, keeping my eyes downcast, until I could feel Kieffer's patience slipping. Even with his infamous self-control, the man had his limits. I could hear him flicking his thumb against his finger under the table. It was music to my ears. That meant his emotions had got the better of him.

Unable to contain himself any longer, he rapped out, 'We received a report that the British have landed three more agents.'

He already knew. That was fast.

'So far, we've been unable to locate these agents. We believe they may have been sent in advance of an Allied invasion. It is imperative that we get more up-to-date intelligence on the Allies' plans. The two of you will be gathering that intelligence for us.'

'How are we going to do that?' asked Charlie.

'You will learn everything you need to know tomorrow morning. Report to 84 Avenue Foch at ten o'clock. Come separately. If anyone asks, you can say you were called in to answer some questions.'

'Does that mean I go to work at Le Chat Noir as normal?'

'Yes, of course.'

I placed my hand on my stomach in what I hoped looked like an unconscious gesture. It had the desired effect. I could see him reining in his annoyance.

'Unless you are not well enough?'

Sometimes it was an advantage to be a woman, especially in our game.

'I'll be fine.'

'Good. Then I'll see you both tomorrow.'

'Very good.'

Charlie rose and offered his arm to help me up. I could see the mixture of irritation and concern on Kieffer's face. Not that he was concerned for my health but rather that I might prove more of a liability than an asset. Which was, of course, precisely what we wanted.

'Lean on me harder,' muttered Charlie, keeping hold of my arm as we made our way out of Maxim's.

Outside, he hailed a taxi. 'The American Hospital.'

An interesting choice. The American Hospital was the only truly independent hospital in Paris, especially in the current situation. It ran on private donations and treated Allied prisoners of war, the Germans allowing it to do so because it saved them the cost of doing so themselves. Rumour had it that some of those POWs made it out to safety when they'd already been certified dead by the hospital, their records falsified. Why Charlie wanted us to go there was a question yet to be answered, but I certainly wasn't going to ask it in front of an unknown taxi driver. You never knew where loyalties lay.

I could see the driver peering at us both in the mirror as he drove off. 'You like that restaurant?'

There was an undertone to his words. 'Not especially,' I said.

Our eyes met in the mirror. He looked as if he was calculating a risk. Then he spat out the window of his cab. 'Full of fucking Nazis.'

At least we knew where he stood.

'I'm afraid so,' said Charlie.

He looked at us both again. 'Perhaps you prefer music?'

'I especially love "La Marseillaise".'

With that, he beamed and fiddled with his radio, moving through Radio Paris and Radio-Vichy with their constant diet of propaganda broadcasts until, crackling across the airwaves, I heard the familiar words, *'Ici Londres... Les Français parlent aux Français...'*

London calling... Frenchmen speaking to Frenchmen...

Radio Londres. The station operated by the Free French from London and strictly banned here since the Germans had realised how it bolstered the spirits of its listeners, exhorting them to rise up and resist the enemy.

The driver sighed happily. 'They can't stop me listening to it. If a Nazi gets in, I just switch stations.'

'How do you know we're not Nazis?'

He gave me a gap-toothed grin in the mirror. 'I can tell. You learn a lot in this job. I'm good at reading people.'

'Is that so?'

We looked at one another. I leaned forward. 'Then maybe you'd like to help us.'

'In what way?'

'Oh you know, taking a message here and there. Passing on any information you think might be useful.'

The taxi driver picked at his teeth, steering us through the streets towards Neuilly with his other hand, all the while listening to the broadcast from London.

'Before we begin, some personal messages,' said the announcer.

My ears pricked. These personal messages were usually coded messages for the Resistance and agents in the field. As ever, they made no sense unless you were the intended recipient.

The driver chuckled, repeating one. 'Jean has a long moustache. And Hitler has, how do you say, only one ball? I can do as you ask.'

'That's wonderful,' I said, only half-listening. The announcer was repeating his latest message. 'The black cat is unlucky.'

I flinched. The black cat. *Le chat noir*. Coincidence? I thought not.

'We're here,' said Charlie, getting out and holding the door for me. As he paid the driver, I saw him slip his card in among the notes. 'If you see or hear of anything, you can get in touch with us here.'

The driver handed him his card in turn with his name on it, 'Henri Carrière,' then made the sign of the cross. 'God bless you both.' As he drove off, he roared at the top of his voice, '*Vive la France!*'

I looked at Charlie. 'What are we doing here?'

'Two reasons. One is insurance. We'll make sure Kieffer gets to know of your visit just in case he develops any doubts about your story. The other, bigger reason is inside.'

With that, he made for the front door of the hospital with me hard on his heels. 'We're here to see Dr Jackson,' he announced to the receptionist. 'Tell him the Yankees are going to win this time around.'

After a short wait, a young doctor appeared. 'Dr Jackson asked me to meet you and take you to his office.'

'What the hell are we doing here?' I muttered as we followed the young doctor down what felt like endless corridors.

Charlie simply shook his head. The inference was clear. No talking until we got to wherever it was we were going, which turned out to be an office at the other end of the building with a sign on the door that said, 'Sumner Jackson MD, Chief Surgeon.'

The young doctor knocked on the door. A voice inside called out, 'Enter.'

As we entered the office, a tall man with heavy eyebrows rose from behind the desk dressed in a white coat. He looked more like a gangster than a surgeon. 'Sumner Jackson,' he said. 'Good to meet you.'

'And you, sir,' said Charlie. 'I've heard a lot of good things.'

'We don't have much time,' said Jackson. 'Please come with me.'

We followed him down yet another corridor to a door marked 'Theatre'.

Inside, there was a room full of sinks from which double doors led into an operating theatre. There, huddled behind the operating table, stood Amalie, along with the two other agents.

'Are these your people?' asked Jackson.

I looked at the three of them. They didn't appear to have had any sleep. How they had managed to wash up here was a mystery that could be resolved later. For now, I simply wanted to get them out of here and to somewhere they could rest. 'Yes. They're with me.'

'There's a hospital laundry van waiting through the back doors,' said Jackson, indicating the exit from the operating theatre. 'It will take you three to my apartment at 11 Avenue Foch and drop you off at the trade entrance. My wife will be there to meet you.'

Avenue Foch. The same boulevard that housed the head-quarters and offices of the Gestapo, including their torture chambers. This was either a brilliantly daring plan or utter madness.

'I suggest you two return the way you came,' he added. 'Then make your way to the apartment separately. It's right on the corner, the ground floor. You can't miss it because there's a French flag in the window. My wife is Parisian, born and raised.'

'Thank you,' I said. 'We'll do that.'

I glanced at the dark circles under Amalie's eyes. Her chin was still up, her mouth determined. *That's my girl*, I thought, even though I wished to God she wasn't here. Although wherever she'd been didn't seem much better. She looked thin, her wrist bones visible where they poked out from under the Breton jumper someone had given her. The others were in a similar state. They could all do with a good, square meal as well as that rest, or they'd make a fatal mistake the moment they stepped out on a Paris street. But there was no time to rest. No time to do anything but keep them on the move if they wanted to stay alive.

The black cat is unlucky.

Was it a warning?

Only one way to find out.

'Welcome to Paris,' I said. 'Welcome to the network.'

FORTY-THREE

The doctor's wife was kind. 'Don't worry. We take turns at the window, watching to see that no one is coming. I'll make sure you're not disturbed.'

She had the practical air of the nurse she was and the haunted gaze of someone who'd lived a double life for far too long. She'd given Amalie her own room, one at the back of the apartment looking out on to the courtyard and gardens at the rear of the building. The Gestapo were further up the street. I wondered if they had a garden too. Probably far too busy torturing people to tend to plants.

As soon as we were alone, Amalie took me in her arms, embracing me as if she'd never let go.

'I've missed you so much,' she said when she finally did.

'And I you, although I wish you were anywhere but here.'

'Christine, I volunteered to do this. If anyone can stay alive in Paris, it's me.'

Her face was ablaze with all the courage and vigour I remembered of old. 'I pray to God you're right.'

'Well that gives me cold comfort. You're not even a believer.'

'Exactly.'

I could smell them now, those candles flickering in the chapel, all apart from the one that was snuffed out, just like all those agents. Just like Amalie, who burned so bright, would be. All at once, I couldn't bear it. 'You must go. Leave now. I'll help you get out of here. We can send you down the escape lines. It isn't safe.'

'You sound just like you did when you wanted Maman and me to run away to Spain. Do you remember? I didn't listen to you then, and I'm not listening now. I have a job to do here, Christine, just like you. And just like you, I'll carry it out to the best of my ability.'

'I know you will.'

I wanted to weep. To fall to my knees and beg her to go. But it wasn't the way either of us did things. Instead, I sat on the edge of the bed and patted the coverlet beside me. 'Sit here then, and I'll brief you as best I can. First things first, we need to get you out of this apartment as soon as possible. We call it Avenue Boche rather than Avenue Foch because there are so many Germans stationed here. The Gestapo has its headquarters at number eighty-four. They interrogate all captured agents there. The sixth floor is where they have their interrogation rooms and cells, while at number thirty-one there's another division of the SS responsible for deporting Jews to the camps.'

The fifth floor was where Kieffer had his office and where he spent his days hunting down agents like Amalie.

Her face barely changed as I spoke. If I'd been hoping to frighten her off, it didn't work. 'I know,' she said. 'I also know that the Paris network has been so badly compromised that it seems impossible for it to carry on. But that's precisely why we must. We can't let them win, Christine. We're so close to an Allied invasion. We need to make sure it happens. And the only way to do that is to beat the Germans at their own game.'

She was impossible. But then, she always had been. Impossibly decent. Impossibly brave. If anything happened to her, I knew my heart would break. 'Promise me something,' I said.

'Depends what it is.'

I laughed. 'There are no flies on you, my friend.'

'Nor on you, *ma chérie*.'

'Just promise me that you'll trust no one. And I mean absolutely no one.'

'Not even you?'

'You may make an exception in my case. Apart from that, the only thing you trust is your instincts, especially because you're the courier. If they tell you to get out of a place, do it immediately. The way agents get caught is by staying somewhere too long. The other way is when someone betrays them.'

'Then there is sheer bad luck.'

'You make your own luck, Amalie. Especially in this game. Check and check again. Watch and listen. I observe the players all the time in the gaming room at the club. The good ones are always watching and listening. The bad ones are too busy thinking about winning or their next move to notice that they're already beaten.'

'What club is this?'

'It's where Suzanne and I are based. Le Chat Noir in Montparnasse. If you ever need anything, you come straight there.'

'I will, but I worry about you too, you know. You don't look after yourself. You never have.'

'There's no need to worry about me. I'm absolutely fine. I have Suzanne there to keep an eye on me, don't forget.'

Amalie didn't look convinced. 'And what about him? That man you're with?'

'Who?'

'Don't play for time. You know who I mean. The handsome American. The one who looks at you as if he's madly in love with you. Which he obviously is.'

There was no fooling Amalie. Not that I was stupid enough

to try. 'Don't be silly. He's a colleague. OSS. We're working an op together. Officially, he's supposed to be Irish and educated in America.'

'What kind of op?'

'I can't tell you that.'

'Of course not.' She smiled, a smile full of infinite tenderness and regret. 'So here we are, circling around one another, unable to tell each other too much. And yet there is so much I want to say to you. So much to tell.'

'Once this war is over, we'll have all the time in the world to do that.'

Her eyes clouded. 'Will we though?'

I wanted to throw my arms around her, to tell her that of course we would, that this was merely an interlude before the world would once more be sane again. But Amalie knew me too well to believe any of that, and I loved her too much as a friend to lie.

FORTY-FOUR

My fingers scrabbled for the right place, pressing, until, finally, the wall swung open. We stared into the hidden room we'd last seen when Madame Joey showed it to us before she left. No network had meant no one to conceal here. Now, though, we were back in action with agents to protect.

'It's better than the apartment on the Avenue Foch,' I said. 'Sooner or later, the Gestapo are going to notice the comings and goings from there.'

Suzanne walked over to the tiny window, standing on tiptoe to peer out of it. 'I agree, but is here any safer?'

'It has to be. Madame Joey managed to get away with it for long enough. She smuggled all sorts of people in and out of here. She even hid Sarah among the girls. No one ever spotted a thing, except Kieffer that one time.'

'Exactly. It only takes one time. And things have changed. You're directly in the gaze of the Gestapo these days. Rest assured they'll keep a closer eye on you now that you're one of their own.'

'That could work in our favour. If they keep their eyes on me, they won't be looking elsewhere.'

Suzanne folded her arms. 'True.'

I waited her out, knowing that she had to say yes.

'Very well,' she said. 'They can come here for a few days, but we need to move them on as quickly as possible. We still don't have the car back, so we'll have to think of another way to get them here. Something the Gestapo won't spot as out of the ordinary.'

As was so often the case, the simplest method was the best. We carried them out under the noses of the Nazis.

When another van called at the apartment, it brought with it three empty wine barrels among a consignment of full ones. Our own cellar man unloaded them all when they were delivered back to us, rolling each barrel down just as he always did. Once the cellar door was safely locked and bolted, we opened up the barrels and helped the agents out, Amalie groaning in pleasure as she stretched, finally released from the confines of her temporary wooden prison.

'Thank goodness. I thought I might be stuck in there forever.'

I looked at her arching her back and shaking the life back into her limbs. Part of me wished I could just keep her bundled up in that wine barrel until the war ended.

'Follow me,' I said, leading them past our basement office, through another storeroom door and up the back stairs to the hidden room. They looked around in appreciation, at the beds made up for them and the food laid out on the table.

'You'll be safe enough here, but we're going to have to move you again in a few days.'

The taller of the two men stepped forward. 'We cannot thank you enough for everything. The name's François, by the way. I'm the new organiser. And this is Ambrose, our radio operator. I think you know our courier, Tania.'

Tania. Her code name. It didn't exactly trip off the tongue.

'I'll be back with some more food for you. In the meantime,

I suggest you make yourselves comfortable. The bathroom is halfway down the stairs. That door we passed on the way up. We'll let you know when we think it's safe for you to set up your radio.'

I locked the storeroom door after me as I emerged. It wouldn't stop the Germans kicking it down, but it might just buy them a little more time if it came to it. Not that it would come to it. Not if I had anything to do with it. There was only one real way to keep them safe and that was to get deep inside the Gestapo as quickly as we could and find our traitor. But there was something else I needed to do, just as urgent. Something I could barely acknowledge, even to myself. Especially to myself. And there was somewhere I needed to be. Or rather, someone I needed to see. Without even thinking, I reached for my coat.

FORTY-FIVE

I took the backstreets to Charlie's apartment, the scarf wrapped around my head as before, my coat buttoned to the neck. I walked as briskly as I could without breaking into a run, my strides covering the ground, footsteps echoing the drumbeat in my head. Still, I stopped in a doorway down the street to watch and wait until, satisfied the street was empty, I crossed over to his building. He didn't look too surprised to see me.

'Come on in. Scruff here's been missing you.'

The dog wagged its tail, jumping up to give me a lick.

'See what I mean? Here, boy. Wrap your teeth around that.'

He threw a bone down on the kitchen floor, and the dog leaped on it eagerly.

'You can't call it Scruff.'

'Why not?'

'For one thing, he is actually a she, and that is no name for a lady.'

We both looked at the dog, gnawing away at the bone as if her life depended on it.

'She looks like an Alsatian–collie cross to me. A working dog. Not too many sheep for her to round up in Paris, unless you count the collaborators. In any case, what are you going to do with her?'

'I'm going to keep her of course. You know me. I like to collect waifs and strays.'

'Yes. I mean, no. No, I don't. Didn't know that.'

'Come to think of it, you're a bit of a waif and stray yourself, aren't you, Christine?'

He was far too close for comfort now. Dangerously close, in fact. 'I have no idea what you mean.'

'I think you do. It's that look you have about you. I noticed it the moment I saw you. Sure, you act all sophisticated, but there's this lost look in your eyes, as if you landed in a place you never meant to be.'

My heart was hammering so hard I thought he must hear it. Or feel it. He was pressed up against me now, his lips inches from mine, one hand cupping my chin. 'I'm right, aren't I?'

'Yes.'

It was a yes to everything. To his question, to him, to this whole crazy thing. Yes, I wanted him. I needed him. It was why I'd practically run here. Yes, yes, yes, yes. And then the old doubts started creeping in, up my spine, clutching at me with their talons. No. I wasn't good enough. Not for this. Not for love.

As if sensing that, he kissed me, a kiss that was at once gentle and electrifying, sweeping away all my doubts as, this time, I let the surge take me with it, swirling around us both, pulling me down into a place where all thought dissolved and at last I was free.

Free to let go, to let my body respond to his, tangling together in a glorious, never-ending tumble of pleasure, my heart opening along with every other part of me.

'I love you,' he whispered.

As swiftly as it opened, my heart clammed shut, back into its shell. I could feel my body shrinking from his, tightening back into a ball of shame. 'Don't,' I blurted. 'Don't ever say that again.'

'Why not?'

His hands held me, along with his eyes. In them, only patience. Compassion. Maybe even understanding.

'I don't deserve it, that's why. I'm tainted, Charlie. Sullied.'

'Christine, I don't care what you've done. What you do. I never have. You've saved hundreds of lives by doing it, that much I do know.'

'Yes, but I also took one.'

'We've both killed people in the line of duty.'

'This wasn't in the line of duty. It was before the war. Believe me when I say I had to do it.'

'I believe you. Want to tell me about it?'

I was about to shake my head, but all at once, the words were spilling out, mingling with tears of relief. At last someone was listening to me. Someone I cared about. Not since Tom had I been able to tell anyone the full story, and now here I was, stuttering and stumbling at times, unable to look at him but knowing that he was hearing what I had to say.

When at last I was finished, he pulled me down onto his chest, stroking my hair as my mother had once done, saying nothing, although I could feel his heart beating under my cheek, steady and reassuring, his ribs rising and falling in the same rhythm.

He pressed a kiss on the top of my head. 'I love you even more now.'

At that, the dam burst. I howled for the pain and the shame that had haunted me all these years, for the girl I'd been and the woman I'd become. I cried, too, for all that I'd lost. My home. My country. My family. My chest heaved with sobs until, at last, I was spent, my eyes swollen and ugly but with a new smile on my face. 'It's gone,' I murmured. 'This feeling I always had. I was so angry, you see. My heart hurt with it at times. But now, there's nothing.'

'Nothing except peace.'

I raised myself on my elbow, looking into his eyes, those beautiful, clear eyes, so wise and yet so accepting. 'Now you know everything about me,' I whispered.

'Not quite everything.'

The gleam of wisdom gave way to something else I loved about him. That spark of mischief. *Loved.* That word again. Only this time it felt right. 'Oh yes?'

'Yes.'

His hands caressed me once more, demanding now, every part of me answering him. Rising in me, a cry of pure abandon as I felt myself soaring somewhere I'd never been, giving all of me and taking all he gave in return. Then a deep blanket of contentment falling over me, cradling me so I felt completely safe. There, in his arms, I knew I'd come home. He was me, and I was him. If this was love, then it was all I'd ever wanted.

And so was he.

FORTY-SIX

NOVEMBER 1938, THE EAST END, LONDON, ENGLAND

He barely made a splash as he dropped over the side and into the waters, which swirled and then closed, inky dark, over him. The chains we'd wrapped around him had done the trick. He sank like a stone, heading for the murky bottom of the Thames, which was where he belonged, in among the filth and rubbish that littered its bed.

'Come on, Chrissie,' said Tom. 'Let's get out of here.'

I looked at my brother, sweating in spite of the November chill, the dank air plastering his hair to his forehead under his cap along with the perspiration. 'I want to make sure he doesn't come back up.'

Tom took my hand in his big, capable one. I could feel the callouses on his palms from the hours he spent mending cars and bikes at the garage where he worked. He was a good soul, Tom. I wished he still lived at home. Then it might never have happened.

'He's not coming back up, Chrissie. I made sure those chains were good and tight. But we have to get out of here before someone spots us and wonders what we're up to.'

I glanced around the docks. Over the water, I could hear a voice, probably from one of the boats at anchor, but here among the warehouses, there was nobody in sight. Not that you'd expect to see anyone at 2 a.m. It had taken me that long to run and rouse Tom, begging him to come with me back to that alleyway, somehow making him understand between my incoherent babbling that it was urgent. I would never forget his face when he saw our stepfather lying there.

'God Almighty, Chrissie, what have you done?'

'I had to, Tom. The bastard was going to do for me. He already... you know...'

I saw realisation wash across his broad, handsome face, and then his fists clenched. He looked at our stepdad slumped in the gutter and then spat on his head. 'He had it coming to him. But we've got to get rid of him, Chrissie. Or they'll come after you once they work it out. The police aren't going to listen to you, and he's dead. You've got motive. Everyone knows what he was like.'

I stared at him, at the muscle twitching in his cheek, visible even in the gloom. 'I know. What are we going to do?'

'We'll do what you normally do with a piece of rubbish like this. We'll throw him in the river.'

The Thames harboured many secrets, especially around here. With any luck, they'd never find him.

Together, we wrapped him in the sacking Tom had brought and heaved him along the alleyway towards the docks, my heart hammering not so much with the exertion as the thought that at any second someone might appear. Luckily not even the night watchman wanted to leave his cosy hut and venture out into the fog that had descended, its frigid tendrils curling around us as we dragged him to the riverside and tipped him over as gently as we were able. The waters were high, which helped. They swallowed him whole without too much effort.

Now we were walking as fast as we could from the scene so

as not to attract attention, Tom almost carrying me, his arm tucked under mine. I couldn't match his stride, and, in any case, my knees had gone as it began to dawn on me just what we'd done. What I had done. I swiped the tears away as we went, furious with myself, with that bastard who'd made me do it. With the whole world. With my mum who'd let him treat us all like dirt. No, that wasn't fair. He'd bashed all the life out of her a long time ago.

We were standing a couple of doors from the house now, the street silent, although I knew that if I so much as coughed, a curtain would twitch somewhere. Funny how a sneeze would bring them to the window but my mum's screams were ignored. It was only the old couple over the road who'd ever shown us any kindness, but they were too frail to do anything but offer us the odd smile and gentle word.

'Right, Chrissie, you listen to me. You go on in and act as if nothing's happened. You get up at the normal time and pretend to go to work, but you take a suitcase with you. You're up before everyone else so no one will notice. Leave a note for Mum telling her you've met someone and you're eloping, then come over to my house. I'll hide you there until tomorrow night. Then we'll put you on the Night Ferry from Victoria.'

I stared at him, trying to take in what he was saying. 'The night ferry?'

'It's a boat train to Paris. Some of the boys I know have, shall we say, had to use it. I'll send a message to one of them. Get him to meet you off it.'

'Paris? But I don't speak a word of French.'

'Then maybe it's time you learned. You can't stay here, Chrissie. Sooner or later, someone's going to start asking questions then put two and two together. I won't see you hang for that piece of shit. Not if I can help it.'

Tom might have had his moments, but he wasn't a bad lad. The closest he'd ever come to being arrested was when he stood up to Mosley's Blackshirts a year ago. As far as I was concerned, he had a heart of gold. If he thought this was the best thing to do, then I'd go along with it. Besides, I didn't exactly have any other options.

'Paris it is.'

FORTY-SEVEN

JANUARY 1944, PARIS, FRANCE

From the outside, 84 Avenue Foch looked like any other building in this salubrious street, lacy wrought-iron balconies running outside its tall windows, from which, so the other residents said, they could hear agonised screams shattering the peace of the otherwise quiet neighbourhood. All was silent now as I trudged up the stairs to the fifth floor behind a uniformed SS guard, past the other offices used by various sections of the SD, including the Gestapo, their doors firmly shut.

Charlie was waiting for me, looking surprisingly relaxed as he sat on a chair in front of Kieffer's desk. The room was cramped, the windows smaller than those of the lower floors with their high ceilings and generous proportions. I glanced around, taking in the mandatory photograph of the Führer, the large desk behind which a mirror was hung at eye-level, presumably to unsettle those sitting in front of it. Then there was Kieffer himself, half-rising to shake my hand, his own pudgy with power.

'Please, sit.'

I took the other spare chair, dropping my bag beside it. Although the guard had searched it, he'd failed to spot the camera hidden inside my box of matches. If there was any opportunity to photograph a document or even the inside of this building, I fully intended to take it.

Kieffer was sporting an avuncular smile as he looked at me. I'd heard he favoured a more intelligent approach to his interrogations than the usual brutality, trying to win his victims over with affable words and what appeared to be kind gestures rather than instruments of torture. A clever ruse, especially when prisoners were already half-broken. But I wasn't his prisoner, and I intended things to stay that way.

'Would either of you like coffee?' he asked, still smiling.

I declined, as did Charlie.

'In that case...'

The smile disappeared as, businesslike now, he pushed the dossier in front of him across the desk to me. 'Open it.'

I flipped it open to see a photograph of Suzanne staring up at me. Beneath the photograph, typewritten notes on her, including a biography and details of her movements since we'd arrived in Paris. I flicked through those too, careful not to let any reaction show on my face, aware that Kieffer was watching me keenly. At last, I reached the end, noting that the last report on her was dated two months back. Clipped to the final page, another photograph, this time of Suzanne talking to a man I didn't recognise.

The photograph was taken through a café window. Suzanne wore that closed look I knew all too well, while the man was caught in the full flow of what was obviously an impassioned speech. He was well dressed. Middle-aged. Not a typical *résistant*. Which made me wonder who exactly he was. I scrutinised his face, thinking that perhaps I half-recognised him. Then again, there were so many men who looked like that.

'Interesting,' I said.

'Isn't it?' Kieffer tapped the photograph. 'You, of course, know this woman.'

'Well, she is my cousin as well as my boss.'

'Indeed. That is why you're the perfect person to keep an eye on her. You see, we think she may have something to do with the Resistance. At least, we know that her predecessor, a Madame Josephine, did. We have Madame Josephine in custody. She was picked up in Marseilles, helping some airmen escape. Didn't take long for her to tell us everything she'd been up to here in Paris. Of course, a little bribe helped. Once a whore, eh?'

I stretched my lips into a smile to match his. 'Indeed.'

So Madame Joey had sold us out. Or, at least, that was Kieffer's story. Having met the woman, I very much doubted she'd done anything of the sort.

'I'm curious,' said Charlie. 'Just because this Madame Josephine helped the Resistance, why do you think this other woman does? One doesn't necessarily follow the other.'

His tone was as genial as Kieffer's.

Kieffer sat back, spreading his hands, the picture of reason. 'I don't. What I mean is, I'm not yet certain. But it pays to be careful, don't you think? Especially as we still haven't found those three British agents I mentioned.'

'Ah yes,' I murmured. 'You did say something.'

'I also said that I thought they are here in advance of an Allied invasion. We know that the Allies like to send in their people to lay the ground, as it were. They did so in Sicily last summer before they invaded. That's why I want you to find out everything you can about any invasion plans.'

'How do you expect us to do that?'

The smile was gone, replaced with a gimlet-eyed stare. 'I expect you to do whatever it takes. You will keep a close eye on this woman and keep a record of her every movement. Where she goes, who she meets. What she says. I want every detail, or I'll be forced to get them out of her myself. I'm sure you understand what I'm saying.'

So much for Mr Nice Guy. 'I do.'

It wasn't so much an implication as a threat. Get some dirt on Suzanne, or he would arrest her and torture her until he got some for himself.

Kieffer studied me for a moment as if I were an interesting specimen. 'Your friend here thinks you'll be useful to us. I'm not so sure. It's up to you to convince me, otherwise you may find yourself in the same situation as your, ah, cousin. Under investigation. And we wouldn't want that, would we?'

I could feel a lump forming, hard, in my throat. One of outrage rather than suppressed tears. I swallowed it back as unobtrusively as I could. 'No.'

Kieffer snapped the dossier shut, replacing it in a drawer. 'I expect you both to keep your eyes and ears open at all times regarding this woman and in your business dealings. You will report back to me instantly on anything that requires my immediate attention. Otherwise, I expect a weekly report on any intelligence you've managed to gather.'

I glanced at Charlie, who was brushing an imaginary fleck from his trousers. 'Of course.'

If only Kieffer knew that further down this very street, those agents he was so keen to find had been hiding under his nose. Dr Jackson and his family were brave, but I feared their luck could run out at any moment. The SD were no slouches when it came to gathering information. Sooner or later, someone would betray Sumner Jackson and his wife. Sooner or later, someone would betray all of us.

At that moment, there was a muffled crash from somewhere above us, followed by another and then a heart-stopping scream that trailed off into silence, the only sound in the room the ticking of the clock, its hands sweeping away the hours just as surely as the Nazis snuffed out yet another life.

FORTY-EIGHT

I glanced at Kieffer.

He shrugged. 'We keep our prisoners upstairs,' he said. 'Sometimes they get frustrated or a little upset.'

I bet. 'Can we see them? I'd like to see what an agent looks like. It might help me spot one. That is what you have up there, isn't it? Agents for the Allies?'

He looked as if he might balk at this request and then shrugged. 'I don't see why not.'

If nothing else, it was another chance for him to drive his message home. Deliver the goods or we might end up like those poor bastards in the cells.

He led the way out of his office and up a narrow staircase to the floor above, which was little more than an attic. The ceilings were lower here, the guardroom I glimpsed as we stood outside in the corridor even smaller than Kieffer's office. A row of cells extended along from the guardroom, each with an observation hatch in an otherwise ordinary-looking door. At the far end of the corridor, there was yet another door, from behind which we could hear more gut-wrenching screams and groans.

'What is going on in there?' Kieffer snapped at a guard. As if he didn't know.

'I believe Hauptsturmführer Braun is interrogating a prisoner,' the guard mumbled.

Kieffer muttered something under his breath.

There was silence now from the room at the far end of the corridor. I wasn't sure if that was a good or bad thing. Either the prisoner had passed out, unable to bear the pain, or Braun was even now holding his head under water in their infamous *baignoire* or torture bath as the poor bastard choked and gasped for breath. He could even be dead. Which might be a blessing.

Trying to hide his irritation, Kieffer indicated one of the cell doors. 'Look in here,' he said. 'You can see we take care of our prisoners.'

I peered through the hatch he was holding up, swallowing hard to cover my sharp intake of breath. Jacques was sitting on the single iron bedstead, the only piece of furniture in the room, his head bowed and shoulders slumped. I wanted to call to him, to shout out and tell him not to give up, that we were going to get him out of there one way or another, but to have done so would only have put him in even more danger. Instead, I pretended to drop my bag, spilling its contents, fumbling against the door as I scrabbled to pick it up, exclaiming all the while to cover the message I tapped out on the door.

Three dots and one dash. V for victory. I hoped he would understand, that he'd realise only a comrade in arms would send a message like that.

As I rose to my feet, brushing past the hatch again, I caught the briefest glance of his head now raised, his face turned towards the door. It was enough.

I turned to Kieffer. 'Silly me. Yes, I can see how you take care of them, thank you.'

I longed to pull out the camera, but it would have been suicidal to do so. Instead, I tried to ignore the acrid taste of bile in my throat, fighting back the waves of nausea and sheer rage that were threatening to engulf me. Jacques's face told me all I needed to know. And there were others like him here and in Fresnes Prison although, compared to the ones who'd already been sent to the camps, they were the lucky ones. We had to stop this now. To work out how the Germans were on to each drop so fast. Otherwise, these cells and all the others would be full of people like Jacques, men and women prepared to die for freedom. I didn't want them to have to pay that ultimate price.

We followed Kieffer back down to his office, where he took his leave of us. 'I look forward to your reports,' he said, giving me a long, hard stare. 'I'll be in touch with further orders. Remember you are to call me at once if you hear anything at all about those British agents, and I expect you to keep a very close eye on your cousin. Discreetly, of course.'

'That won't be a problem.'

'Good. Well, thank you for coming.' The genial Kieffer was back, shaking our hands as if we'd just indulged in small talk over tea. It took everything I had not to wipe my hand on my coat. At least there was no guard this time to lead us back down the stairs.

I pulled my matchbox camera from my bag the minute Kieffer had shut his office door. The same matchbox that had spilled on the floor in front of him along with the lipstick container that unscrewed to hide messages. The Nazis might think they were winning this war, but we still had plenty of tricks up our sleeves.

'Cover me,' I whispered to Charlie as I started snapping away.

There was a low murmur of voices when we reached the second floor and what sounded like radio traffic. I nudged Charlie. 'Hear that?'

He nodded. We paused on the landing, listening hard. The door to what looked like another warren of offices was open, and the sounds of radio traffic were coming from there. I noticed the plaque on the door: Section IV.

All of a sudden, the door swung wider, and a man in plain clothes stepped out. Behind him, I caught sight of a radio operator at work. There was something about him that rattled my brain, but there was no time to stop and stare.

We moved in tandem, taking the next flight of stairs at an even pace as the man stared after us. Mercifully, he didn't call out or challenge us, but my heart didn't stop its tattoo until we were out in the street and a few blocks away. There, I let out the snarl I'd been holding back behind my teeth. 'That bastard. Did you see Jacques's face? They've obviously worked him over good and proper. It was all I could do to stop myself punching Kieffer.'

'I'm very glad you didn't, or you would probably have been joining Jacques in those cells. Christine, we can only get these guys by playing their game better than they do.'

'Yes, but we don't yet know what their game is. We're no closer to finding out who the hell is betraying agents like Jacques.'

'On the contrary, we're a hell of a lot closer. Kieffer's taken us on. That gives us the chance to play him.'

'It does, but he's still testing us. All that stuff about wanting me to keep an eye on Suzanne – that could be real, or it could be a double bluff. Doesn't matter. We're in the door. Now all we have to do is convince him. And what about the second floor? They're obviously transmitting from there.'

'They are, and I'd love to know what exactly it is they're sending. Did you see the radios they had?'

I stopped dead. 'My God. Of course. I thought they looked familiar. Those were our radios. You were right. They're using them to transmit messages.'

'And I'd wager they're sending those messages to London, playing us back. That's why they keep sending agents over. The

Germans are pretending to be radio operators for the network here and telling them it's safe to do so.'

We looked at one another. 'We have to warn them. Let London know what's really going on.'

Charlie took my arm. 'We do, but face to face, through Colonel Olivier. You saw for yourself we can't trust any SOE radio comms now that we know the Germans have a whole section dedicated to playing us. Funkspiel, they call it. The radio game.'

Only this was no game.

'Section IV,' I murmured.

The section that was luring our people to their deaths.

FORTY-NINE

I could feel Suzanne's eyes on me as I pulled up my chair, assessing my every move. I knew that look on her face. It was the same as the one she'd worn when she was evaluating a student. 'You seem different.'

I resisted the urge to pat my hair into place or tug at my clothing. I'd taken a long look in the mirror before leaving Charlie's apartment that morning. Nothing that would give me away. Except, perhaps, the smile on my face. 'I do?'

'Yes. You look radiant.'

I hastily wiped away that smile. 'Any news on the safe house?'

'Marcel may have something to report later. He's waiting for one of his contacts to get back to him.'

The agents were safe in the hidden room for now, but they needed to start rebuilding the network, and they couldn't do that here with all the Germans coming and going. Even so, I wished I could keep them in there forever. Or at least Amalie. But there was something even more pressing I needed to discuss. 'Good. I have something to report too, as it happens.'

'Oh yes?'

'We had a meeting with Kieffer yesterday.'

'How did it go?'

I hesitated, not quite sure how to put it. 'Kieffer has you in his sights.'

Her eyebrows shot up. 'Since when?'

'Since we got here, it seems. He has a whole dossier on you. Probably me as well. We are quite high profile after all. Standard Gestapo operating procedure. Except that they arrested Madame Joey the other day in Marseilles. According to Kieffer, she talked.'

'I don't believe it.'

'Nor do I. I think he was bluffing, but he definitely suspects you have some connection to the Resistance. Maybe me too. He asked me to spy on you and report back. It's evidently some kind of test.' I hesitated again, feeling my way. 'There were also these photographs of you meeting someone. A man. Quite recently.'

'What kind of photographs?'

'They were obviously taken through a café window. You were talking. Nothing more.'

Suzanne laced her hands behind her head, gazing into the middle distance. Finally, she appeared to come to some kind of decision. 'Christine, you're going to have to trust me on this one. That meeting had nothing to do with our work here, but I can't tell you what it was about. It's personal.'

'Right.'

Something stopped me telling her about Section IV. The same something that prompted me to ask her about the man in the photograph. Their meeting had to be significant for the SD to have it on file, and yet she hadn't mentioned it to me. Until that moment, I'd trusted Suzanne with my life. I still did, to a point. But there was now a question mark in my head.

'I'll let Charlie know he needn't worry about it then.'

'Listen, Christine, when all's said and done, you work for SOE. Not the Americans.'

'I thought this was a joint op.'

'It is.'

'Then that's exactly what we're doing. Carrying out a joint op. We share information.'

'So long as that's all you're carrying out.'

'I don't know what you're talking about.'

She pulled out a cigarette and lit it, lighting another from it before passing it to me. 'I know you, Christine. Better than you know yourself, I sometimes think. You've changed since you met that man. All I want you to do is be careful. Protect yourself at all times. Even from him if necessary.'

I took a drag. 'It won't be necessary.'

'You can't be certain of that. In this job, you can't be certain of anything.'

I felt the same rebellious kick inside as I had when a school-teacher told me off. Yes, Suzanne had taught me a lot, but I'd learned even more on the job, including when to trust my gut. Right now, it was warning me to also keep quiet about my rela-tionship with Charlie. No one need know, least of all Suzanne or anyone connected with our work. This was between me and him. I spent my life trying to extract other people's secrets. Now I had one of my own to keep. Another one.

'Actually, that's something I wanted to talk to you about. Do you remember when you recruited me and you promised that any trace of those witness statements would be wiped clean? I want your assurance that actually happened. I don't want to land back in London when the war's done and find a bunch of coppers waiting for me.'

For a moment there, I was Chrissie again, the East End breaking through in my voice as well as the trickle of fear that crawled down the back of my neck. I would never stop looking over my shoulder. Right now, it was for the Nazis, but behind them, lurking in the shadows, was the knowledge that someone out there knew what I'd done. Not just one person either but a few, including the very people who employed me. Then there was my brother, Tom. Not that I thought he would ever betray me. I didn't even know where he was now, or whether he was still alive. A sixth sense told me he was, but I was beginning to think I could no longer trust my gut.

'I can promise you've nothing to worry about, Christine. That's all forgotten. In the past. Your slate is clean. What I want you to do is keep it that way.'

I threw back my head and blew a perfect smoke ring. Another thing Tom had taught me, along with how to land a big fish. 'If you've any concerns about my work, I'd rather you told me now.'

'Christine, your work is exemplary. As I often say, you're the best.'

'Then what's the problem? You don't like to see me happy, is that it? You'd rather I was still that sad kid from Shadwell who'd lost everything and had to start again? Or maybe it's this Christine you don't like. The one sitting here now. The thing is, Suzanne, you helped create this Christine. You and Madame Joey and all those men I've worked over. But I'm not prepared to be her anymore.'

There, at last, I saw it. The tiniest flicker that told me I'd got through to her. That Suzanne wasn't immune to emotion after all. 'What are you saying?'

'I'm going on this mission with Charlie, and when I get back, things are going to be different. No more sweet-talking those bastards while they paw at me. I can't do it any longer. I don't want to.'

Suzanne ground out her half-smoked cigarette in the crystal ashtray that sat on the desk, the one luxurious item in this other-wise utilitarian office. 'It's your job, Christine.'

'No. My job is to extract information from the enemy which

can be used to help us win this war. The way I do that is up to me.'

She sat staring into the middle distance for a moment, her gaze unfocused, a faraway look on her face. This was a new Suzanne too. One with an air of vulnerability I'd never seen before.

When at last she spoke, it was hesitantly. 'I was about the same age as you were when I stood up to my father. It was the day I took my power back. From then on, I never let a man touch me unless I wanted him to. It's your body, Christine. More importantly, it's your soul. Your mind. And it's your right to do what you want with them. Or not, as the case may be.'

I gaped at her, transfixed. Even her features appeared different. Softer somehow. 'Was that the day Marcel got shot?'

'Yes, it was. My father sent someone to stop me leaving. He never did his dirty work himself. Still doesn't. He's a bit like Kieffer in that. I was adamant I wasn't coming back, so he pulled a gun. Marcel pushed me aside and took the shot. Luckily, it hit him in the leg because he was moving. The man was aiming for my heart, you see. My own father had ordered him to shoot to kill if there was no other way of stopping me.'

Her hands were shaking as she tucked away a tendril of hair that had escaped her chignon. I wasn't the only one with a past that came back to haunt me. But I wanted to lay those ghosts to rest. To build a new future with the man I loved. I never thought I could love anyone the way I loved Charlie. His were the only hands I wanted on me. His bed the only one I could bear to share.

'I'm so sorry,' I said. 'That must have been horrific.'

A bleak, fleeting smile. 'No more horrific than what happened to you.'

I rose. 'I'll go and check on the agents. They'll be delighted to learn they should be getting out of here soon.'

Suzanne sat straighter in her chair and picked up her pen. 'You do that. I have this report to complete. And, Christine?'

'Yes?'

'Let your friend do what she has to do. I know you feel responsible for her just as I do for you, but it's her life. Her choice to join SOE. You can't shield her from that. Or from whatever the fates might have in store.'

I took a deep breath. 'I know. It's not easy, is it?'

A more heartfelt smile this time. 'It's never easy, but then you and I don't like things too easy, do we?'

Words that seemed prophetic when I remembered them later. Words that rang out with my own screams in my head.

FIFTY

'We have more orders from Kieffer,' Charlie murmured in my ear, his chest to my back, spooning me. 'He's insisting I set up a meeting with the middleman I told him about to do business with the British. Tomorrow. He wants me to tell them I have a new supply of copper and I can get it to them fast. You're to come along too. Kieffer wants you to stay away from the club for a few days.'

'He does? How odd. How am I supposed to keep close tabs on Suzanne?'

'The whole thing is odd. I wonder what he's really up to.'

I rolled over so I could see his face. Three weeks since we'd been in Kieffer's office. Three weeks and one day since that first unforgettable night. A night we remembered by spending the subsequent ones together, wrapped in each other's arms, finally falling asleep once we were spent from hours of lovemaking, limbs heavy, hearts filled with one another. Although right now my heart was contracting into a ball of doubt.

'Whatever it is, we're going to have to play along. At least for the moment. It's probably another of his tests. There's just one problem – you don't have a middleman.'

'I know, but Colonel Olivier is bringing in someone from London. He'll supply us with fake orders, along with everything else we need to convince Kieffer. If the British place a big order for copper, it's a sure sign they're gearing up for something big like an invasion. They need it to manufacture ships and aircraft, as well as for ammunition.'

London. My throat started to tighten along with my heart. They weren't so much doubts now as fully-fledged fears. Something felt very wrong. Was I being set up by my own too? 'I'm not so sure I should come with you to this meeting,' I said.

'Why ever not?'

I could hear it now, in my head. The crack as his skull split open, the splash as we tipped him into the water, the gurgle as it closed over him. 'You know. It's all very well dealing with people from SOE, but this person from London could be anyone. He might know about me. For all I know, I'm still on some wanted list.'

He leaned back so he could look at me, his eyes searching my face. 'Christine, you told me they'd wiped any trace of that from the records. That it was the price of you agreeing to work for them.'

'They promised they would, but how do I know they did it for certain?'

'Oh, baby.' He stroked my cheek with his thumb, wiping away a traitorous tear. 'You trust Suzanne, right? You think she would renege on the deal?'

I kissed his thumb as it traced my mouth. 'No, I don't. Not really. But it's always a possibility.'

A question hovered between us, unspoken.

'Do you really trust anyone?'

His eyes were guileless, clear, shining with sincerity. For a man who could deceive the Germans so brilliantly, he was incapable of lying when it came to me.

'I trust you,' I whispered.

He kissed away the tears this time, murmuring to me all the while. I could feel myself melting into him once more, no longer sure where I started and he ended. I'd never known such pleasure or felt such pain. It couldn't last forever. Nothing ever did. At least, not for me. But I still couldn't hold back even if I wanted to. My heart was made of glass as far as he was concerned, hiding nothing, transparent and yet tough enough to contain the white-hot passion I felt for him while being more fragile than ever.

Afterwards, as I lay staring at the ceiling, watching the lights from outside chase the shadows across it, mingling so they formed shapes, I fancied I could see my mother's face among them. She was looking at me in the way she had before my stepfather came into our lives, before she could no longer raise her head. Unconsciously, I reached out a hand as I thought I heard her whisper my name, 'Chrissie.'

'Who's Chrissie? Is it you?'

I must have whispered back to her without even knowing it. Or perhaps Charlie heard her too. 'It's what my mum used to call me.'

'I like it.'

'It's Christine now. I haven't been Chrissie for a long time.'

Not since I'd laid out that sleazy hotelier on my very first night here. I'd come a long way since then. Too far to ever go back.

'Chrissie. Christine. Whatever you want to call yourself. In fact, how about you call yourself my girl?'

I carried on staring at the ceiling, mesmerised. The shapes were still there, but my mum's face had disappeared. Maybe it had never been there at all. Was I seeing as well as hearing things? A burst of incredulous laughter flew from my lips. 'Your girl?'

'Yes. My one and only girl.'

'I should hope so.'

At that moment, a ball of fur burst through the door and landed on top of me, licking my face.

'I'm not so sure about being your one and only.'

'You see? Even my dog wants you to say yes.'

Laughing and spluttering, I gently pushed the dog to one side. She responded by wagging her tail and licking my hand. 'OK, OK, I'll be your girl. Whatever that means.'

'Is that a yes?'

I slid across the bed, took his face in my hands and kissed him hard. 'Yes, I'll be your one and only girl. Apart from your dog. On one condition.'

'Anything.'

'We call the dog Betty.'

'Sure. Betty it is, but why?'

'It's my mum's name.'

FIFTY-ONE

Colonel Olivier met us in the main chapel, emerging so soundlessly from the shadows I thought at first he must be an apparition.

'Follow me.'

This time, he led us not into the side chapel but through the door at the side of the altar into a robing room, and from that into the sanctuary beyond. The inner sanctum of the convent, a place reserved ordinarily for the priests and nuns. But these were extraordinary times, and we were on no ordinary mission.

We followed him along a corridor lined with images of the saints, stopping in front of a heavy oak door which Olivier opened, ushering us through into a room dominated by a large refectory table, a portrait of the Pope taking pride of place on the wall.

A tall, slim man stood beneath the portrait, his fair hair and complexion offset by a pair of bright-blue eyes. Those eyes were regarding us both now with keen interest. 'Dick Ward,' he said in impeccably plummy tones, striding forward to shake my hand. 'Delighted to meet you.'

'Take a seat,' said Olivier, indicating the chairs set around the table, on which a couple of folders were neatly set. This was evidently the nerve centre for the SIS network here in Paris.

'Let's get down to business, shall we?' said Ward, sliding into the chair in front of which the folders were placed and addressing me. 'Although I work for the Secret Intelligence Service, I'm also seconded to the Supreme Allied Expeditionary Force, which will carry out the invasion of France, otherwise known as Operation Overlord. As such, I liaise closely with double agents sending disinformation to Germany.'

Charlie nodded at him. 'Good to see you again, sir.'

'I understand you've been tasked by the SD to get evidence of a planned Allied invasion in the form of orders for copper and other materials.'

'By Josef Kieffer, no less. He wants to debrief us straight after this meeting. Of course, he'd be delighted if we brought back even harder evidence such as dates, places, that kind of thing.'

Ward looked at Charlie and then at me. 'Kieffer's a wily one, as I'm sure you've realised. He's been in this game long enough to be able to sniff out an agent who, for want of a better phrase, is attempting to double-cross him. We need to be careful to feed him the right kind of information.'

I couldn't help but butt in. 'Which is?'

'Just enough to make him feel he's getting value from you both and can trust you without giving him so much he becomes suspicious. It would be foolhardy, for example, to go back to him with what you claim are the precise plans for the invasion.'

'Of course.'

'So we'll give him what he asked for and just a little more.' Ward opened one of the folders in front of him. 'In here we have prepared confirmation letters, along with details of large and urgent orders for copper that would indicate an invasion is imminent. As you can see, these orders need to be fulfilled within the next ten days. They're authorised by the Ministry of

Supply, and those are genuine stamps which will pass any German inspection. To sweeten it, we've added an extra order for rubber to make ski bindings. You might want to mention to Kieffer that the British were keen to know if the copper components would suffer in sub-zero temperatures.'

'So that the Nazis think the planned invasion might take place in Scandinavia?'

'Precisely. Our agents have already fed them the story that there is a Fourth Army gathering in Scotland, poised to invade Norway along with the Soviets.'

'That all sounds perfect. May I take a look?'

Ward passed the folder to Charlie then addressed me. 'I understand that you've already had an encounter with Admiral Canaris, as well as Kieffer. Part of my job is to liaise with Bletchley, and the Ultra intercepts indicate that there's a lot of pressure on the Abwehr from Berlin to perform. At present the intelligence they're producing is considered disappointing. They're also suspected of anti-Nazi sentiment. According to the intercepts, the SD are hovering, just waiting to take over.'

I instinctively liked this quietly spoken man. He was charming, yes, but there was grit beneath the charm. 'That's what Canaris said too. I assume you'd like us to find out what's really going on and if the SD have any imminent plans?'

'Correct. We'll continue to send as much information as we can to aid you, but there's nothing to replace human intelligence. We're hoping that what you take back to Kieffer today will start to build enough trust that you can get some useful information. Although I know he's a tough nut to crack.'

Charlie looked up from the folder, glancing at me. 'There's something else we wanted to share with you, sir. We have evidence that the Germans are using our radios to transmit back to London. They call it Funkspiel. Playing us back. Pretending to be the Paris network when, in fact, they've all but obliterated it.'

Ward glanced at Olivier. 'What evidence?'

'We saw it with our own eyes at 84 Avenue Foch. On the second floor, there's a division called Section IV. We heard radio traffic and saw the radio sets they were using. They were ours.'

'Are you sure about that?' asked Olivier.

'Completely sure. It's why we waited until we could meet face to face to tell you. We believe all radio communications between the network and London could be compromised. That's why new agents are being picked up immediately by the Germans. We only managed to rescue the last three who were dropped in by the skin of our teeth.'

Ward remained silent for a moment or two, digesting this information. 'The question is whether or not we tell SOE.'

I stared at him. 'What do you mean? Of course we must tell SOE.'

An uncomfortable silence fell around the table.

'I'm not sure that would be a good idea,' said Ward.

'Why not?'

He cleared his throat. 'Look, I'll level with you. We suspected this might be the case. I'm sure Lieutenant Russell has told you that. What we also suspect is that SOE might already know as well.'

'If they know, why the hell are they still sending agents over?'

'Because it suits them to do so,' said Olivier. 'It's all part of the game.'

'For Christ's sake,' I exploded. 'This is not a game. These agents are being arrested and tortured. One was shot in front of my own eyes. A young woman, running for her life, gunned down in cold blood by the Germans.'

'I realise that,' said Ward, his charm failing to soothe me. 'Unfortunately, we think that SOE are happy for their agents to be captured and interrogated, because then they might give up information which supports Operation Bodyguard and the

great deception. All of them have been told that the invasion
will take place this spring at Calais. If they divulge that under
torture, it will convince the Germans even more that this is
indeed the plan and that talk of a summer invasion in
Normandy is just a decoy.'

I could scarcely believe what I was hearing. 'That is
unspeakable. Are you telling me that SOE are knowingly
sending agents over, possibly to their deaths, just to support one
big lie?'

'Not just one big lie,' said Ward. 'The most important lie of
this war. Although I agree with you in your assessment of their
tactics.'

'So why don't you stop them?'

'We will now that we have your evidence as well. I'll call a
meeting with the head of SOE as soon as I get back to London.
That does not, however, help those agents who've already been
arrested. Or the ones they just sent over.'

'We have the ones they just sent over,' I said. 'We're keeping
them safe at Le Chat Noir.'

Without saying a word, Ward passed a copy of a decrypted
message to me.

Confirm the black catt has three kittens, it read.

I read it twice through and then looked up at him. 'This was
sent from Avenue Foch?'

'We believe so. The tell-tale sign is the lack of checks.
They've added one – the deliberate misspelling of "cat" – but
missed out the second. It was what was happening with other
recent messages too. That's what alerted us.'

Every legitimate SOE message contained two deliberate
mistakes so that London would know they were the real thing.
Except, apparently, they hadn't spotted the omission in this one
or any of the others.

I read through the message again. Just one deliberate

mistake. It was glaringly obvious. 'Was there a response to it from London?'

'Yes.'

He passed me a second message. On it was one word: 'Confirmed.'

'Oh my God,' I whispered. 'It was them all along. Our own people, they were the traitors, not the Germans. Sending all those agents to be tortured. To their deaths. And they've done it again. They've given up the three we're hiding to the Germans. Given us up as well. SOE were the ones who betrayed us. The entire network destroyed by our own HQ. No one else. They were lambs to the slaughter, and all to make sure the Germans believed a big lie. When did you get these?'

'A couple of hours ago.'

I stared helplessly at Charlie. 'What the hell do we do now?'

He looked at the others then at me. 'Absolutely nothing.'

FIFTY-TWO

'We have to get back there straight away.'

Ward poured me a glass of water. 'To Le Chat Noir?'

'Yes. Of course. We can't radio, and it's far too dangerous to try to call if the Germans are watching. They'll have tapped all the phone lines as well as running the radios. There's no way to warn them.'

'We don't know that,' said Ward. 'We don't even know for sure that they mean Le Chat Noir.'

'Of course they do. What else could "the black cat" mean?'

I stared at him, feeling the impotent rage rising in me once more. It was the rage that had simmered since the day my step-father raped me, kept alive by all the other men who thought they could do the same or take advantage of me in some other way. If only I'd been born a man. Then perhaps they'd take me more seriously. Although, if I'd been born a man, I wouldn't have been able to use what I had to garner intelligence, not to mention the confidence of those same men.

'What are you suggesting?' I snapped. 'That we simply sit here and wait to see what the Germans are going to do?'

'Lieutenant Russell's right. There's nothing else we can do,' said Ward. 'Except watch and wait or we'll blow their cover along with everyone else's. We can, however, alert our people on the ground here. Colonel Olivier, see to it that an urgent message goes out to the MI6 Paris network. We need them to stand by just in case.'

Ward rose from his seat. 'Perhaps you would prefer to sit somewhere more comfortable while we get hold of our people? It may take a little time. I believe the sisters keep a reception room for us as well?'

Olivier nodded. 'They do. Allow me to show you.'

I was itching to leave now and get back to the club as fast as possible, but it made sense to wait until we knew what reinforcements we could call upon, if any. 'Thank you.'

'There's just one more thing,' added Ward, withdrawing an envelope from the second folder and handing it to me. 'I believe you wanted to know the whereabouts of your family. You'll find all the information you need in there.'

I took the envelope, feeling it burn through my fingertips as I held it, desperate to know what it contained and yet terrified at the same time.

Charlie and I followed Olivier from the room into another anteroom, where armchairs were arranged next to the unlit fire, around a coffee table on which yesterday's newspapers had been neatly stacked. English newspapers. Ward must have brought them with him. The headlines blared up at us:

London cinema hit: Seven die.

BOMBS IN ORANGE SHIPS.

Phone murder 'political job'.

In my mind's eye, another headline: *British agents betrayed by their own.* I still couldn't believe it. Not the Germans after all, but our own people, ruthlessly using us, no doubt brushing it off as collateral damage. They not only knew the Gestapo were going to pick up our agents the moment they landed, they actually wanted them to. It was beyond belief. Well, I wouldn't let them do it again. Not this time. Not to Amalie. Or Suzanne.

I kept my eyes fixed on the door, waiting for one of them to reappear, to confirm that their messages had got through, that their agents were ready to back us up if necessary. On the mantelpiece, a carriage clock ticked, sounding louder and louder as the minutes passed.

I could feel Charlie's eyes on me. 'Aren't you going to open it?'

I stared at the envelope in my hand. Open it and I would know, one way or another, what had happened to Mum and Elsie. Possibly Tom too. But there was comfort in not knowing. Or at least a crumb of hope. And I wasn't sure I could take any more shocks today. I felt sick to my stomach, my head whirling with all that I'd heard.

'Here.' He took it gently from me. 'How about I open it and then you read what's inside? It's opening it that's the hardest part, isn't it?'

'I suppose. A bit like Pandora's box. My mum told me that story too. It's a Greek myth, you know.'

'I do.'

'I forgot... you must have studied all the classics at school. The myths and legends. I love all of those. I used to read them in the library as well.'

'You're stalling.'

'I know.'

'I'm opening it. Here you go.'

FIFTY-THREE

Before I could stop him, Charlie slit open the envelope with his thumb and was holding it out to me. I gazed at him, my heart lodged in my throat, a ringing sound in my ears. I felt as if I was falling from a great height down a deep, dark well. It had been so long. What if they were dead? Then at least I'd know. I'd be able to start mourning them. To move on. Then again, hadn't I done that already?

No. Not really. I'd just put my old life in a box, a bit like Pandora, and it was high time I opened it again.

I pulled a single sheet of paper from the envelope and unfolded it. The words danced in front of me like ants, running around the page. I took a deep breath and focused. Read it through and read it again. Then I looked up at Charlie.

'They're dead. My mum and little sister were killed in the Blitz. A bomb landed right on the house. At least it must have been quick. No news of Tom except that he joined up. Maybe no news is good news.'

I choked back a sob.

'My God, Christine, I am so sorry.'

I held up a hand to stave him off as he reached for me. I

couldn't bear anyone touching me right now, least of all Charlie. It was my fault they were dead. An eye for an eye, wasn't that what it said in the Bible? Except in this case, God had taken two of the people I loved most in revenge for one vicious brute.

I tore the piece of paper into tiny pieces, watching them flutter from my fingers, imagining the bombs dropping on the East End, on my mum and Elsie. They must have been so scared, hearing them dropping all around. Death might have been quick, but they would have known it was coming.

I could feel the back of my throat burning. Tried to swallow back the nausea. No use. I rushed from the room, spotting the sign on the toilet door, bursting through it just in time, feeling my guts lurch as I kneeled over it and retched.

At last I was done, my throat and gullet red raw, stomach aching, empty. I wiped the sour taste from my lips, splashing my face, staring at my chalk-white reflection in the mirror. Eyes like lumps of coal stared back at me.

'Bloody hell, girl. You look like death warmed up.'

At least I was still alive, unlike Mum and Elsie.

I swilled water around my mouth and spat it out, reapplying my lipstick and pinching my cheeks. It didn't make much difference, but it would have to do. Not that there was any fooling Charlie. He rose as I re-entered the room and helped me to my seat, kneeling in front of me to take my hands in his.

'Christine, look at me. This wasn't your fault. I can see it on your face. I know what you're thinking. But it wasn't you who dropped bombs on that street knowing there must be civilians down there. It wasn't you either who started this war in the first place, although you've done so much to fight for your country. For all of us. You're a heroine, my darling.'

My tongue felt thick in my mouth as I forced out the words. 'No I'm not. I wasn't there to protect them, was I? What kind of heroine leaves her own family to die? Not to mention her friends? Look at me, sitting here safe while any minute now

Kieffer's men could be dragging Amalie and the others from behind that bloody picture. That's if they haven't done so already.'

'From behind a picture?'

'Yes. There's a concealed room there. Madame Joey used to use it to hide downed airmen and other people she was helping escape. Jewish families and the like.'

'If she managed to keep all of them hidden, then chances are they'll get away with it this time as well. The Germans must have searched the place before. They didn't find anything then. And we don't even know if that's what they're planning.'

'Oh come on, Charlie. "The black cat has three kittens. Confirmed." SOE might as well have taken them to the door and asked them to arrest our agents. How could they? It's unconscionable. To send them over expecting that they would be caught. Setting them up so they would be. And then hoping they'd crack under torture just to keep up this charade we're playing with the Germans.'

Charlie took my hands in his. 'It's not a charade. You know this is deadly serious. You've laid your own life on the line with Kieffer, for God's sake. If he even suspects for one moment what we're really up to, he'll have us in his damn cells faster than you can blink. This is all or nothing, Christine. The biggest roll of the dice since the war began. We manage to keep the Germans in the dark about the real invasion and we'll catch them on the hop. That means hundreds of thousands of lives saved. Our boys taking those beaches and then marching on to Paris instead of being cut down before they even get a chance to land. Liberation, Christine. Victory. For us.'

I let out a bitter laugh. 'Victory. What does that even mean anymore? Have we really won if people like Amalie and Jacques die? If my own mother and little sister are already dead and my brother is somewhere out there, fighting, if he's not also dead in a ditch somewhere too? Tell me, who wins out of that? Not me, that's for sure.'

Charlie pulled his handkerchief from his pocket and carefully wiped away my tears. At this point, I was surprised I had any left. Too much water had passed under too many bridges for me to shed any more tears. I could still see that first one in my mind. The bridge over the Seine my first night in Paris. The waters had swirled, oil slicked and murky then. If only I'd heeded that as a warning.

FIFTY-FOUR

Ward was back, still calm and in control. 'I've managed to get through to Jim.'

I wanted to shake him. 'What's he going to do?'

Ward looked at me and then at Charlie. 'He'll get over there, along with your other people, and assess the lay of the land.'

'For Christ's sake, they should be going in there and getting them out before the Germans can. I'm leaving. We need to help them now.'

Charlie took hold of my hand once more. 'We can't do that, Christine. We have to see this through without blowing our cover. If you go rushing in there right now trying to extricate everyone, Kieffer will start asking questions. He'll know that we intercepted the messages. Let Jim and Colonel Olivier handle it, along with Suzanne.'

He was right. Of course he was. Unbearably, horribly right. 'So we just have to wait?'

'We do.'

I took a deep, shuddering breath and glanced at my watch. More than two hours since Ward had received those messages.

Two hours in which anything could have happened. Kieffer moved fast. We'd seen that with all the drops. But there was nothing I could do. This was the life I'd chosen. One that meant tough choices and even tougher results. The worst part was knowing that I was powerless. That this would play out regardless, and I had to rely on others to make sure Amalie was safe.

'What about Marcel? Can't we try and get hold of him as well? He knows everyone, including the top brass in the Gestapo and the Abwehr.'

Ward frowned. 'Marcel?'

'Marcel Aragon. He's our fixer here in Paris.'

'Excuse me one moment.'

Ward was back within minutes, another dossier in his hands. He handed it to me. 'Is this the man you know as Marcel Aragon?'

I looked at the photograph inside. 'Yes. That's him. Are you saying he has another name?'

Ward flipped up the photograph. Beneath, the usual typed notes. A name leaped out at me: 'Marcel Guiet'. I turned the page, looking at more photographs of Marcel, one in the company of a younger Suzanne and another with a man whose face rang bells. I pointed to him. 'Who's he?'

'That's Paul Boulain,' said Ward. 'A known Gestapo double agent. Marcel has been on to him for some time, sending us reports on his activities as well as keeping an eye on him until the time is right to eliminate him. Boulain believes Marcel is as pro-Nazi as he is.'

'Wait, are you saying that Marcel works for you? I thought he was simply a part of the Resistance working with SOE.'

'Marcel has been working for us as an embedded agent since 1935. When SOE came along, it made sense for him to take on his role as a local *résistant* and help you too.'

'So he's been spying on us for you all this time?'

'He's been spying on the Germans and their collaborators while serving his country.'

I glared at Ward. 'We're not collaborators.'

'I know that.'

All at once, it dawned on me where I'd seen the other man before, this Paul Boulain. Another surge of nausea. Oh Christ, not again. Was I sickening for something? I took a deep breath. 'Do you remember that photograph Kieffer showed us in his office?' I asked Charlie. 'The one of Suzanne talking to some man?'

'I do.'

'It's him, isn't it? The man in the photograph. Paul Boulain. Kieffer said nothing about him being a Gestapo agent. He didn't even tell us his name. What the hell was Suzanne doing meeting him? Please don't tell me she was in on it with London. That she knew all along. I don't think I could bear that.'

'I don't know,' said Charlie grimly. 'But we're sure as hell going to find out.'

FIFTY-FIVE

1.30 P.M., 19 FEBRUARY 1944, PARIS, FRANCE

Kieffer was waiting for us as we entered the lobby of the Ritz, sitting apparently at ease in an armchair, a cup of coffee in front of him. There was nothing for it but to go and join him.

'Well, how did it go?'

I picked up the pot of coffee and poured a cup for Charlie and then myself.

'It went well, thank you,' said Charlie. 'They were keen to place large orders, as you suspected.'

'But of course.'

Kieffer was enjoying this. And it wasn't just because he'd been right about the orders. He was holding something back. I could see it playing across his face, the glee of someone who's about to reveal something. I sipped my coffee as nonchalantly as I could, waiting him out. Charlie, too, appeared totally at ease, although I could feel his foot tapping next to mine under the table.

Finally, Kieffer could hold back no longer.

'You may wonder why I'm here instead of at the office. I thought, with everything going on, we would have more peace to talk here.'

If he expected us to swallow his bait, he had another think coming. 'Good idea,' I murmured, signalling to the waiter, who glided smoothly over. 'Could I see the lunch menu please?'

I had no stomach for anything, but it might help get rid of Kieffer. If he insisted on joining us, at least that would suggest he wasn't immediately staging a raid.

'But of course, madame.'

'I'd like a menu as well, thank you,' said Charlie. 'I need the energy,' he added, dropping a wink at Kieffer.

I almost choked on my coffee. I could see what Charlie was doing, pricking the bubble of Kieffer's self-importance. The man evidently thought he had us in his thrall, gagging to hear what he had to say. Truth was, we were, but neither of us would give him the satisfaction. That look of glee had faded, to be replaced by something nastier. He was relishing this, and I hated him for it.

'It's a pity we didn't have time to give our guests lunch before they departed.'

I looked at him over the rim of my coffee cup, feigning ignorance. 'Your guests?'

'Yes. The ones you saw in our cells. We've emptied them out, ready for the next batch.'

'I see.'

'I'm afraid there's no lunch menu where they're going.'

Charlie's foot was no longer tapping. He sat dangerously still, his gaze fixed on Kieffer. 'And where would that be?'

'They've been relocated to Germany.'

No doubt to somewhere like Dachau. The camp where Amalie's father had disappeared without a trace. I no longer held out any hope that he was still alive, although I suspected she might, in her heart of hearts. And now Kieffer had sent Jacques to a death camp, along with the other *résistants* and agents he held prisoner. The Nazis might deny or play down their existence, but I'd seen the evidence and it sickened me.

It was with a real effort that I kept my composure and affected disinterest. 'More coffee?'

'I believe Madame Josephine has been transported too.'

I kept my hand steady as I poured the coffee, although, for half a second, I was tempted to pour the hot liquid all over Kieffer's hand and see how he liked it. The Nazis liked to pour boiling water on their victims or hold their heads down in it as they tortured them, along with stubbing out cigarettes on the same hands they'd broken under hammers once they'd ripped out all the fingernails. I didn't know which was worse – a Nazi who carried out torture with his own hands or someone like Kieffer, who delegated his dirty work while pretending it didn't happen, sanctioning inhuman degradation and signing execution orders he'd get others to carry out.

'Is that all?' I asked, handing Kieffer the sugar bowl, fighting as hard as I could to keep my hand steady. This was no debrief. Kieffer had a whole other agenda.

'Not quite. Have you heard of Admiral Canaris?'

'Name sounds familiar,' drawled Charlie.

I shook my head. 'Doesn't ring a bell.'

'Ah, well. Canaris is the head of the Abwehr. I should say former head. The Abwehr was abolished by decree from the Führer. As of yesterday, it no longer exists, and we are in charge of all intelligence and counter-espionage activities.'

Shit. Those bastards had got their wish. Kieffer caught my stare and I hastily looked away, affecting indifference. 'Oh. Right.'

He stroked his moustache, enjoying his moment. 'There is one other thing I wanted to tell you, and that is you no longer need to keep an eye on your cousin. I think we have everything we need.'

I looked at him, seeing the anticipation, the cruel delight of a cat about to devour a mouse. 'Excellent.'

Kieffer wiped his mouth with his napkin, pushed back his chair and rose to his feet. 'You'll be hearing from me.'

I smiled up at him. 'I look forward to it.'

Beside me, Charlie grunted something similar. The moment Kieffer had disappeared through the door, he reached out and took my hand. 'He's on to us.'

'I know.'

FIFTY-SIX

No candles this time. They'd all burned out. I hoped it wasn't a sign. The chapel felt colder and darker without them. It was Olivier who once more greeted us and led us through the robing room. At the end of the corridor into the sanctuary, I thought I glimpsed a nun carrying a lit candle. Or perhaps that was wishful thinking. Even if she set every candle in the chapel alight, it wouldn't shift the shadows of Kieffer, this war, what could happen to Suzanne, Amalie and the others, to all of us.

The moment the door shut behind us, I rounded on Ward. 'Well, have you got them out of the club yet? Are they safe?'

'They're still in Le Chat Noir. Your colleague has been informed of the danger, as has Marcel. So far, the Gestapo has made no move to raid the place.'

I wanted to take him by his immaculate lapels and shake him. Hard. 'They may not have made their move yet, but they will at any moment. Kieffer is on to us.'

Ward frowned. 'How do you know?'

'We just saw him. At the Ritz. He couldn't wait to come and tell us that he's emptied his cells and transported the prisoners, ready for a new intake.'

'His implication was clear,' added Charlie. 'Along with his intent. He's made us and he wanted us to know that. I suspect he's hoping to force us into making a false move. Then he'll swoop and snatch us all up at the same time. He's no fool.'

'Evidently.'

'Which means,' I went on through gritted teeth, 'we need to get them out of there now. We can't wait until Kieffer's lot decide to come calling.'

'We're trying to set up an escape line for them with the aid of our people,' said Ward. 'I believe you have an agent called Jeannette.'

'I do,' said Charlie.

'She's working with Jim to come up with a safe route out of Paris. From there, we'll attempt to exfiltrate the agents back to London. I agree that it's far too dangerous for them to stay. For you to stay too. The problem is that the Gestapo are searching every vehicle going to and from the club, which is going to make getting them out of there very difficult indeed.'

'There's another problem,' said Charlie. 'Kieffer told us that Canaris has been sacked by Hitler. The Abwehr no longer exists. It's been taken over by Kieffer's lot. Which means it's only a matter of time before they arrest Canaris on some spurious charge.'

Ward lit a cigarette. It was the closest I'd ever seen him to being mildly rattled. 'Yes, but as you say, Kieffer is on to you anyway, so this mission is dead in the water.'

We'd failed. Except we hadn't. It was SOE who'd failed us. We may not have penetrated the Gestapo and the Abwehr, but what did that matter when one no longer existed and the other had been fed our own agents by our own people?

'I suppose it is, but it still leaves Charlie and me exposed. It also means we have no access to the Abwehr's double agents and they won't be sending disinformation for us back to Berlin.

I assume Canaris's plan to broker a peace deal is also dead in the water.'

Ward glanced at Olivier. 'He may still have other plans. And we still have our own double agents feeding disinformation. What we have to do now is get you all safely to London. There will be no more agents dropped in for the Paris network for the moment. Instead, they'll be sent from other networks in France to rebuild it once we're sure it's safe to do so.'

No more sending agents to their deaths. At least that was something.

'The two of you need to return to the Ritz and carry on acting as if everything is normal,' said Ward. 'Leave the rest to us. If Kieffer gets so much as a whiff of what we're planning, he may well jump the gun.'

'What I don't understand is why he hasn't raided the place already. Or arrested us.'

Charlie reached for his coat. 'He'll have his reasons. Kieffer always does.'

I had no doubt those reasons included catching us in the act. It would be quite a coup, arresting multiple Allied agents. Too bad we weren't going to let it happen.

'Good luck,' said Ward. 'I'll be returning to London on the next plane, but Colonel Olivier here will liaise with you.'

It would take more than luck to outfox Kieffer and his men.

As soon as we were out of earshot, I leaned close to Charlie and murmured, 'Leave the rest to us, my arse. I trust that man about as much as I trust Kieffer right now.'

'I agree. It's down to you and me, kid. With a little help from our friends.'

I smiled into his eyes. 'That'll do for me.'

FIFTY-SEVEN

We took a circuitous route back to the Ritz, making sure no one had followed us from the chapel. To anyone watching, we looked like a couple who'd taken a long stroll through Paris, stopping every now and again for a kiss, all the while checking over one another's shoulders to see if we were being tailed. If Kieffer thought he'd got us worried, he had another think coming.

As we approached the reception, my stomach plummeted. The concierge greeted us with a smile that looked slightly strained. 'A message for you, madame. And one for you, sir.'

I opened mine to see it was from Suzanne: 'Stay where you are. The cat is not well.'

I passed it to Charlie. 'We need to find out what's happening. We may have to move even faster.'

In turn, he handed me his message: 'Lighting a candle for you at 4 p.m.'

'Does that mean what I think it means?' I asked.

'Yes. We need to be back at the convent then. Looks like they already made some plans after all.'

I glanced at the clock above the reception desk. 'We've only got half an hour.'

The concierge cleared his throat. 'If I may, there is also this package for you.'

The moment he handed it to me all wrapped up in ribbons, I knew by the weight that it contained a gun. 'Thank you. That's very kind.'

'Not at all, madame.'

The look on his face said it all.

'Excuse me one moment.'

Safely in the ladies' room, I undid the ribbons and then opened the lid of the box embossed with the name 'Lanvin'. The pistol hidden beneath the scarf inside was couture of a different kind and far more useful right now. I tucked it into my belt and then rebuttoned my coat, making sure no bulge was visible. I had no doubt there would be eyes on us the moment we left the hotel, unless we managed to shake them off.

I was still trying to work out a route that might outwit even Kieffer when I rejoined Charlie at the concierge's desk.

'Madame, if you would follow me.'

It appeared Charlie had been discussing that very issue with the concierge because just a few moments later, he was leading us through a back corridor and down some steps to a door, which he unlocked. 'This is a tunnel that leads beneath the Place Vendôme,' he said. 'It is for the use of our VIP guests should they need it.'

I glanced at Charlie and then ahead, where I could see the beginning of the tunnel lit up by the lamps that ran its length. 'Where exactly does it emerge?'

'It leads to the parking lot. From there, you can get to the backstreets beyond without being observed.'

'I see. Thank you.'

Charlie shook his hand, and the concierge dropped us a little bow. 'It is I who should thank you on behalf of France.

Good luck. I'll leave this door unlocked in case you should need to return this way.'

I heard him shut it behind us as we started down the tunnel. A small act of heroism among so many. For him, for Amalie and all the rest, we had to keep going. No matter what.

FIFTY-EIGHT

We'd only been gone a couple of hours but the chapel looked and felt completely different. The smell of incense now filled the air, candles flickering in every window as well as on the altar. I could have sworn I saw a nun's habit disappear around the far door as we entered. They'd obviously just finished their prayers. I hoped they'd said one for us. Make that several.

Jim was waiting for us in the side chapel, a look of relief washing across his face as we entered. 'I thought you were never coming.'

Charlie slid into the pew beside him. 'Good to see you too. How's my dog?'

'Your dog is just fine. I wish I could say the same for your friends.'

He looked at me and my heart sank. 'What do you mean?'

'I mean that we have it on good authority Kieffer is planning to raid Le Chat Noir tonight. We need to get your people out of there now.'

Cold terror gripped me, squeezing my heart like a vice. I forced myself to stay calm. 'Do we know what time?'

'Sometime around ten. When the club is at its busiest. I

guess he's hoping to kill two birds with one stone and arrest anyone who doesn't check out at the same time.'

'He's hoping to humiliate us,' I said. 'He knows the agents are in there so he's going to make a public show of Suzanne and anyone else he suspects helped to hide them. Including me. Then he'll close down the club and throw everyone he can into his filthy cells. The ones he's emptied in readiness. That way he looks even better in Berlin's eyes.'

'Then there's no way you're going anywhere near the place,' said Charlie. 'We're not handing him another agent on a plate, least of all you.'

'There's no way I'm staying away from the place,' I said. 'Suzanne and Amalie are my friends. The other agents and staff are my responsibility. I have to make sure they get out of there alive. All of them. Without Kieffer getting his hands on anything.'

'How the hell do you plan to do that?'

I stared Jim down. 'I thought you were the man with the plan.'

'We have transport organised, and our people can get you all out of Paris to an airfield. The problem is still getting them out of the club.'

I gazed sightlessly at the statue of the Madonna and Child. *Think, Christine, think.* We had so little time. But if the gods were actually with us, there was a way. An incredibly risky, daring way. The only kind that would work. 'I have an idea.'

Jim made a snort of what sounded like impatience, but Charlie gave me an encouraging nod. 'Go on.'

'They're expecting us to try and smuggle them out so why not do the opposite? We dress them in staff uniforms and have them working, not out front but behind the scenes. Amalie could easily pass as a cook. She ran her own café. The men are a little harder, but they could be kitchen porters or cellar staff. At the right moment, just before Kieffer's raid, we cause a diversion. Something big enough that will have everyone running around in chaos. An explosion or a fire perhaps. That's when we evacuate the building, and Amalie and the other two slip out with the other staff. If we have Jeannette and her people close by, they can get them away before Kieffer and his men spot them. Us too.'

Jim was looking at me with grudging respect. 'It could just work.'

'Have you got a better plan? Because I don't. I say we go with it.' Charlie was already on his feet. 'And I know just the man who can help.'

'You do?'

'Remember that cab driver? The one who took us to the American Hospital? We can get him and his fellow cab drivers to block the street outside the club, pretending they're there to collect customers when this sudden explosion happens. I vote we go with an explosion. It's easier to rig and control. That way, the Gestapo can't get close with their cars and won't be able to follow any vehicle they see leaving.'

'That's genius,' I said. 'As for the explosion, I'm pretty nifty at setting charges. Came top of my class.'

'I have no doubt.'

The adrenaline was back, coursing through my veins, and I could see it was the same with Charlie. We were made of the same stuff. It was one of the many reasons it felt so right to be with him.

'Looks like you two have this all sewn up,' said Jim. 'How about I get my hands on those explosives for you? We have a guy here who can supply us.'

'Sounds good to me. I'll go back to the apartment and get a message to Jeannette.' I could see the trepidation in Charlie's eyes as he turned to me. 'What about you?'

'I'm going back to the club.'

'I thought you might say that.'

'I have to. We need to act as if everything is normal. Kieffer would expect me to go to work even if he no longer wants me to spy on Suzanne. If I don't, it's yet another reason he might start to get suspicious and bring his raid forward. Besides, I need to warn Amalie and the others and get them kitted out. I also need to fill Suzanne in on the plan.'

'You sure that's wise?'

I knew Charlie was thinking of the photograph of Suzanne talking to Boulain, the Gestapo contact, just as I was. 'There's nothing else I can do.'

In my soul, I didn't believe Suzanne was a traitor. Or maybe it was that I didn't want to believe it. I still had no alternative. This would be the ultimate test, not just of friendship but of loyalty. SOE had already failed us on that score. I could only hope she didn't let us down too.

'Come back with me first to my place,' said Charlie. 'Let's make sure we have everything ready before you go to the club. Please, Christine. You know it makes sense.'

There was something in his voice that I'd never heard before. It sounded almost as if he was pleading. Whatever it was, it struck a chord deep within me. Much later, I would recognise that chord for what it was. For now, all I knew was that I would follow Charlie to the ends of the Earth.

'Try and stop me,' I said.

FIFTY-NINE

We were extra careful as we approached the apartment, lingering in a doorway at the end of the street, scanning it to make sure there was no one watching from the shadows, or from another door or window where they could suddenly appear.

'Looks clear to me.'

'You sure about that?'

Before I could answer, Charlie had turned his back to the street and was kissing me for all he was worth. Finally, he drew back, although his eyes wouldn't let mine go.

'Just making sure?' I murmured.

'Something like that.'

Inside the apartment building, the concierge hovered. 'A young lady dropped this off for you.'

Charlie took the note she was holding out. 'Thank you.'

As he opened the apartment door, a streak of fur shot at us, whimpering in delight.

'Hey, Betty. Hey, girl. I've missed you.'

She was smothering Charlie in dog kisses, her tail wagging furiously. I laughed. 'I see I have competition.'

'Afraid so.'

She sat, tail still wagging, looking from Charlie to me as he read the note. 'It's from Jeannette. She'll be here in forty minutes. I've no doubt that old bat of a concierge read it too, so she can let her in. That gives us a good half hour.'

'For what?'

'For this.'

Twenty-five minutes later, I lay sweat-slicked beside him, stroking the hair back from his forehead before dropping a kiss on it. The adrenaline was pumping, fuelling our fire. The same adrenaline we'd take into battle with Kieffer. Funny how close the two felt. Or perhaps not funny at all. 'I'll take a quick shower before Jeannette gets here.'

'Must you?'

'You're insatiable.'

'For you, yes.'

Another kiss, this time on his mouth. It tasted of salt. Of me. 'Hold that thought.'

When I opened the bedroom door, it was to see Betty lying there, guarding it and us. 'Good girl.'

She threw me a look then leaped on the bed. As I started to run the water, all I could hear was Charlie laughing under her onslaught.

The water was tepid as I pivoted under it, soaping myself where he'd touched me, feeling the fire start to rise once more in my belly. Was it my imagination, or was my belly a little rounder? My dress had seemed tighter when I last wore it.

I did a swift calculation. I was late. And I was never late.

'Oh my God.'

I felt my belly again, gently stroking it, wondering if there was a tiny person in there, growing day by day. A person who'd look like me and Charlie. A baby. Our baby. I couldn't believe it. Nor could I believe that I was grinning from ear to ear even as I felt another surge of nausea. That too. Along with feeling more tired than usual, now that I thought about it. Of course. It was all starting to make sense.

Then another thought struck me. How would Charlie feel about this? I had no idea.

One thing was for certain, I was keeping this baby, no matter what. Another person to love. Someone of my very own, besides Charlie. I had a feeling he'd be as happy as I was, but I'd long ago learned not to count on anything, least of all another human being.

I heard a knock at the door above the sound of the shower still running then voices in the hall. By the time I emerged from the bathroom, Jeanette was busying herself in the kitchen. I'd have to hug the news to myself for the moment. She smiled at me, completely unabashed by my appearance – I was draped in nothing more than a towel. 'We have a long night ahead,' she said. 'I thought coffee would be a good idea.'

'Great idea,' I muttered, making a beeline for the bedroom to find Charlie was almost dressed, Betty supervising his every move.

He planted a kiss on my shoulder. 'That suits you.'

I automatically dropped the towel and reached for my clothes, glancing up at his sharp intake of breath. I could have sworn those were tears glinting in his eyes.

'You're absolutely exquisite, my darling,' he said. 'The most beautiful woman I've ever seen.'

I dropped my head again, unused to the sincerity of his words, aching to tell him but knowing this wasn't the time. Men complimented me all the time with empty phrases, but this was different. It came from Charlie. From his heart. I opened my mouth. To hell with timing. But when I looked up, he was gone.

I could hear voices from the kitchen and smell the coffee now brewed. I removed the red dress from my bag then pulled it over my head, smoothing out its creases before reaching for one of Charlie's sweaters and tugging it on over the top. I then strapped on a leg holster and tucked my gun into it. It could double up to strap the explosives into place too. A quick look in the mirror to smooth my hair and apply lipstick to a mouth that couldn't stop smiling. My eyes, too, shone in a way that no cosmetic could ever highlight.

'Face it, girl, you're in love,' I murmured. And not just with one person anymore. With the promise of a future. Our future. With any luck.

The woman in the mirror smiled back at me.

'OK. Deep breath. You've got a job to do.'

She looked at me again, sombre now, the seriousness of what lay ahead wiping away any trace of a smile.

SIXTY

In the kitchen, Jeanette handed me a coffee. Charlie was on the telephone, listening intently. Finally, he replaced the receiver. 'The delivery should be here in twenty minutes. Jim has organised one of the cabs to take you to the club.'

'Just the one cab?'

'Every single one that's available. He found our man, who was apparently only too happy to help. He's bringing all his cab buddies who hate "those bastard Boches", to use his own words.'

Jeannette looked puzzled.

'It's part of the plan,' I said. 'We're going to get the cabs to block the streets around the club so the Gestapo can't easily get close and can't follow an escape vehicle either.'

'An excellent idea. May I suggest you also use one of those cabs as an escape car? If the others are moving at the same time, the Gestapo won't know which one, if any, to follow. Otherwise, they're bound to radio ahead and catch a particular car at a roadblock. Not so easy when you have dozens of cabs that all look the same.'

I beamed. 'Jeannette, you are brilliant.'

'Not at all. We're a team. You made the initial plan. I just added a suggestion.'

'Well it's a fine one. Thank you.'

There was another knock at the apartment door then. Charlie raised a hand to signal silence and moved to it soundlessly, pulling out his pistol and standing by the lintel before calling out, 'Who is it?'

'Special delivery from the Yankees.'

'When did they win the world series?'

'1941.'

Charlie unlocked the door. 'Good answer.'

The man standing there looked so quintessentially French I almost burst out laughing. His beret was perched on his head at precisely the right angle, the waxed tips of his moustache bristling with patriotic pride. He handed Charlie the box he was carrying. 'For you, I believe. Be careful. It contains plastique.'

'Nobel 808?'

He nodded. 'Six pounds along with safety fuse and blasting caps. I'm afraid I couldn't obtain pencil charges so you will have to detonate it manually. Good luck.'

With that, he slipped out of the apartment, leaving Charlie to place the box on the kitchen table and carefully remove the lid. Inside, lumps of green plastic explosive were nestled next to the safety fuse and blasting caps.

'I can make them up,' I said. 'We need to soften the 808 in hot water first. Too bad about the pencil charges, but we'll just have to work around that.'

Jeannette looked dubious. 'How are you going to get them into the club?'

'Under my skirt of course.'

Charlie shook his head. 'No. No way. Far too dangerous.'

'Do you have a better idea?'

'No, but that doesn't mean you should do it.'

'I can strap the explosives to my leg. This skirt is full enough. They won't show at all.'

'What if the Germans search you going in?'

'Why would they? I work there.'

I sounded more confident than I felt. Deep down, I was terrified and not just for me. Plastique was stable enough until there was a detonator in it. I'd set the fuses once I got there, but even so, it was a hugely risky plan. In my experience, those were the best kind. The ones that usually worked. In a war where life was cheap and freedom a dirty word, insanity was an asset. At least it kept the enemy on their toes and hopefully wrong-footed at every turn.

My hand drifted to my stomach, but I snatched it away before the others could notice. *Concentrate, Christine. All the more reason now to make sure this goes off without a hitch.*

I placed the plastique gently in the sink full of hot water Jeannette had boiled up on the stove. Together, we worked it, moulding it into lumps small enough to strap to my legs while remaining large enough to cause a decent explosion. Charlie, meanwhile, pored over a rough plan we'd drawn of Le Chat Noir, mapping out the best spots to place the explosives so they caused mayhem without too much carnage.

'If we set one in the storeroom at the back of the bar and another in the hallway here, they should go off without blocking any exits or blasting through walls,' he said. 'Then we can put two by the cellars so that gives plenty of smoke for the agents down there to get out.'

'What about the others? We have enough plastique here to make six.'

'How about we put them by the front door and at the top of the first flight of stairs? That way, we can set them off just as Kieffer and his men try to enter the building. I can detonate those and the others on the first floor. Marcel can take the other two by the cellars. The distraction caused should give us enough time to get the agents into the cab.'

'I think we should split them up into two separate cabs. Or even three. That way, if one or two are caught, the other still has a chance.'

Charlie chewed the end of his pencil. 'We could send the cabs in three different directions. Then they can drop the agents at a prearranged place which I think should be here.'

He tapped at the map of Paris spread out beside the plan of the building, drawing a circle around the American Hospital. 'You use this anyway, Jeannette, as an escape line. It's a tried and tested route. I'll try and get word to Sumner Jackson, but even if he's not there, you know the back entrance to the hospital wing that he uses and the roads out of there.'

'I do,' said Jeannette. 'We can get the car in position at the back of the hospital. Your Hispano-Suiza. I brought it back as good as new. It's fast and more powerful than many of their vehicles, which will give us a head start. It will also confuse the Gestapo even more if we switch vehicles. The taxis can circle back into the city centre and, if they're searched, there will be no evidence of anything.'

'With any luck, Kieffer won't even realise what's going on until it's far too late.'

Charlie squeezed my arm. 'Don't underestimate him. Kieffer's been in this game a long time.'

I smiled, staring into his eyes. 'So have I.'

SIXTY-ONE

I could feel the lumps of plastique brushing against my thighs as I strode as smoothly as I could up the street to the club. One trip or stumble and that would be the end of me, never mind my legs. The end of both of us. I scarcely dared breathe, never mind look around for lurking Gestapo. My friendly taxi driver had dropped me off a couple of streets away so I could get the lay of the land.

'I will go and organise the other drivers,' he said as I carefully exited the cab. '*Bonne chance!*'

I would need more than luck if I was to pull this off. Skill and a miracle maybe.

The street appeared to be clear as I approached the club entrance, but I could feel eyes on me, probably from one of the buildings opposite. The Gestapo were well versed in the art of apparently appearing from nowhere. We already knew they had men in position watching this place round the clock. It was another reason not to draw up in the taxi. The last thing I wanted was for them to search me or the cab. Now I had to rely on our friendly driver gathering his fellow cabbies to help. A stab of nostalgia as I imagined London cabbies on the job. They'd have been here in a flash too.

Inside the club, everything seemed to be ticking along as normal. I made my way down to the basement office, moving through the storeroom to what looked like a cupboard door but which actually opened into the dank space that was our nerve centre. Suzanne looked up, startled, as I entered. Her head was bent low over her desk, almost touching that of Marcel.

'I thought I told you to stay away.'

'Nice to see you too,' I retorted. 'No, please don't come too close.'

I took a step back as she rose, shrugging off my coat and lifting my skirt to reveal what was underneath. The two of them stared at the plastique strapped to my legs.

'Perhaps you could explain?' murmured Suzanne.

'I'd love to, but first could we get this stuff off me? Don't worry, the detonators are in my bag, but they're still made up and ready to blow, so we need to go carefully.'

Marcel kneeled in front of me, studying the plastique. 'Allow me.'

He peeled each one off with steady hands, placing them one by one on the desk until they were all removed. Only then did I allow myself to start shaking, my whole body trembling with the effort of getting them in here without blowing myself up, along with the entire operation.

'We have a plan,' I gasped, taking a breath and then another, my heartbeat slowing to near normal. 'Kieffer is planning his raid for ten o'clock, so we must get these in place before then. Charlie mapped out where we should place them for maximum effect and minimum damage. He – along with you, Marcel – will detonate them just as Kieffer arrives. They should cause enough chaos so that we have to evacuate the building. In the meantime, we need to disguise the agents as staff. Amalie can be a cook. The men a kitchen porter and a cellar man so they don't arouse suspicion by speaking too much.'

I was aware I was gabbling, but I had to get it all out. I glanced at my watch – 7.48 p.m. We had so little time.

'With any luck, there will be dozens of cabs blocking the streets outside so that Kieffer can't drive up. He also won't be able to chase an escape vehicle easily because we'll use the cabs for that too, putting an agent along with one of us in each. The rendezvous point is the American Hospital. We have an escape line planned from there so we can be extracted to the airfield to fly home. I'm afraid Kieffer is on to us, so we'll all have to leave.'

Suzanne was looking at me as if I'd taken leave of my senses. It was only then that I remembered the photograph of her with that man, Boulain. Too bad. It would have to wait until later. Besides, she had no opportunity to alert anyone. In just over two hours, Kieffer would be here. We needed to be gone before he arrived. Then there was that sense in my bones that Suzanne was no traitor. I'd have to trust that too. As for Marcel, I already knew his bona fides.

'Well, what are we waiting for?' I snapped. 'We need to find them staff uniforms. Fill them in on the plan. You go and do that while I set the charges.'

'I'll give you a hand,' said Marcel.

Suzanne pulled her pistol from the top drawer and tucked it in her waistband. 'I always knew you were my best student.'

'You're a great teacher.'

For a second, our eyes met. I remembered the most important lesson she'd ever taught me. Trust no one. The same lesson I'd taught Amalie. Should I really trust her? Too late. We were committed to this plan.

I slung my bag over my shoulder and lifted up two of the lumps of plastique, holding one in each hand. 'Suzanne, you lead the way. Marcel, get the other two.'

For now, it was me in charge. This was my op. Get it right and we all lived to fight another day. I wouldn't even think about getting it wrong. It simply wasn't an option.

SIXTY-TWO

She looked the perfect picture of a chef, her hair tucked into a cap and her apron wrapped around her, concealing her weapon underneath.

'Don't forget there are also kitchen knives there,' I muttered. 'Just in case.'

Amalie reached for one of them and began chopping the pile of vegetables on the counter. 'I won't forget. And don't you forget to be careful.'

'When have I ever been that?'

Her smile was fleeting. 'Not often enough.'

I took a step closer and squeezed her shoulder. 'Don't worry about me. You just concentrate on the plan.'

'You can count on me.'

If only I could depend on everyone else to do their bit, we might just pull this off. Upstairs, Charlie was busy laying detonation cord. Kieffer was due at ten o'clock precisely. One thing you could rely on with the Germans was punctuality. I glanced at my watch again – 9.29 p.m. There were just a couple of the girls in the salon, the others already occupied in their rooms, safely out of the blast range. The two male agents were in position and primed, one hovering close to Amalie while the other pretended to lug the crates of wine and beer back and forth from the bar to the cellar, under strict orders to make sure he was back downstairs when the explosives were scheduled to blow.

I drew one of the heavy curtains aside, peering down into the street below. I could see four cabs already driving up and down the street with some more at each end, parked so that they blocked the intersections. 'Take that, Kieffer,' I muttered.

'Let's hope he does. Right in the balls.'

I whirled round to see Suzanne watching me. She gestured towards the upstairs office door. 'A quick word?'

I stepped inside. This was my chance. As I opened my mouth to speak, she held a warning finger to her lips. I followed her gaze as she looked up towards the ceiling light. Her meaning was clear. Someone had bugged the office. I could take a good guess who that might be.

'I was talking to a Monsieur Boulain last night. He's bringing some friends in this evening. VIP guests. I'd like you to greet them.'

Her meaning was clear. Boulain was the advance party, and she wanted him picked off before he could help Kieffer do his worst.

'Of course,' I said. 'I'll make sure I'm right by the door so I can welcome them. What time are we expecting them?'

'Any moment now.'

'Very good.'

She reached into her desk and handed me a sleeve dagger, which I slid into place, the pocket sewn into my dress there precisely for that purpose. I patted the pistol at my waist for reassurance. Two guns. Six bombs. Six agents, not counting Marcel. Against God knows how many Gestapo, along with their SS soldiers. We weren't exactly evenly matched. Granted, Jim and Jeannette would be outside in waiting taxis, hidden from view, ready to receive the agents and drive off in different directions. So much that could go wrong there too.

I plastered my professional smile on my face. 'Better get down there then,' I said brightly, for the benefit of anyone listening. 'It wouldn't do to keep our customers waiting.'

Suzanne dropped me a wink. 'Quite.'

She was a crack shot herself. If there was anyone I wanted by my side right now, it was Suzanne. Time enough later to find out why she'd been working Boulain. The very fact she'd warned me he was turning up was already helping clear the lingering clouds of suspicion in my mind.

Nine forty. Boulain would be here any minute, Kieffer soon after. Through the glass panes in the door, I could see more cabs appearing, filling up the street. Then a small party of men approaching, one looking irate as he addressed the doorman. Seconds later, I was greeting them. 'Gentlemen, good evening.'

I recognised Boulain at once, but it was the man alongside him who made me take a step back. Braun. What was he doing with him? Then there was his other guest, Eugene Schumann. His eyes met mine then slid away. This was some advance party.

'What is happening in this street?' demanded Braun.

'I'm not sure what you mean.'

'Taxi cabs everywhere. We had to park two streets away and walk.'

Excellent. The blockade was working. 'Really? My goodness. I had no idea.'

'Do you have a telephone?' snapped Braun.

'Yes, we do.'

'Show me where it is. I must telephone my office and get them to clear this street at once.'

I gaped at him, mind whirling, heart racing. Charlie was

upstairs setting the detonators. If I took Braun up there now, he might spot him or the cord. But there was no way I could refuse. There was nothing for it but to lead him upstairs to the office, talking as loudly as I could, while Boulain and the others headed for the bar. At least they'd be in the right place when the bomb went off. I kept up my distracting chatter, my eyes darting left and right as we mounted the stairs. No sign of Charlie, although I thought I caught a glimpse of safety fuse being yanked out of sight.

Mercifully, Braun was too intent on making his phone call to notice and too irritated by my incessant monologue to do anything but head straight for the office door. I rapped on it once and then again, expecting Suzanne to call out.

'Just open it,' huffed Braun.

When I did, it was to find the room empty. I hid my surprise and pointed to the telephone. Where the hell was Suzanne? Being in here alone with Braun was making me nervous. Having him in such close proximity to Charlie and the explosives was only ratcheting up my anxiety.

'Shall I leave you to make your call?'

Anything to get out of that room and shut the door on him.

'No need. Stay.'

I pretended to tidy some paperwork as he dialled, rapping out his orders before slamming down the receiver. Shit. Now what?

I thought I heard a knock from the floor above. Held my breath. Braun didn't appear to notice. He clearly had something else on his mind, something which, as I saw the ghastly glint in his eyes, filled me with sheer terror.

'Come here.'

Heart hammering, I watched as Braun strode past me and locked the door before turning on his heel and repeating his command.

'What for?' I stammered.

He sighed. 'Don't be stupid. This is what you do, isn't it? I want you to come here and pleasure me.'

I stared at him, at that mouth twisted in a snarl, into his bloodshot, rheumy eyes. Behind him, I glimpsed the clock on the wall – 9.55 p.m. Kieffer would be here any minute.

Another, louder sound from upstairs. This time, Braun glanced at the ceiling. Shit. I had to keep him in here at all costs. If he caught Charlie, he'd shoot him on the spot.

'What is it exactly you want me to do?' I prevaricated, playing for time.

He began to unbutton his trousers. 'Come here. That's an order.'

I weighed up my options. There was no way I could get to the door without having to go within inches of him. And I had to keep him in here, whatever it took.

My eyes flicked to the clock again. Four minutes. Four minutes until Charlie set the bombs off. I didn't have four minutes. Braun was reaching inside his trousers now, pulling himself out.

'No.'

He stared at me, eyes bulging. 'What was that?'

Then he lunged, his hands reaching for my throat, closing around it as the spittle rained down on my face. 'Bitch. Whore. You will do as I say.'

The world spun, red mist descending. Not again. Never again. I could see stars as the room darkened, my vision as choked as my breath. Had to distract him. Keep him away from Charlie. Two minutes. Couldn't do it. His hands, squeezing the life out of me. Writhing and squirming, kicking out, trying to break free. Braun's face in mine, mouth gurning, fingers like a vice. Then a curious calm descending. The deep peace of acceptance. I was dying. Maybe it wasn't such a bad thing.

No. I had to live. For me. For Charlie. Most of all, for our baby. I jerked my arm, feeling the dagger drop into my palm, hearing his grunts, his insults as foul as his breath on my face.

'You dirty slut.'

He punched me in the stomach – hard. I gasped as pain shot through me, doubling over to try and protect my womb, the new life within it.

Another blow to my belly, one that sent me reeling backward. And then I was howling in rage, sounding more animal than human, lunging forward, hearing Braun's insane insults, his words dying on a gurgle as I plunged the dagger into his heart and twisted it not once but twice, smiling in satisfaction as the spittle at the corners of his mouth turned pink with his own blood.

It was only when he slumped at my feet, his blood already pooling, that I realised what I'd done. Kieffer would be here any minute. Nine fifty-nine. Thank God. Charlie was safe. He could set them off.

I hobbled to the office door and wrenched it open, grabbing the lump of plastique I'd stuck by the window in the hall, shoving it down Braun's open trousers before slamming the door behind me as I ran for the stairs, hearing the blast when I was halfway down, feeling the heat at my back driving me on. He'd done it.

'I love you,' I mouthed.

More blasts from the first floor. People emerging from the salon and the bar, running for the doors, faces white with shock. Smoke everywhere. Shouts and screams. Above them, Suzanne's voice calling out, 'Stay calm. This way.'

People thrusting past me, among them Boulain. I took my cue from Suzanne, directing staff out the rear door, the customers out the front. Might as well kill two birds with one stone and dispatch a few Nazis at the same time.

More shouts from the street. It sounded like Kieffer and his bully boys arriving. My eyes streamed, my stomach aching.

Bang. The final one going off. Bravo, Marcel.

Cries now of agony. One or two caught in the blast. *Good.*

I raced for the rear door and out into the rear courtyard where the staff were gathered, gazing in confusion at the smoke pouring from the building.

I could see the two male agents, François and Ambrose, but not Amalie. I grabbed François by the arm. 'Come on.'

The two men followed as I sprinted down the alley, a sliver of a street that led to the wider one beyond, emerging to see a taxi waiting, another behind it.

'Get in.'

I thrust Ambrose into the first and François the second, catching a glimpse of Jeannette as she pulled Ambrose to the floor of the cab. No sign of Charlie. No time to waste.

I spun on my heel, racing to the back of the club again, my eyes frantically scanning the crowd. Still no Amalie. No Suzanne either.

More shouts from the building. Then the sound of gunshots. *Shit. Shit. Shit.* I shoved my way through, wrenching open the back door, diving into the building, feet pounding down the back stairs to the cellars and the kitchen.

She was lying on the floor, the lump of ceiling that had hit her on the head lying in smithereens all around her.

'Amalie. Oh God, no. Amalie, can you hear me?'

I checked her breathing, her pulse, feeling the warmth of air on my finger and the flutter of her heart under my fingers. She was alive. That was something. Now to get her out of here.

I hoisted her under her armpits, her head against my belly, dragging her as gently as I could towards the door, knowing there was no way I could lift her, especially not in my condition.

'Here, let me.'

Marcel's voice in my ear, his arms taking over from mine, hoisting Amalie over his shoulder, leading me with him out through the smoke and dust into the fresh air, the cold making me shiver once more. Or perhaps it was the shock.

'We have to get her into a taxi,' I muttered, seeing her stir as she slid to her feet, looking around, dazed. 'Amalie, come with me.'

Together, we led her back down the alleyway. There was no cab waiting. I looked up and down the street. Nothing.

From behind us, more shouts, this time commanding. Kieffer's men.

'Where's Suzanne?'

Marcel jerked his head towards the front of the building. 'Out front keeping them at bay as best she can.'

At that moment, a cab crawled into view around the corner, speeding up as it saw us standing there. My heart rose further as I spotted Charlie in the back.

'Get in.'

I half-shoved Amalie inside then felt hands also pushing me in.

'Go,' said Marcel. 'It's too dangerous for you. Go with them.'

'What about Suzanne? And you?'

'We'll be fine. But you need to go now. They're shouting about finding a body.'

'Braun.'

'You can explain later.'

'He's right,' said Charlie, reaching out a hand to pull me into the cab, wrenching the door shut behind me as the driver sped off while I, too, flung myself to the floor.

We lay there, huddled in a heap, one of my hands stroking Amalie's poor head, the other clinging to Charlie. I could feel the cab lurching as he took the corners fast, speeding towards the American Hospital. We'd got them all out. Now all we had to do was get them to the airfield and they were free. My heart soared like one of those planes into the skies, bound for

England. I risked raising my head to look at Charlie, seeing him flash me that smile, the one that told me everything was going to be alright.

A screech of brakes.

The taxi slamming to a halt.

Then a voice, shouting in German. 'Halt! Everyone out.'

SIXTY-THREE

Another screech of tyres as the driver thrust the cab into reverse, shooting up the street the way we'd come. A burst of gunfire. Then another. The taxi lurching and spinning, listing to one side as a tyre was blown out. The driver hurled the cab round the corner. Another blockade ahead of us. No other cabs in sight. It was all going wrong.

'Get out,' yelled the driver. 'Run.'

I raised my head. He'd managed to stop right by another alleyway, blocking it from this end.

I flung open the door. 'Go on,' I shouted to Amalie. She was already halfway up the alley when I started after her, Charlie right behind me. That was when I felt the bullets whizzing past, heard them ricocheting off the walls. I turned, trying to get a clean shot at them, but it was no use. They were crouched behind the cab, firing at us from behind it.

More bullets. A groan from Charlie. I turned to see the red stain spreading across his torso under his jacket.

'Charlie. Here. Lean on me.'

His face was grey, his weight slowing me down as I dug in my heels, pushing harder, the end of the alleyway in sight.

Amalie swivelled to see what was happening then ran back to
help me, a bullet missing her by inches. I could see them
shoving the cab out of the way, thrusting their guns in the
driver's face, shouting at us to stop.

'No bloody way,' I grunted as we staggered out into the next
street, looking wildly up and down it.

Another cab miraculously appeared around the corner,
accelerating as the driver saw us. I caught sight of him too. Our
man, Henri. Thank God.

We piled into it, laying Charlie out on the back seat, and I
crouched beside him, holding his hand.

'Charlie. Oh please no. Charlie, please don't die. Stay
with me.'

Amalie called out, 'The American Hospital. Please hurry.'

My tears fell on Charlie's face, sobs tearing at my throat. He
was deathly white, the life fading from him even as I watched.
No. Not Charlie. I couldn't bear to lose him too. I had to keep
him here, with me. With our baby. 'Hang on,' I murmured.
'We're getting you to hospital. It'll be alright.'

'Don't worry,' shouted Henri. 'I know these streets better
than those bastard Boches. Hold on tight.'

He put his foot down, taking the corners at breakneck
speed, but as we wove in and out of the backstreets, I could see
we were running out of time. Charlie's breathing was turning
shallower, the gaps between his breaths longer. All the blood
appeared to have drained from his face even as it carried on
seeping from his wound, an ever-spreading stain no matter how
hard I pressed on it with both hands. Where were the gods
when you needed them? He was like one of those candles in the
chapel, burning down, down, until there was no light left,
nothing but a whisper of smoke until even that, too, was gone.

'Come on, Charlie. Please. Please don't go,' I whispered,
dropping a kiss on his forehead, his lips, so cold now. I felt them
move under me.

'I love you.'

'What? What did you say? Stay with me, Charlie. Please. You can't leave me. We're having a baby. You're going to be a daddy. I need you to be here. I love you, Charlie.'

A soft sigh and then nothing more.

I stared wildly at his face, laying my cheek against it, listening for the sound of his breath, hoping against hope.

'We're here,' shouted the driver.

'Christine. We're here. Let's get him out.'

No point. I raised my cheek from his, stroking his eyelids, his forehead, focusing on the roughness of his stubble, the softness of his lips. The lips I would never feel again, the voice I would never hear. Those eyes that had shone so bright now extinguished. All that remained was love. My love for him. For our child. His love for me too. I could feel it, even as I saw his spirit leave him, a wisp of ethereal smoke, just like those candles.

'It's too late,' I whispered. 'He's gone.'

SIXTY-FOUR

The back door of the hospital burst open, the figures that emerged running towards the cab. I saw Jeannette lean into the taxi, taking in the scene, her eyes widening in shock. Then she was issuing commands. 'Let's carry him in. That's it. Gently.' Her arm dropped round my shoulders to guide me in too. I recognised the operating theatre where they were laying Charlie on the table.

'I need you all out of here,' said Dr Jackson as he pulled on a pair of gloves.

'I want to stay.'

I knew there was no point. I'd felt his last breath, his life ebbing away as I held his hand. I still wanted to believe that Sumner Jackson could somehow pull him back, but I wasn't going to leave Charlie on his own, no matter what. I think Jackson must have known all of that because he didn't object, simply handed me a mask and an apron.

I watched him gently examine Charlie before shaking his head. It was then that it finally hit me like a physical blow. I sank to my knees, sobbing. He was really gone.

'I'm sorry,' said Jackson. 'Even if you'd got here quicker,

there would have been no way to save him. The best we can do for him now is take care of him.'

His eyes travelled down, to the top of my legs. 'You're bleeding.'

'I... What?'

I looked too, seeing the stain, feeling the dull ache low in my belly along with a sharp, tugging pain, knowing what it meant. 'The baby...'

'You're pregnant?'

'I... was.'

My hands folded over my belly, trying to hold it in, to stop our baby leaving me too. It was hopeless. I knew that. But still I tried, as I had with Charlie. Was that what we'd done? Made a deal with the devil? We'd lied to Kieffer about this, and now it was actually coming true.

Too many thoughts now, my head dizzy with them. The world tilted around me. I could feel Dr Jackson gently leading me to a bed then handing me a cloth, helping me up so I could clean myself in the bathroom.

'It's very early on in your pregnancy so there's nothing much I need to do. You may bleed for a week or so, but it should get lighter. If it doesn't, get some medical attention. I'm so sorry, my dear. You've suffered two great losses today. Would you like me to make the arrangements?'

I stared at him, taking in what he was saying, the implication. There was no way I was leaving Charlie here, in a war-torn country overrun by Nazis. God knows what they would do with his body if they got hold of it. No doubt by now they had a shrewd idea what had really happened at the club and to Braun. 'He's coming with me.'

There was no other option. I was getting on that plane too. With Charlie.

Jackson looked at me then quietly removed his gloves,

pulling the sheet up to Charlie's neck. 'I'll leave you with him for a moment.'

Outside the operating-theatre door, I could hear voices talking and then arguing, growing more insistent. I blanked them out, knowing that this might be my last chance. Mine and Charlie's.

'I love you, you know that,' I murmured, laying the back of my hand on his cheek, feeling it growing colder as every minute passed. 'I also know that you love me. But this is it, isn't it? Pain. The price of love. And my God, does it hurt. It's a price I'm happy to pay for you. You're the best thing that ever happened to me. And I will always love you. Always. Don't you ever forget it. Now you go look after our baby. Tell him or her all those stories you read in that library of yours.'

For half a second, I thought he might open his eyes and flash that wicked grin, telling me it was all a joke. That he was just kidding.

Wishful thinking. Or desperate wanting.

I placed my lips on his for one last time. One last kiss. A kiss I wanted to go on forever.

A discreet tap on the theatre door. Suzanne put her head around it. 'Christine, I'm sorry, but we need to talk.'

I reluctantly rose from Charlie's side and followed her into the corridor. 'I'm so glad you got here safe,' I mumbled, taking in the sight of Jim as well. He looked as if he'd aged ten years, his face sagging in shock and grief.

'May I see him?' he asked.

'Of course.'

It felt as if everything was happening in a dream. Or rather, a nightmare. Faces floating in front of me, faces I knew. Not one of them the face I longed with all my heart to see. That face no longer even looked like the one I loved so much. The spark, the very soul of Charlie, had fled. In its place, a mask bearing the features of the man who meant everything to me. Now there was nothing. No more laughter. Or love. No future with him. No child to raise together. I gazed at Suzanne's mouth moving, not really taking in what she was saying.

'Jim has organised another plane,' she repeated. 'You can travel on it with Charlie back to London.'

'What about Betty?' I whispered.

'Betty?'

'Charlie's dog. Our dog. She's at his apartment. We can't leave her there.'

Betty, the one remaining link I had with him. Our surrogate child. Our only child now.

'Christine, listen to me. The Gestapo are looking everywhere for you. They know it was you who killed Braun. Boulain has already told them he went upstairs with you. Unfortunately, you didn't quite blow him to bits. It was evident he'd also been stabbed. We need to leave now. I can go on the plane with the other two. Marcel is heading south, to the escape line there, once he's made sure all the girls and staff are safe. Jim is in the clear, at least for now. We can't risk all our lives for a dog. I'm sorry.'

'She's not just a dog. She's Charlie's dog. Our dog.'

I knew I sounded like a child. I didn't care.

'It's OK,' said Jim. 'I can go back and get her.'

He was holding on to the theatre door, or perhaps it was holding him up. His face was chalk white now, his eyes great pits of sorrow. I realised then that I'd misjudged Jim. He was, after all, Charlie's friend.

'I'll bring her to you, but you must promise to leave for the airfield now. Dr Jackson has said he can take care of Charlie so he's ready to travel. You can sit with him all the way, Christine.'

'OK,' I whispered. Ready to travel? He was gone. They were both gone.

I was suddenly too exhausted even to utter another word. All the fight in me had seeped away, shock spreading through my veins, replacing it. I could see Amalie casting me worried looks. I didn't care. There was nothing to worry about now except Betty. Amalie and Suzanne would be alright, one way or another. But it was Betty who'd leaped all over Charlie, making him laugh, smothering him in her dog kisses. The kisses he would have bestowed on our baby. I needed her by my side. Charlie needed her too. He'd loved us both, possibly not quite equally. I could live with that. What I couldn't live with was losing that dog too.

SIXTY-FIVE

This time the airfield was to the north-east of Paris, the moon sitting low and fat in the sky above it, its light filtered by the clouds that stubbornly refused to shift. It was a stroke of luck that there was a full moon tonight. Apart from that, luck seemed to have deserted us. We were huddled in the lee of a dry-stone wall, keeping low so our silhouettes blended with the deep shadows. The night was oddly still, without a breath of breeze to blow away those clouds, while a soft drizzle persisted, soaking us all to the skin.

There was no sign of Jim. I'd be damned if I left there without Betty. I couldn't bear to look at Charlie's body wrapped in a white sheet. We'd placed him as gently as we could by the wall.

'They're sending one bigger plane for all of you,' Jeannette had announced when she'd met us at the rendezvous, before leading us across to the spot where we sat now. 'A B-24.'

The Carpetbaggers were coming to get us. That was fitting. The US Army Air Force squadron attached to OSS. It was thanks to the agents they dropped into France that we were here now. If it wasn't for Jeannette and the others, we'd never have made it out of Paris alive. I had to hand it to them – their operation was seamless. Dr Jackson had led us out of the back door by the theatre to an ambulance where I'd watched as they carefully carried Charlie into it on a stretcher before I'd climbed in beside him, sitting as close as I could so he would know he wasn't alone.

The others had sat with their heads bowed while I stared sightlessly out of the rear window as the streets of Paris flashed by, saying a silent farewell to the balconies and the boulevards that I loved. And where I'd fallen in love for the first and last time. Once or twice, we'd passed German patrols, my heart lodging in my throat each time. I'd felt Suzanne squeeze my hand and thrown her a grateful glance. Other than that, we'd sat silently, not daring to speak. And then the ambulance had juddered to a halt. A roadblock.

We'd just been able to hear the driver arguing with the soldiers as we'd ducked low, demanding to be allowed to go on his way, that this was an emergency. I'd closed my eyes and muttered a silent prayer, one my mum had taught me. If they insisted on searching the ambulance then all was lost. They were hunting all over Paris for us. If they caught us now, like this, Kieffer would show no mercy. We'd be as dead as my beloved.

Then, with a lurch and a final shouted order from the Germans, we'd been on our way. Maybe someone up there, or even my mum, had heard us. Eventually my heartbeat had slowed to normal. Not that there was a normal anymore. There never would be again, at least not for me.

At last we'd reached the edge of the city. 'Everyone out.'

The ambulance doors had opened and we'd scrambled down, François and Ambrose carrying the stretcher to the farm truck that had been waiting, hidden among the trees behind a bombed-out factory building.

As we'd climbed into the truck, my foot had caught and I'd

stumbled. For some stupid reason, it had brought tears to my eyes.

'Here.' I'd felt Suzanne's arm under mine, helping me up. She'd given me a quick hug. 'Be brave, *ma chérie*. He would want that.'

I'd looked at her wordlessly, trying not to drown in the agony that was flooding through me, threatening to pull me under to a place from which I'd never return. All I'd been able to do was huddle on the floor of the truck, hidden among the sacks of grain and crates of beet along with the others, feeling every bump and rattle as we'd thundered along tracks and back lanes, staring at the stars and the moon as they appeared and disappeared through the scudding clouds, wishing I was up there. With him.

And then we were here, at the extraction point.

The moon was rising higher, edging the clouds with silver, lending them an unearthly light as it hovered behind them once more. Any moment now it would break through, above the cloud line, illuminating the landing field. The rain had finally stopped. The heavens no longer wept for Charlie. As for me, I couldn't cry anymore. I was frozen, numb to everything but the need to see Betty safe and to know that I was bringing them both home.

'Where the hell is Jim?' I muttered. It was ten minutes to midnight. The plane would be here soon after.

That was when I heard it – the drone of an engine.

As one, we scrambled up, legs stiff with the hours of waiting, shaking ourselves off like dogs. It was coming in lower and lower. Any minute now we'd see it beneath the clouds.

Come on, come on. I'm not leaving without her.

Lights. Not from the sky but from the field beyond. It looked like torches.

Christ, no. Not again. How the hell did they find us?

Then a bark, just the one, and a ball of fur leaped the wall and raced up to me, tail wagging, licking my hands, my arms and any other part of me she could reach.

'Betty. Oh, my darling Betty, you made it.'

Jim panted as he, too, scrambled over the wall, shining his torch up now, flashing it on and off in a prearranged signal. 'Are they here yet?'

In answer, the drone grew louder, the plane breaking through the clouds, its sleek silver underbelly right above us, banking as it turned to make a semicircle then came in to land, its tyres ripping across the field, bouncing once, twice before finally taxiing to a halt. François and Ambrose turned to lift Charlie then stopped in their tracks. Sitting, guarding him as if her life depended on it, was Betty, baring her teeth.

'Come on, Betty. Come on, girl,' I murmured. The others were already running for the plane. And still Betty growled, hackles raised. There was no way anyone was going to interfere with her master.

All of a sudden, she stopped, dropped to her belly and lay there, staring at something we couldn't see. The two men lifted Charlie and carried him to the plane, Betty trotting beside them just as she'd kept pace with her master, looking for all the world as if she was walking alongside an invisible someone. Someone I loved with all my heart.

That sense stayed with me as we strapped ourselves in and I held Betty on my lap. She gave my face a lick then jumped down to lie beside Charlie, resting her head on her paws so she could watch over him once more.

'Look after him,' said Jim as he slammed the hatch shut and the co-pilot sealed it.

Then we were taxiing back down the field, bumping over ruts until, finally, we were rising higher and higher, France shrinking beneath us before the clouds blanketed her from view and we turned, heading for England. For home. Except it wasn't my home any longer. I wasn't even sure I had a home anymore.

I glanced at Suzanne and then at Amalie, her head wrapped in a bandage where Dr Jackson had tended to it, just as he'd tended to me. I was glad they were here, relieved we could travel together. We belonged together. We were renegades, all of us. The kind of people who never quite settled. It was what had sent us out here, to fight as we did, along with a burning sense of duty. And yet I would have settled with Charlie and our baby. Our family. The one we'd never have.

Was any of this worth it? I had no idea. Certainly not for Charlie. Never again would he see the moon rise, so close it seemed I could touch it through the plane window, a perfect silver orb guiding us across the waters, back to safety. Although there was no real safety either, in a world where your own betrayed you.

I could see Amalie out the corner of my eye, trying to catch some sleep, exhausted but alive, no thanks to SOE. How many others had died because of their cockeyed plan to deceive the Germans? They would argue that thousands more lives would be saved, and they might be right, but at what cost? I only had to glance at Charlie's body to know the price.

I reached out a hand and stroked Betty's ears. She barely moved a muscle, so intent was she on guarding Charlie. Now that was loyalty. A shame our lot couldn't do the same. Perhaps if they had, he would be here now. Alive. With me. Holding me in his arms. Laughing up at me from beneath Betty's onslaught. Cradling our baby in his arms.

I felt something in my chest unravel, a tight knot that had been there forever. As it loosened, the tears began to flow once more, and I let them. I cried for me, for Charlie, for all that we'd lost and everything we'd wanted. The life we could have had. The life we never would. I cried for the only man I would ever love. The man I would never see again. And the child he would watch over forever from somewhere beyond the stars.

SIXTY-SIX

20 FEBRUARY 1944, LONDON, ENGLAND

'Lieutenant Russell's parents are flying in to bring him home. They specifically asked if you would be there.'

I raised my eyes from the tea I'd been listlessly stirring. It felt like a lifetime since I'd sat at another table with Ward, Charlie beside me. Now it was Suzanne sitting there in his place. Not that anyone could ever take Charlie's place. 'When are they arriving?'

'This afternoon. At Harrington airfield. We have transport waiting to take you there.'

'What about Betty?'

'Betty?'

'My dog. Charlie's dog. She'd want to be there.'

Ward glanced at Charlie's London boss, a man named Pearson, who placed a hand on my arm. 'That won't be a problem.'

If either man wondered why I was so grief-stricken over a fellow agent, they were too tactful to say anything. Then again, it was probably blindingly obvious to anyone who'd seen us together. There were some things you couldn't hide. True love was one of them.

'Do you want me to come with you?' asked Suzanne.

I shook my head. 'No thank you. Betty and I can handle this.'

She was upstairs in the room right now, probably chewing her way through the furniture. Ever since they'd taken Charlie's body away in another ambulance, once we'd landed, she'd looked completely lost. I suspected I did too. I'd watched them wheel what looked like a stretcher to the plane then lift Charlie on to it with infinite care. Then they'd stood back and saluted him. We'd saluted him too, shoulders back, heads erect. Hearts breaking. At least in my case.

'It's alright, girl,' I'd murmured to Betty as we'd watched it drive away from the airfield. 'They'll look after him.'

I wasn't even sure I could go through that again, but for Charlie's sake, I had to.

With leaden legs, I took the stairs to my room, avoiding the lift in case there was anyone else in it. I couldn't cope with small talk or niceties. Not now. Maybe not ever again.

As I unlocked the door to the room, I called to Betty. She didn't respond. Heart in my mouth, I stepped in, my eyes searching for her. She was curled up on the rug beside the bed, eyes open but vacant. When I bent to pat her head, she didn't even raise it, never mind wag her tail.

'You miss him, don't you?' I murmured. 'So do I, girl. So do I.'

I buried my face in her fur for a moment, breathing in that dog scent. For half a second, I thought I could smell Charlie too, where his hand had ruffled her. Stupid. I was imagining things. I clipped her lead on to her collar. 'Come on, Betty. It's time to say goodbye.'

She looked up at me with mournful eyes as if she under-stood then trotted beside me out to the waiting car. All the way to the airfield, she lay with her head in my lap, only raising it when we drew to a halt outside a hut. I could see B-24s lined up alongside the runway, and uniformed men and women marching purposefully between the huts, but my eyes were drawn to the vehicle parked by the runway too. A hearse with a coffin in the back of it that contained Charlie's body.

'Come on, Betty,' I said. 'Let's go keep him company.'

As we emerged from the car, a USAAF colonel appeared from inside the hut, accompanied by another, distinguished-looking man in a suit. The colonel saluted. 'Colonel Heflin, United States Army Air Force.'

The other man shook my hand. 'John Winant, United States Ambassador to Great Britain. I'm very sorry for your loss.'

Out the corner of my eye, I saw someone get out of the front seat of the hearse. It was Pearson, Charlie's London boss. He walked over to stand by my side. 'I accompanied Lieutenant Russell from the morgue here. I didn't want to ask you to do it.'

I nodded absently, surprised but pleased that Charlie had such a send-off. Then it struck me. Of course. His stepfather was someone big. He must have pulled strings to get a plane over here.

As if on cue, the roar of engines overhead drowned out Pearson's next words. We all watched as a transport plane made a perfect landing on the runway, taxiing to a halt a few feet from where we stood.

I was stroking Betty's ears once more, soothing her. 'It's OK, darling. Just a plane.'

She sank to her belly with a whimper and lay by my feet as the plane door opened and steps were wheeled up to it. Moments later, a man and woman appeared in the doorway and began to descend the steps as we walked forward to meet them. The hair under the man's hat was white, his face kindly if a little stern, but it was Charlie's mother I hardly dared look at.

When I did, it was to see two grey eyes looking back at me. Charlie's eyes. Although her hair was greying too, I could see strands that were still the same colour as his. For one insane second, I wanted to reach out and touch it. They both wore good but simple clothes, her black coat as elegant as her hat. But it was the way they carried themselves that spoke of their breeding. They had the same quiet confidence as Charlie, as far from arrogance as possible. It was one of the things I'd loved most about him.

I held out my hand, but she ignored it, wrapping her arms around me instead. 'My dear. I'm so glad to meet you even if it is under the worst of circumstances.'

I could feel her heart beating against mine. I had the sense that was the same as Charlie's too. Loving. Generous. Above all, full of courage. She held me at arm's length, studying my face. 'You're just as Charles described. Quite lovely.'

'H-He told you about me?' I stammered.

'He wrote me lots about you. I have some of the letters here. I thought you might want to read them too.'

I could see her eyes brimming just as mine were. She handed me a packet of letters tied with a ribbon, and I tucked them into my handbag. 'Thank you.'

Her husband introduced himself. 'John Morgan. And who is this?'

Betty looked up and wagged her tail.

'This is Betty. She's Charlie's... Charles's dog. Well, our dog really. She sort of adopted us.'

Morgan patted her. 'She has good taste.'

I heard rather than saw the hearse glide up and park right by us, gulping in a breath, my fingers tightening on Betty's lead. An honour guard marched up and moved into place, saluting, while four more soldiers hoisted the coffin from the hearse and carried it up the steps, draped in the Stars and Stripes, as a bugler played taps. I felt Betty straining at the lead, desperate to run over to where she knew Charlie was. Then she broke free, slipping her collar and dashing up the steps into the plane to lie next to Charlie's coffin, head up, daring anyone to come near. She was guarding her master to the last.

I didn't know whether to laugh or cry. It was such a solemn moment and yet Betty had lightened it. Then I felt a gentle hand on my arm.

'Let her go with him,' said Charlie's mother. 'We'll take good care of her.'

I couldn't speak, a fiery ball of pain and grief rising from my gut and filling my gullet, burning right through me. He was gone. But I longed, in a selfish way, to hold on to any part of him I could, including Betty.

'You know, Charles loved you very much,' she added. 'He told me you were the woman he was going to marry. The future mother of his children.'

I gaped at her. 'He did?'

'He also told me that your mother was killed and that your home was destroyed by a German bomb. I want you to know that you always have a home with us. I know I can't replace your mom, but believe me, we're always here for you. Aren't we, John?'

Blinded now by tears, I had a blurred impression of him nodding while she carried on smiling at me, even though her heart must have been breaking too. There was no way I could add to that by telling her about the child we'd almost had. I would keep that secret for us both. One last secret.

I pulled out my handkerchief and dabbed at my eyes, then handed her Betty's lead and collar. 'You're right. She should go with Charlie. With you. I can't look after her in any case. I have no idea where I'm going next.'

It was true. I wasn't even sure if I wanted to stay with SOE, not after all of this. Living in a hotel room was no good for Betty. She'd be better off with them. All these things I told myself as Charlie's mother gazed at me with tenderness.

'Thank you,' she whispered. 'I promise we'll take great care of her.'

The colonel stepped forward. 'Sir, ma'am, the plane needs to leave. We're on a tight turnaround.'

This was it. The final goodbye. Another hug and Charlie's parents proceeded up the steps, retaking their seats at the front, his mother waving at me through the window. Almost before I knew what I was doing, I sprinted after them before the hatch could close, racing up the steps and into the plane, bending down to stroke Betty one last time. She looked at me as if she knew then licked my hand, tasting the salt from my tears, licking those away too.

'Goodbye, Betty,' I managed to choke out. 'Be a good girl. Look after him.' I touched the coffin behind her. It felt smooth. Cold. *It's just a box, Christine.* A box holding Charlie. 'Goodbye, my love.'

Words echoing into eternity.

'Ma'am, you need to leave now. We're ready for take-off.'

The co-pilot gently took my arm to help me to my feet and guide me back out down the steps. The hatch slammed shut, steps pulled away, the engines roaring once more. I saluted as I watched the plane accelerate back down the runway then lift its nose and soar into the sky, a beautiful bird taking my boy home to his final resting place.

SIXTY-SEVEN

I didn't want to go back to the hotel just yet, not without Betty. Couldn't bear to read Charlie's letters yet either. Instead, I leaned forward and spoke to the driver as we neared London.

'Can you take me to Glamis Road in Shadwell please? It's near the docks.'

'I can, miss, but a lot of that area has been bombed out. Is there a particular address you want on that street?'

'Number forty-one.'

'Very good, miss.'

As we drove through the East End streets, I could see the devastation. Houses now nothing more than piles of brick and shattered timbers, to say nothing of the lives they'd once contained. Entire streets reduced to rubble along with schools and hospitals. I wondered if the pilots had even once thought of the defenceless people they were targeting as they released their bombs. I doubted it. But then, our boys did exactly the same. So many lives destroyed. Was it worth it? I wasn't sure anymore. Just as I was no longer sure I wanted any part of it. Not after all that had happened.

'Just here on the right,' I said to the driver, who obligingly turned up the street and then stopped. I knew already that our house, Mum's house, was gone, but it still didn't prepare me for the great gash in the terrace where it had once stood. The houses either side of it were gone as well, what had once been their yards still piled high with what remained of people's lives and homes. I thought I saw a child's ball poking out of the mess that had once been our neighbour's kitchen. Their little boy was about Elsie's age, maybe a year or two younger.

'Will you be alright, miss?'

'What? I— Yes, I'll be fine.'

The driver looked dubious but said nothing more as I paid him and stepped out into the street, drawn towards the shell of what had been my home, a house I'd loved and hated in equal measure. It was the place where I'd been born and where my dad had dangled me on his knee. It was also the place where my stepdad had terrorised us all, the shouts of happiness turning to screams of terror once he moved in. I stared at the door lying on the ground, remembering him slamming it in rage when he staggered home from the pub. Fragments of paper clinging to a bit of wall that still stood, the pattern on them instantly taking me back to the bedroom I shared with Elsie, how I used to make up stories about the faces we fancied we saw in them.

Something glinted in the watery sunlight. I darted forward, scrabbling at the rubble, pulling lumps of stone and brick aside so I could unearth it.

One of my mum's pans that she'd scoured for hours until they shone, the same size and shape as the one I'd brought down on my stepfather's head. I could feel the weight of it in my hand, heavier than I remembered. Had I really done that? It seemed now like it had all happened in a dream. I even imagined I could hear Tom calling out to me just as he'd done that night.

'Chrissie.'

I wasn't dreaming. It was Tom grabbing me by the arm,

tugging me away from the bomb site that had been our home. 'Chrissie, get away from there. It's not been cleared properly. It's dangerous.'

I stumbled as I half-turned, throwing out my arms to break my fall, feeling Tom steady me. 'Christ. It's you. It's really you. What the hell are you doing here?'

'I could ask you the same.'

He looked older, but he was still recognisably Tom, apart from an empty sleeve where one arm was missing. He saw me glance at it then look away. 'Invalided out. Some might call it a lucky escape.'

'How did it happen?'

I was still trying to take in his face, his eyes, his voice.

'Grenade out at El Alamein. Stupid here was charging a German machine-gun nest.'

I stroked his shoulder where his arm had been. 'That was incredibly brave of you. But how is it that you're here, today of all days? I didn't plan this. I was... somewhere else. It was a last-minute decision. A lucky one, as it turns out.'

We smiled at one another, neither of us quite believing what we were seeing.

'I'm staying in that house over there.' He jerked his thumb at the terrace behind us, towards a house a few doors down. 'Remember the old couple who live there? They took me in when I turned up just like you. My place was bombed out too. Both their boys were lost years back at Passchendaele, and I wanted to be close, see, in case you came back. You're the only person I have left in this world, Chrissie. Couldn't believe it when that cab stopped and you got out.'

He'd been waiting for me, looking out for me just as he always did. I tried to speak, but all I could do was heave out a sob and then another. I heard him murmuring as he stroked my hair, his good arm holding me tight. 'It's OK, Chrissie. You let it out, girl. Have a good cry.'

At last, I raised my tear-streaked face. 'Promise you'll never leave me again.'

'I never did. You're the one that left.'

'I had to.'

'I know.'

I gazed at what had been our home. 'How can you bear it? Always looking out on the place Mum and Elsie died.'

'I don't think of it like that. I think of them still alive, Mum happy without that bastard. That's who she was after you'd gone, Chrissie. Happy again. Told the police when they came knocking that he'd probably fallen off a bar stool or something.'

'Did they ask about me?'

'Yes, and Mum said you'd run off with your sweetheart. One or two of the neighbours tattled, and she told them where to get off. They were jealous of you, Chrissie. Everyone was.'

'Me? But why?'

'Because you're beautiful, sis. You always have been. I tried to get word to you through the boys in Paris but heard nothing back.'

'He never turned up, your mate, to meet me,' I said. 'Don't worry. I made my own way.'

Shock and then anger flitted across his face. 'I'm sorry, Chrissie. I didn't know. You must have had a hell of a time.'

'I did at first, but it toughened me up. Comes in handy these days.'

He looked at me, apparently taking in for the first time the WAAF uniform I'd worn to see Charlie off, my cap perched on my head. 'Well, look at you. So you joined up?'

'It's a long story. One I'll tell you over a pint if you like.'

He gave me his remaining arm. 'You're on. Let's go down the pub and you can tell me all about it. Oh, and Chrissie?'

'Yes?'

'Welcome home.'

SIXTY-EIGHT

I kicked off my shoes and stretched out on the bed with a sigh. It had been a long day. Saying goodbye to Charlie and Betty. Finding Tom again. I was wrung dry. No more tears to shed, of sadness or happiness. I reached for my handbag and pulled out the letters. It was now or never. If I left it, I might never read them. It was almost too much to bear.

There were three of them, bound together with a white ribbon by Charlie's mother. I carefully unpicked the bow and put it to one side, then pulled the first letter from its envelope. The first few lines were the usual affectionate words from a son to his mother. Then a paragraph further down caught my eye.

> *I wanted you to be the first to know I've met someone very special. Her name is Christine, and I think she could be the one. You always told me I would know when I met that person. You were right, Mom. I just know.*

I felt my vision misting over, blinked and carried on reading.

She is beautiful and brave. Intelligent and well read. She is everything I always wanted. I think she's a lot like you.

It was no use. I was sobbing once more, gulping in the air to steady myself. I folded that letter and tucked it back into its envelope before turning to the next.

Dearest Mother,

I hope that you and Pops are well. I'm just fine and eating splendidly, you will be glad to hear. It's strange to think that back home everything more or less carries on as normal while people here are suffering so much. I can't tell you too much about it, as you can imagine, but it hurts to see the gaunt, frightened faces all around me. I know that I'm doing the right thing by being here.

I also know that I'll be doing the right thing when I ask Christine to marry me. I haven't found the right moment yet, but when I do, I hope you will be as happy as I am. You will love her as much as I do. I'm sure of that. If she says yes, then she will make me the happiest man in the world, just as you and Pops are so happy. You have been the most wonderful example for me. I wanted you to know that. I realise that my father wasn't the kindest of men, but Pops has more than made up for that. He is a fine man, Mother, and I want to be just as good a husband to Christine.

I stared at his words, hardly taking them in, reading them through twice more to make sure. I was still in shock when I pulled out the last letter. It was unopened, addressed to me.

My darling Christine,

If you're reading this, then you'll know that I'm gone. I asked my mother to make sure this got to you in case the worst happened, because I want you to know just how much you mean to me, which is everything.

I think I fell in love with you the day I met you, although I was probably too stupid and stubborn to realise that at first. I'm so sorry for that as I am for all the times I was too much of a coward to tell you the truth. You are the most magnificent woman I've ever met, beautiful inside and out, and nothing would make me happier than for you to consent to marry me. It breaks my heart to know that, if you're reading this, it's too late for all of that and more.

I watch you when you're sleeping sometimes and imagine our life together. Making a home and filling it with children. Our children. Doing normal things that ordinary folk do, away from all the madness of war and what we do. Loving one another as I know we do, in good times and bad. That's what makes a real marriage, don't you think? The one I was afraid at first to even contemplate, probably because of what happened with my own parents. I can't tell you how much I regret now holding back, knowing how I really felt about you. How I will always feel about you. Yes, even now that I'm gone.

You told me once that you feel tainted, but nothing could be further from the truth. You are pure courage, pure beauty and, for me, pure love. Think of me when you look at the stars at night. I'll be somewhere up there, shining just for you. I love you, Christine. I always have, and I always will. Please carry me in your heart and remember me sometimes. If a spirit can remember, then mine will never forget you.

Your loving,

Charlie xxx

I stared at those kisses, tracing them with my finger as I'd once traced his lips, those soft lips that had met mine just as every part of Charlie had embraced me. He was me, and I was him. Always would be.

I got up from the bed and flung open the window, staring up at the night sky, making out the stars one by one, wondering which was Charlie. There he was, the brightest star, the one shining close to the moon. Venus, the planet of love. That was Charlie, shining still. Venus, another name for Aphrodite. I thought of that rose in the Jardin du Luxembourg, the blood welling where its thorn had pricked me. Pain. The price you paid for love. A price worth paying.

'I will always love you,' I whispered. 'Always.'

Above me, the stars twinkled, multiplying through my tears. The brightest might be shining up there, among them, but he was also here, in my heart.

A LETTER FROM AMANDA

I want to say a huge thank you for choosing to read *The Paris Spy's Girl*. If you enjoyed it and want to keep up to date with all my latest releases, just sign up at the following link. Your email address will never be shared, and you can unsubscribe at any time.

www.bookouture.com/amanda-lees

Before I write a word of my WW2 books, I spend many hours researching the real people and stories behind them, relying where I can on primary source material and first-person accounts. In this case, the facts remain controversial to this day, exposing as they do an especially murky part of SOE's history. While they continue to be disputed, my sympathies lie with those who were discredited and their stories disbelieved to cover up inconvenient truths. What is certain is that the agents of the SOE, MI6 and the OSS, along with the Resistance, possessed courage beyond measure, along with a spirit that transcends everything.

Christine is based, as are all my characters, on an amalgamation of people who actually lived and carried out her work. I want to pay special tribute to one because she epitomised the 'cool, lonely courage' which was the hallmark of these agents. Marie Christine Chilver, otherwise known as Agent Fifi, was only revealed as the *agente provocatrice* who tested wartime recruits when her documents were declassified in 2014.

Her cover name was actually Christine, and her vital work ensured that agents who might have succumbed to temptation, and betrayed themselves and others in doing so, never made it to the field. Latvian on her mother's side, the family's property was confiscated by the Russians, something for which Marie Christine eventually obtained compensation. She went on to found an animal sanctuary in Latvia after the war while living quietly in Gloucestershire with her friend Jean, a retired SOE officer.

Agent Fifi's work may have raised eyebrows along with unwarranted gossip, but it was as vital as the work carried out by other agents, and she performed brilliantly. While SOE indicated that, in order to perform her task, she had to 'get herself "picked up" by the man', there is no evidence in her declassified files that her tests ever turned into assignations or affairs. In fact, the most 'intimate' activity recorded in Fifi's file is her time spent at a man's hotel, hemming scarves.

Although in real life she never married, the love affair between the characters of Christine and Charlie in this book represents the passionate, sometimes sadly short-lived relationships that happened in the fevered atmosphere of war. Charlie is partly based on a real-life character too, and you may recognise the nods to a famous father along with other hints in the story. I read many letters sent between sweethearts during the war before I wrote the final chapter. Their heartbreaking poignancy resonates even now, all these years later.

On a personal note, I couldn't resist including my own dog, a rescue just like the dog in the book, and naming her after my mother. She sits beside me as I write, accompanies me on walks as I work through plot points and is every bit as protective as Betty.

My mother, the real Betty, was also remarkable, a tiny Glaswegian with as much courage as any SOE agent who set off for the jungles of Borneo after she trained as a nurse and ended up running the hospital in Hong Kong where I was born. Her love story with my father, who'd served in military intelligence, ended far too soon when he died while I was still a toddler. I think of them both when I write these books as I know they both served people, and their country, with enormous pride.

My dearest wish is that you fall in love with these people and their complexities as I did, reading long into the night of the remarkable things they did to ensure our freedom. It's an honour to bring their stories back to life and to you, and I gain as much from writing them as I hope you do reading them.

I hope you loved *The Paris Spy's Girl,* and if you did, I would be very grateful if you could write a review. I'd love to hear what you think, and it makes such a difference helping new readers to discover one of my books for the first time.

I love hearing from my readers – you can get in touch through social media or my website.

Thanks,

Amanda

facebook.com/AmandaLeesAuthor

x.com/amandalees

ACKNOWLEDGEMENTS

I get as much joy from writing the acknowledgements as I know some readers get from combing them for titbits and clues. Let me spare you any guessing by telling you that a book is always a team effort and I have the most wonderful team – or perhaps army – behind me.

First, there is my agent and friend, Lisa, who has brilliant instincts, an earthy sense of what works and a heart of gold along with a dress sense that outshines us all. I owe her so much, along with her amazing posse in Patrick, Zoe, Jamie and Elena.

Then there's my wonderful editor, Susannah, and the team at Bookouture, who not only get my books out into the world but make sure they have gorgeous covers, are superbly produced and come in all kinds of formats, including audio. Behind the scenes, they crunch data, perform publishing wizardry and weave marketing magic. Peta, Saidah, Kim, Noelle, Sarah, Jess, Jenny, Alex, Melanie, Mark, Ruth, Richard, Lauren, Marina, Alba and so many others, you're all fabulous, and if I've left anyone out, forgive me. There's simply so much talent under your roof.

I also once again want to thank my author buddies – Karin, Vanessa, Anne, Victoria, Lisa, Martyn, Susi, Anna and, again, too many more to mention who've been endlessly supportive, along with the book bloggers and reviewers who do so much, especially Robyn, Christine and Dee. And if I've inadvertently left out any names here, apologies once more. I appreciate you all.

As ever, there is my constant inspiration, my daughter. I love you, and I am always proud of you.

Next, the friends and family who've been there for me through times dark and light – Julia and Phil, Andrew, Sean, Josa, Guy, Nina, Barb, Christian, Jackie and Sam, Sumaira, Marianne and Margaret, Clare, Natalie and everyone else who has helped in any way or cheered me on.

Above all, everlasting thanks to the women and men who served, and gave their lives in service for, their countries and our freedom. We will never forget you.

PUBLISHING TEAM

Turning a manuscript into a book requires the efforts of many people. The publishing team at Bookouture would like to acknowledge everyone who contributed to this publication.

Commercial
Lauren Morrissette
Jil Thielen
Imogen Allport

Cover design
Debbie Clement

Data and analysis
Mark Alder
Mohamed Bussuri

Editorial
Susannah Hamilton
Nadia Michael

Copyeditor
Laura Kincaid

Proofreader
Anne O'Brien

9 781837 906277